"Is that w   For me to leave?"

"No. I'm sorry I snapped at you." She extended a hand to him and Holden took it without hesitation.

"I'm sorry, too," he admitted. He sank onto the couch, pulling her down beside him. "What's wrong between us, Merry? We never used to have trouble talking in the past."

She shrugged. "I feel like I don't know who you are anymore, Holden."

"I'm the same person I've always been."

"No, you're not. You've changed." She turned to look at him carefully. "All I know is that ever since you arrived there's been this...tension between us."

"I know. I feel it, too."

"I want everything to be the way it was when we were kids. We could talk about anything back then," she said on a sigh. "I miss those talks."

Holden pulled her into the crook of his arm and held her protectively. The blinds on the patio weren't fully closed and she could see the Christmas tree standing out there, leaning a little.

"But we're not kids any longer, Holden," she said at last.

"No, we're not. And that's a good thing. Because of this." And he lowered his head and kissed her.

Dear Reader,

If you come to Minnesota for the holidays, bring warm clothes. In this land of 10,000 lakes—all of them frozen in December—winter sets the perfect stage for those who dream of a white Christmas. You can cross-country ski, skate, snowmobile or even snowshoe your way to Grandma's house. Of course, Jack Frost will probably be nipping at your nose, but a cup of hot chocolate in front of a crackling fire will help you forget his bite.

I have to confess that if it weren't for Christmas, I'd say, "Bah humbug" to Old Man Winter. I prefer to stay indoors when the temperature drops and the snow falls. Yet, come December, I find myself catching snowflakes with my tongue and drawing pictures on the steamed windowpanes. I'll stand on a ladder in the frigid outdoors to string colored lights along the roof and trudge through thigh-high drifts of snow in search of that perfectly shaped Scotch pine at the tree farm. Chalk it up to the wonder of Christmas.

Because there *is* something wonderful about the holiday season. The world becomes a nicer, more romantic place in December. For a few short weeks, the spirit of Christmas warms even the coldest of hearts. Blessings are counted, hopes are renewed and people are reunited—with old friends, distant relatives and loved ones. It's the perfect time for falling in love—or rekindling a first love, as my hero and heroine discover in this book.

You might not be able to take a sleigh ride across a snow-covered meadow this holiday season or catch snowflakes with your tongue, but you can let the spirit of Christmas into your heart. Spend this December with the ones you love, and as my heroine would say,

"Be Merry!"

Pamela Bauer

P.S. Whether it be December or any other month of the year, I love hearing from my readers. You can write to me at:

Pamela Bauer
c/o MFW
P.O. Box 47888
Plymouth, MN 55447

Pamela Bauer

MERRY'S CHRISTMAS

Harlequin Books

TORONTO • NEW YORK • LONDON
AMSTERDAM • PARIS • SYDNEY • HAMBURG
STOCKHOLM • ATHENS • TOKYO • MILAN
MADRID • WARSAW • BUDAPEST • AUCKLAND

ISBN 0-373-70670-7

MERRY'S CHRISTMAS

For my dear friend Barbara Schenck
who asked all the right questions.

With special thanks to

Andrea Sisco who graciously shared her
professional expertise with me

and

Keith Wenger who kept my manuscript
from falling into a black hole in cyberspace.

PROLOGUE

Twenty years ago

"YOU CAN COME OUT NOW. They're gone."

The attic was dark except for the shaft of light coming up through the stairway and the faint moonlight pushing its way through a small, uncurtained gable window. Holden hoisted his lanky frame onto the wooden floor, carefully pulling up the ladder, then closing the trapdoor behind him.

"Merry, did you hear me? I said you can come out now." This time his voice was stronger, more encouraging.

Still no answer. The only sound was the faint strains of "Joy to the World" that played on the stereo two floors below.

Holden peered into the shadows. He knew Merry was hiding there somewhere. In the short time she'd been in Rosie's foster care, she'd made a habit of seeking refuge in the attic of the two-story farmhouse. Holden didn't understand why.

It was crowded, dusty and smelled like old shoes. And it was home to all sorts of bugs he preferred not to think about, including the hairiest spiders he had ever seen.

Merry didn't care. She had read *Charlotte's Web* a dozen times and thought of spiders as her friends. Holden suspected she went to the attic hoping to find some secret message written in one of the many webs spun in its corners.

She also liked to rummage through the trunks and put clothes on the old wire dress forms Rosie no longer used. She'd given each one a name, and Holden often caught her talking to them as if they were real people.

"Come on, Merry. You know you can't stay up here all night," he said with as much patience as he could muster, considering his mind was filled with images of huge black creatures tap-dancing all over his body.

Finally a muffled sob broke the silence. Then he heard her say in a defiant tone, "I'm not a charity case and I don't need their crummy presents." Crummy was hyphenated by a hiccup.

The floorboards squeaked as Holden crawled toward her. He prayed that the webs he encountered along the way were uninhabited. Rosie said spiders, like bears, hibernated in the winter, but he didn't believe her. He knew they lurked in the corners and between the cracks in the floor.

As he expected, he found Merry sandwiched between two dress forms. "They brought mostly baby things. Some dolls and games. A fire truck. That kind of stuff," he said, squeezing in beside her.

"I don't care what they brought. I don't want any of it," she said stubbornly.

"Because of what happened with your real mom and dad?"

Again there was silence. Holden could hear her trying to smother her sniffles.

"Are you crying?"

"No! I told you I don't cry. Only babies cry. I'm not a baby."

But Holden knew that tears were filling her big brown eyes. They were in her voice, and he could feel her shoulder trembling against his. "I won't tell anyone, Merry."

It was a long time before Merry spoke again, and then she said in a small, trembly voice, "They're getting a d-d-divorce."

"Is that why you didn't get to go home for Christmas?"

"There w-was no place to g-go," she stammered. "My dad's gone away on business and my mom's still s-sick."

Anger flared in Holden. All Merry had talked about since he'd known her was her mom and dad coming to get her in time for Christmas. It was the one present most of the kids who lived with Rosie wanted—their real parents with them for Christmas. Not glow-in-the dark paint sets or Barbie dolls or any of the other toys the ladies from the church dropped off every year.

Only most of the kids at Rosie's had learned that it was better to wish for toys from strangers than to hope that parents would keep their promises.

But Merry was not like the other kids. She was so trusting, so full of hope.

But then, she was only nine and had been in foster care less than three weeks. Holden was thirteen and knew better.

"So I guess that means you'll be staying here at Rosie's for a little while longer," he said in a calm, matter-of-fact tone.

"I don't want to. I can take care of my mom. I know how," she said in a voice that made Holden's insides feel all squiggly.

"You shouldn't have to be cooking and cleaning house at your age. You're just a kid."

"But I want to go home! I don't want to be a foster child," she declared emotionally, fighting back the tears.

"Just because you didn't get to leave today doesn't mean you're going to be here forever," he said, consolingly. He put his arm around her and pulled her closer. She turned her head into his shoulder and stopped fighting the tears.

Listening to her cry, he didn't have the heart to tell her that fathers "away on business" had a habit of disappearing and never being found again, and that sicknesses had a way of never getting cured. In the three years he had been in foster care, only two kids had ever returned to their real parents for good. The rest had either been adopted by strangers or transferred to other foster homes.

"It'll be all right, Merry," he said softly as she sobbed into his sweater. "Being a foster kid ain't so bad. There are worse things that could happen to you." Someday he would tell her about those things, but not now.

When her tears were spent, she straightened. "I suppose now you think I'm a baby for bawling my eyes out."

Holden let his arm fall back to his side and said simply, "Everyone cries once in a while."

"I bet you don't."

"I've learned how not to."

"Will you teach me?"

"You don't need to know how. It's okay for girls to cry."

He didn't want to talk about his feelings and quickly changed the subject. "Listen to me, Merry. You can make it here. Rosie's not so bad. Actually she's pretty neat for a foster mom."

Merry didn't say another word. Holden took her silence to mean that she knew he spoke the truth. Finally he asked, "Are you ready to go downstairs?"

She sighed. "I guess."

He reached for her hand. "Hold on to me so you don't fall."

She slid her small, warm hand into his. "You won't tell anybody about my mom and dad, will you?"

"Parents getting divorced is nothing new around here."

She stopped and tugged on his hand. "You have to promise me, Holden, or I'm not going downstairs."

"All right. I promise. But I'm telling you, divorce is no big deal. It happens to almost everybody who gets married."

"Well, it's not going to happen to me, 'cuz I'm never going to get married. Not ever," she stated firmly.

"Me, neither."

"Good, 'cuz it's dumb."

"It sure is."

There was a pause before she said, "Emily Parker doesn't think so. She says girls are supposed to get married. That's the way it works if you're not a weirdo. Girls marry boys so they'll take care of them."

As quietly as he could Holden lifted the trapdoor and lowered the portable stairs. "You won't need a husband to take care of you, Merry. Besides, I'll always be there for you if you need me," he told her as he guided her to the top step.

"Even when I'm old?"

"Even then."

"Good. Because I swear, I'm never getting married. Never, ever!"

CHAPTER ONE

The Present

SHE SAT at the Steinway baby grand wearing a sequined red dress that looked as if it came from the exclusive collection of some famous European designer. No one would have guessed that the dress had been created by the pianist's own hands.

It looked too elegant and too expensive. But then everything Merry Mattson wore looked elegant and expensive. Braxton's Department Store had hired her to lend a little class to the bustle of buying and selling, and the place was getting more than its money's worth.

For the past year and a half, Merry had been spending the afternoons playing the piano in the aisle between purses and perfumes on the main floor of the upscale Minneapolis department store. Every time she performed she charmed shoppers with her delightful style of play, her charismatic personality and her beauty. Although Braxton's had six pianists who played at different times in different locations throughout the store, Merry was the one people remembered, the one they came to hear. Instead of sitting inconspicuously playing background music, she attracted attention, sparkling like one of the glittering holiday ornaments that dangled from the twenty-foot Scotch pine at the main entrance.

Traditional apparel for Braxton's pianists was basic black with an occasional touch of white. But Merry wasn't traditional, not in her choice of clothing and especially not in her music. She always wore red, because it was full of emotion, and she always played smooth, flowing melodies that were both soothing and uplifting.

As she began a medley of Christmas carols, several people stopped to listen. Within minutes, dozens of shoppers had gathered around her, utterly enchanted by the sounds she made, by the sheer force of her presence.

Seamless transitions moved her from one song to another. Some shoppers stood quietly as if they were at a concert, while others perused the glass-topped table where cassettes and compact discs of her music were displayed.

When Merry finally lifted her fingers from the keys, the crowd expressed their approval with applause. A boy who appeared to be in his early teens shyly approached her with a copy of her latest recording, *Be Merry*.

"Would you like me to autograph that for you?" she asked, her lips curving into a smile most men found irresistible. The youth was no exception.

"It's for my mom for Christmas," he croaked in a voice that hadn't quite decided which octave it should be. "She's always talking about how much she likes your music."

"So you're getting her one of my CDs. How sweet!" Merry said effusively, causing the boy's face to glow. On top of the piano was a wooden-handled razor blade. Merry reached for it and sliced open the shrink wrap of the compact disc. With a red flow-tip pen, she wrote her signature across one corner of the cover art.

Apparently encouraged by her warm smile, the boy gestured at the empty sheet-music holder and asked, "Where's your music?"

Merry aimed the tip of the pen at her right ear. "It's in here."

"You've got it memorized?"

"No, I play by ear. If I listen carefully to a piece of music, I can hear the melody and then play it."

"Cool!"

Which was the sentiment of many of the shoppers who stood admiring the elegant musician. She autographed several more CDs, then played another medley of Christmas tunes, including a special request from a cane-tapping, white-haired lady who leaned her frail body against the glossy piano like a nightclub chanteuse.

It was a scene that had become familiar to store employees—Merry working her magic with customers. She could put smiles on the faces of the weary simply by running her delicate fingers over the keys. Like her music, she was accessible to her audience, never hesitating to interact with those who crowded around her. When she announced she was about to play her final piece for the day, a collective sigh could be heard. Although her audience was a transient one, Merry knew that some of her package-toting listeners had been there the entire three hours she'd been playing.

One man who'd stood watching and listening for most of her performance was Steve Austin. Wearing a black tuxedo with a red cummerbund, he had carefully kept himself far enough away so that she wouldn't notice him, yet close enough so that he could easily see and hear her.

It came as no surprise to him that others found Merry's music special. She had a way of playing familiar music with a style that was hers alone. The first time he'd heard her play he'd fallen a little in love. There was no other way to describe the feelings she evoked in him. Her music spoke to his heart.

When the final smattering of applause came, he boldly pushed his way through the small crowd still lingering around the piano.

"Need an escort?"

A smile spread across Merry's face. "I thought you were working this afternoon."

"I was. I took off early."

"How long have you been here?"

"Long enough to watch you bedazzle hundreds of tired and irritable shoppers," he answered, adoration written all over his face.

"Everyone loves Christmas music," she said modestly, lowering the fallboard over the keys.

"Everyone loves *your* music," he amended, unable to resist reaching for her hand. His move distinctly proprietary, he whisked her away from the piano and whispered in her ear. "And everyone loves you, including me."

Merry felt his lips gently nudge her ear. It was the closest thing to a kiss she would get right now, for Steve was not one to show affection in public.

"I liked the Rudolph rendition," he told her, holding her elbow protectively as he skillfully ushered her away from the few shoppers who still lingered around the piano.

"I'm not sure Braxton's wants children dancing in its aisles."

"Are you kidding? It's great for business. Maybe you should do a CD of children's music."

"I haven't finished the one I'm working on now," she reminded him, although the reminder was unnecessary. It was because of Steve that she'd produced two compact discs already.

They made a stunning couple as they strolled through the crowded department store, causing heads to turn, mouths to murmur. There were few people who didn't recognize Braxton's Lady in Red and her handsome escort, the popular host of "Let's Shop," the shopping channel featured on cable television.

"Did you come to take me home?" she asked, eyeing his tux. "Or are we off to some gala?"

"No, not home or a gala. I came to take you to dinner."

Her fingers pinched the seam of her sequined dress. "I'm afraid this is all I have except for a pair of jeans and a turtleneck in my dressing room."

He chuckled. "I don't want you to change. You look perfect—as usual."

"We'll be recognized," she warned him.

"Where we're going it won't matter. Keep it on for me, okay?"

Normally she didn't wear the clothes she performed in anywhere but at the piano. Steve's endearing plea, however, had her breaking her rule.

She stopped and looked at him, then began toying with a button on his tuxedo. "So what's the occasion?"

"Can't tell you."

Merry returned his sly grin and tucked her arm in his as they resumed walking. She'd become accustomed to Steve's surprises. It was one of the things she loved about him. That and the fact that he was a true gentleman, taking care of all the little details without a fuss. Taking care of her.

The first time they'd met he'd reminded her of the heroes in the old movies she and Rosie used to watch on Sunday afternoons. His dark hair, graying elegantly at the temples, was neatly trimmed, and he always wore a suit when they were out in public. Until she'd met him, she'd never known that men could be so gallant. He attended to her every need, making sure she never opened a door or crossed a street without his assistance. And he never failed to comment favorably on her appearance.

But there was more to Steve than manners and charm. If it wasn't for his marketing savvy, she wouldn't be where she was today—a rising star with two hit CDs and a third on the way. He had opened doors for her that had allowed her to express her music in ways she'd never dreamed possible.

It was obvious from the limousine waiting at Braxton's employee entrance that this was a very special night indeed. A short while later, when the driver pulled up at the Como Park Conservatory, Merry understood why.

"This is where we met," she said with a knowing grin.

"One year ago tonight." He helped her out of the limousine and up the small flight of stairs leading into the greenhouse. Warm humidity greeted them, a sharp contrast to the dry cold air outside. With the exception of several men in white jackets, the building appeared to be empty.

"Is the place closed?"

"To the public it is," Steve answered, gently guiding her down a narrow walkway lined with red poinsettias.

At the end of the walk was a small table draped in white linen. Red roses, candlelight and silver place settings waited for them. As they took their seats, a violinist strolled in.

"You spoil me," she chastised him gently.

"That's what I'm supposed to do to the woman I'm going to marry," he answered as he filled her glass with champagne.

Automatically Merry's eyes went to the pear-shaped diamond on her left hand. Every time she glanced at the sparkling gem she had to remind herself that this was no dream. She really was engaged to be married to one of the most eligible men in the state.

She sighed and lifted her champagne flute to his. "Everything is so perfect," she said dreamily.

"Almost perfect," he corrected, touching his flute to hers. "It'll only be perfect when the whole world knows you're wearing that ring and we begin to make plans for our wedding."

"It'll all happen. We'll have our engagement party as soon as I get back from California. I promise."

The perfectly white smile faded. "Then you're still planning on going to L.A.?" A frown marred his handsome face.

"I want to tell Holden in person."

"Why? You only see this man once a year at Christmas."

"That's why I have to go. Holden and I have spent every Christmas together since I was nine." Well, almost every one, she amended silently.

The dreamy look in Merry's eyes disappeared. Her relationship with Holden Drake was not a subject she wanted to discuss with her fiancé. Holden had been her best friend when she was growing up, but she knew that even though their relationship had survived twenty years, he was now a part of the past she must leave behind.

Steve sighed. "It's not easy for me to let you go."

"I know. That's why I'll make it a short visit. I'll tell him our news, wish him happy holidays and fly home so we can spend Christmas together."

"A good old-fashioned family Christmas." He smiled at her from across the table, his wonderful, warm smile that made her feel as if she had finally found a place to call home.

It was what she'd wanted all her life. A house filled with people she could call her own. A sense of place. A sense of belonging. She would no longer be one of the lonely souls of this world who found the Christmas season a time of melancholy.

That was why when Steve said, "I'm going to make this the best Christmas you've ever had," she truly believed he would.

"I'M CALLING IT quits. What about you?"

Holden Drake glanced up from the mess of books and papers sprawled across his desk. "Can't. The Manders case goes to court next week, and Mrs. Manders has had a change in heart about accepting the generosity of her soon-to-be ex-husband."

"Does that mean she found out our rock star has been making music offstage with Gina Polina?" Don Fredericks asked as he slipped on his suit coat.

"What it means is more work for me." Holden stretched, his rolled-up shirtsleeves revealing muscular forearms. "Why these Hollywood stars bother to get married is beyond me."

"As my mother would say, don't look a gift horse in the mouth. Their fickle love lives pay our bills," Don reminded him, one hand jingling the change in his pocket.

Holden knew his law partner spoke the truth. If it wasn't for the alimony, palimony and child-support cases of the Hollywood set, he wouldn't be living in a house that overlooked some of the most scenic oceanfront in Southern California.

He'd made a promise to himself when he was a kid growing up in Hibbing, Minnesota, that one day he would live in a place where there was no such thing as a windchill factor. He would have a big fancy house with a couple of fancy cars in the garage and enough fancy clothes to fill two closets.

At thirty-three, he definitely had his share of fancy. A modern spacious home in an exclusive area, a Mercedes convertible and a Land Rover in his garage, tailor-made suits hanging in his closet. He had just about everything a man could want to make him happy. And he was, or at least he was most of the time.

He'd accomplished everything he'd set out to do. He'd earned his law degree and now worked in a partnership with a reputation for winning. He had a comfortable life-style that allowed him to forget he had ever gone to school with shoes that had half the soles missing and worn clothes his classmates recognized as their castoffs. These days, he ate at the best restaurants, vacationed at the finest resorts and left the care of his home to a housekeeper and gardener.

"Before I go, Denise wanted me to ask if you and Shannon are interested in spending next weekend in Tahoe." Don paused in the doorway on his way out of the office.

"There probably won't be a me and Shannon by next weekend," Holden said soberly.

"Uh-oh. What went wrong with this one? I thought you two got along pretty well."

"We did, but she started assuming things are going to happen that aren't."

"You mean like wedding bells?"

Holden leaned back in his chair and sighed. "I don't know what gave her the idea it would ever be a possibility. She's the one who told me that she wasn't looking for anything long-term, that she had her career to think about."

"That's the problem. Look where her career has gone. Nowhere. A couple of bit parts in B movies and a TV commercial."

"Getting married isn't the answer to unemployment." Holden shook his head. "Especially not to someone like me. For Pete's sake, I'm a divorce attorney. I see what marriage does to people."

"You see what *unhappy* marriage does to people," Don corrected.

"Is there any other kind?"

Don chuckled. "Fortunately for us, there are darn few."

Holden rubbed his chin thoughtfully. "You'd think women would be just as disenchanted with the whole marriage scene as men are."

"Not all men are disenchanted."

Holden grimaced. "I hope that doesn't mean you're thinking about walking down the aisle with Denise."

"Diamonds do make great Christmas presents," Don commented with a lift of his brows.

Holden leaned back and folded his arms behind his head. "Maybe around a woman's neck or dangling from her ears. Not on her finger," he said cynically. He leaned forward again and asked, "Are you really serious about Denise?"

"She's a good woman, Holden, and my father always told me that if I ever found a good woman not to let her slip through my fingers."

"Well, tell that good woman of yours I appreciate the invitation, but I'm going to work this weekend."

"Have you made plans for Christmas yet?"

Holden reached for his pen. "I'm glad you reminded me. I better leave a note for Sally to check on my plane reservations."

"Where are you going?"

"London. Merry always complains I work too much when she's here, so I've decided to let her have her way and take a trip this Christmas."

"I thought you said she hated flying."

"She does." Holden smiled. "That's why she only comes out here once a year. But I don't think she'll let a little anxiety keep her from seeing London."

"Are you sure she wouldn't rather be lying on some beach in Martinique or Hawaii?"

"I doubt it. I heard about this hotel in London where they re-create a Dickens Christmas for their guests. Sounds like something Merry would like. Sally offered to make all the arrangements."

"That's because she knows you're a scrooge and would never do it yourself," he quipped. "I'm surprised Merry still spends Christmas with you."

"Old habits are hard to break, I guess." He grinned wryly. "The truth is, we don't have the kind of nostalgic memories most people have of being a kid at Christmas. Neither one of us is particularly sentimental about the holiday."

"Merry must not be if she comes all the way out here to watch you work."

"I don't work on Christmas."

"Holden, you work all the time."

"This year's going to be different. Merry's always wanted to go to London," he reflected wistfully. "I plan on making this Christmas the best one she's ever had. For once, she's going to be happy."

"DO YOU REALLY THINK I'll be able to play it without any mistakes?" The seven-year-old sitting on Merry's piano bench looked up at her teacher with anxiety in her eyes.

"Amber, you're going to play beautifully," Merry said reassuringly, sitting down beside her. "You've played it three times for me and you haven't made a single mistake.''

"But it's easy to play in front of you. You're so nice," the girl said with a shy grin.

Merry slid her arm around her shoulders and gave her a gentle squeeze. "There'll be lots of nice people in that auditorium, and they all want to hear you play 'Silent Night.'"

"Will you be there?"

"Of course. I want to be able to brag to everyone that you're my student," Merry said with an affectionate tug on the child's ponytail. Just then the doorbell rang. "That's probably your dad."

While Amber gathered her sheet music together, Merry went to answer the door. Standing on the stoop was a tall, dark-haired man who smiled at Merry as he came inside. Upon seeing his daughter, he scooped her up into his arms and swung her around in an arc. The young girl giggled as he pressed kisses all over her face.

"Hi, cutiepie. Are you ready to go home?"

"I have to put my boots on first," Amber replied, wriggling out of her father's arms.

Merry watched as the man bent to assist his daughter with her red rubber boots. When he bundled her into her jacket and mittens, Merry couldn't help but admire his gentleness and patience.

"You better let me carry you to the car," he told his daughter. "It's snowing pretty hard and I don't want you to slip and fall on the ice." He lifted her into his arms, thanking Merry for making the time to give Amber the extra lesson.

"'Bye Merry." The young girl waved as she rode out in her dad's arms. "See ya."

"See ya," Merry called back, watching the two as they stepped out into the cold, wintry air. When they were out of sight, she closed the door and leaned against it, wondering if young Amber knew how lucky she was to have a father who loved her.

Merry knew that when Amber played "Silent Night" at the elementary school's Christmas program, her father would be sitting in a front-row seat. And when the program was over and Amber went home, he'd be there to share hot chocolate with her, read her a story and tuck her into bed. He'd plant kisses on her cheeks and tell her how much he loved her.

Merry sighed, wishing she could forget she had a father who hadn't wanted to share anything with his daughter. There'd been no stories at bedtime, no arms to swing her in the air, no hugs and kisses. Her father had never attended a recital or heard her play the piano at all.

For her father had packed up and left when she was only nine. Doubting that he was her father, he'd gone without so much as a goodbye and become lost to her forever.

She shook her head, not wanting to give in to the self-pity that threatened to settle on her whenever she thought about her father. She would *not* think about him. After twenty years of practice, she'd become very good at not thinking about him. Except at Christmastime. Then he had a way of sneaking into her thoughts.

But not this Christmas, she vowed as she turned off the light on the piano and lowered the fallboard. Finally she was going to leave the past behind and start a new life.

There was no place for memories of her childhood, which was why she'd finally redecorated her small town house in September. Gone was the furniture she'd brought with her when she'd moved from Hibbing to the city. Instead of Rosie's sturdy sofa, which had a slipcover to hide the worn spots, a creamy white-leather sectional graced her living room. Gone, too, were the scratched and nicked pine end tables, replaced by wrought-iron and glass. Even the old upright piano had been replaced by a shiny black Steinway.

There was one final connection to her past she needed to break. Holden. She needed to say goodbye to him. Steve didn't understand why she had to go see him in person, but then, her fiancé knew little of her past. He didn't know that since she was nine years old, Holden had been the only person she could ever rely on. Just because they lived in different parts of the country now didn't absolve her from the promise she'd made to her foster mother—that she would always try to be with Holden at Christmas.

It was a promise that had resulted from the one Christmas they had spent apart. It was a long time ago, when she was only fifteen and Holden was nineteen.

Because Rosie hadn't been feeling well, Merry had done everything she could to make Holden's return from his first semester of college extra special. Besides going to school, working part-time at the dry cleaners and helping Mrs. Anderson with her piano students, she had found time not only to bake Holden's favorite Christmas cookies, but to make him a leather jacket.

It hadn't been easy working with the supple leather, but Rosie, with her never-ending abundance of patience, had guided her through all the difficult stages until the jacket looked as good as any in the stores. It was a true labor of love. She had X'ed off the days on the calendar with a red pen, anxiously waiting for him to return. She was doubly excited, because when he'd been home Thanksgiving weekend, he'd kissed her— *really* kissed her—for the first time. Now maybe he would do it again....

But Holden didn't come home that Christmas. The only other people sitting at Rosie's dining room table were the local minister and his wife. At the last minute, Holden had decided to spend the holidays with a girl named Susie Halvorson who lived in Wisconsin, hundreds of miles from the small town of Hibbing, Minnesota.

When Holden finally did show up several days later, Merry refused to give him the jacket. He never would've learned of its existence had it not been for Rosie. He apologized profusely and said it had been a mistake to spend Christmas with Susie. She was already history, just like all the girls before her.

Merry gave him the jacket, but it was a while before she forgave him. Any romantic notions she had about Holden disappeared, however. She knew then that the kissing they'd done only a month before had nothing to do with love; he'd just been teaching her how to kiss, that was all. She didn't care if he ever came home for Christmas again.

But he *had* come home, and before Rosie died, she made Holden and Merry promise that as long as they were single, they would always try to spend Christmas together.

That was the true reason she was going to California. She had made a promise to Rosie, and if there was one thing her foster mother had taught her, it was to always keep her promises.

"YOUR FLIGHT'S been delayed an hour," Steve told Merry as they waited at the departure gate at the Minneapolis–St. Paul International Airport.

Already tense, she took a deep breath. "I hate it when this happens."

He reached for her fingers in reassurance. "It's not a problem with the plane. Apparently there's congestion at the Los Angeles end. Maybe we should have a drink in the lounge?"

She shook her head. "No, it's all right."

"I wish I could come with you. I'd hold your hand for the entire flight." He patted that hand now as if she were a child.

"You're needed at the station," Merry said. "Besides, I've made this trip before. You don't need to worry about me."

He gave her shoulder a gentle squeeze. "How can I not worry when the woman I love is flying halfway across the country by herself?"

"Women fly all over the world by themselves, Steve," she reminded him.

"Not *my* woman," he stated.

Normally she found his possessiveness gratifying; it gave her a sense of security. Today she found it irritating; a fact she attributed to her preflight jitters.

"I still don't see why you have to go all the way out there to see Holden when you could just as easily call him." There was a hint of impatience in his tone.

"He's expecting me for Christmas. I can't just call and say I'm not coming."

"You could invite him to come spend the holidays here."

"He wouldn't come. He hates Minnesota winters."

Steve sighed and lifted her fingers to his lips. "I can't help being selfish when it comes to you. I don't want to share you with another man even if it *is* someone who's like a brother to you. *I* want to be your family."

Merry wanted that, too. All her life she'd wanted to be a part of a real family. Now Steve was finally giving her that opportunity.

She studied his handsome face. He was everything a woman could want—solid, dependable, a successful television personality and a respected community leader. She reached up to smooth a worry line from his forehead. "Please understand. I can't do this over the telephone."

A smile spread slowly across his face. "All right, since I'm going to have you for Christmas, I guess I can let you go for a few days now."

"Thank you." Merry smiled and listened as Steve told her stories of the Austin-family holiday traditions. She wondered if he knew how fortunate he was to have a family to share in those memories. Even though his wife had died several years ago, his three grown children were still a big part of his life. Merry's Christmas memories, on the other hand, were populated with an assortment of people who had come and gone. Apart from Rosie, there was only one person who'd been a regular in those memories, and that was Holden.

For of all of the children who'd been in Rosie's foster care, he was the only one she'd kept in contact with over the years. He was the only friend left from a childhood that had little opportunity for close relationships. He understood her anxiety over the holiday season, because Christmas for him had been just as lonely. But Merry didn't want to think about the lonely Christmases anymore. They were over. Gone for good. She had Steve now. Steady, reliable, faithful Steve. Soon she would have stepdaughters and a stepson, cousins and aunts and uncles. Her future was bright.

As for Holden...well, he'd be fine. He'd never been sentimental about Christmas. He had taken her under his wing whenever she needed to lean on him, but deep in his heart she knew he wanted to fly alone.

So why was she nervous about telling him she was getting married? she asked herself as she boarded the plane. It was a question for which she knew the answer. Even though they had drifted apart, she still wanted Holden's approval. And that was something she knew she shouldn't expect.

No, he would never approve of her engagement. Holden didn't believe in marriage.

CHAPTER TWO

RELIEVED TO HAVE both feet on solid ground again, Merry didn't mind having to make her way to the baggage-claim area alone. On every other occasion, Holden had been there to steer her through the busy corridors. He was the one who always saw that her luggage was retrieved from the moving conveyer belts and stowed in the trunk of his car.

Not this time. This visit was a surprise. Had she called ahead, Holden more than likely would have sensed her anxiety. Since the day they'd met as children in Rosie's foster care, he'd had an uncanny ability to know when something was troubling her.

The subject of this visit was troubling her now and had been ever since she'd accepted Steve's proposal. She knew the time would come when she would have to tell Holden she was getting married.

She felt like a schoolgirl going home to tell her father she had met a boy, which was absurd. Holden wasn't her father or even her brother, yet his opinion was important to her.

That was probably because when she was a teenager Holden had always found something wrong with her boyfriends. Well, he wouldn't find anything wrong this time. How could he?

As the taxi stopped at the iron gates at the entrance of the exclusive housing development known as Eagle's Ridge, Merry rolled down her window and gave the security guard her name.

"Ms. Mattson. I wasn't expecting to see you for a couple of weeks."

"I thought I'd come early and surprise Holden," she answered.

Within seconds, the gates parted and the taxi followed the winding paved road lined with ornately sculpted shrubbery.

As many times as Merry had seen Holden's home, she couldn't help but feel a bit awed by its size and its elegance. Overlooking the ocean, it sat on a hill, a white wonder of modern architecture glowing in an aura of floodlights.

Actually it was too modern for her taste. She loved old homes, like Rosie's farmhouse in Hibbing. Houses with character and warm feelings and familiar aromas. Houses with a history.

Holden hated anything old. He refused even to step into an antique store. To him, old meant poor, and there was no way she could convince him otherwise.

As the taxi pulled up in the circular drive, a heavyset, fiftyish, bespectacled woman wearing an apron over her dress opened the front door. "Merry! What a lovely surprise!"

"Hi, Theresa. It's good to see you. Is Holden here?" she asked the housekeeper as the taxi driver lifted her luggage from the trunk.

"Good heavens, no!" Theresa helped Merry with her bags. "He's working. He seldom gets home before ten or eleven at night. Besides, he's not expecting you for another couple of weeks. Nothing's wrong, is it?''

"No, as a matter of fact, everything's right." Merry followed her into the tiled entryway. "Something smells good."

"Just the usual holiday goodies," Theresa said, hanging Merry's coat in the closet. "Let's put your things away and then I'll fix you something to eat," she said, urging Merry toward the guest wing.

"Are you expecting Holden for dinner?"

"Not tonight, but I can make you something."

"That's not necessary. I ate on the plane."

As the woman led Merry through the beautifully furnished home, she gently chastised her. "You should have called. I would have gotten some fresh flowers."

"It's all right," Merry answered, stepping into the bedroom she always used when she visited. The furniture and carpeting was off-white, and the bedspread had a bold geometric design in white, green and yellow. "Being able to have the windows open will be all the freshness I need," she told the housekeeper as she walked over to the patio door leading to a wooden balcony.

"What I want to know is why you stay in that cold weather when you could live here."

Merry knew that native Californians like Theresa and her husband Bill, would never leave sunshine and warm temperatures for a frigid climate like Minnesota's. She opened the sliding glass door. "This is nice," she said, inhaling the clean smell of the ocean as she stepped outside.

Theresa rubbed her arms and shivered. "It's chilly. Come in or you'll catch a cold." Merry did as she was told and Theresa said, "You still haven't told me why you're here early."

Merry draped her right arm around the older woman's shoulder and held her left hand in front of her face. "Look."

"Ohhh!" the older warmed gushed as she admired the engagement ring. "It's beautiful. Does it mean what I think it means?"

Merry nodded. "I'm getting married."

Theresa hugged her. "Who's the lucky fellow?"

"His name is Steve Austin and he's a wonderful man. I think you'll like him."

"I'm sure I will." She grinned. "So this is why you came to California—to tell Holden you're getting married."

Merry nodded anxiously. "And to deliver my Christmas presents in person."

Theresa's face fell. "You're not coming home for the holidays?"

She wanted to tell the housekeeper that although Holden called California home, her home was Minnesota. "Steve wants me to spend the holidays with him."

Theresa quickly replaced her frown with a smile. "Of course he does. And you should spend Christmas with your fiancé, but I have to tell you, Holden will be disappointed."

Merry felt a stab of guilt. "It's not like we ever did anything special to celebrate Christmas. He usually ends up working on some important case, and I sit alone at the piano, practicing my music."

"That's been true in other years, but..." The housekeeper didn't finish her sentence. "At least you're here now. That's what counts."

"You and Bill will be spending Christmas with Holden, won't you?"

Theresa didn't give her a direct answer, but simply said, "Don't you worry about Holden. He'll be fine. Now tell me about your music. I hear you're becoming quite famous back in Minnesota."

Merry smiled. "Not exactly famous, but I've been getting good reviews and my CDs are selling well."

"I can't tell you how often I hear Holden playing your music," she said, adjusting a tie on one of the drapes. "He listens to it late into the night. Says it soothes him."

Merry felt a delicious warmth spread through her. Holden had always encouraged her to follow her instincts when it came to music. He was the one who'd bought her her very first piano—an old upright he'd found in an estate sale. He'd bought it because it had been painted yellow, the perfect color for someone with a name like Merry, he said. He'd also helped her pay her tuition when she'd wanted to study music at the university.

"I hope you'll play for me while you're here." Theresa looked expectantly at Merry.

"I'd love to. I've written a couple of new songs that are going to be on my next CD. I'll let you be my test audience."

"I'd like that. But first you need to settle in," Theresa said, hanging Merry's garment bag in the closet. "Do you have anything in your suitcase that needs pressing?"

"No, I'll be fine. You carry on with your baking," Merry insisted, uncomfortable with the thought of anyone waiting on her.

"Oh, I've finished for the day. But if you're sure you don't need me, Bill and I were planning to go out for the evening ..."

"Go ahead. I don't need to be entertained."

"Well, if you're hungry, you can help yourself to some of the goodies I've baked for Holden."

Fondly Merry watched her go, then looked about the beautifully furnished room. It was a long way from the farmhouse where she and Holden had spent their youth.

With its white four-poster bed, matching armoire and ensuite bathroom, the room made her feel as if she were in an elegant hotel. It had all the luxuries and conveniences money could buy, yet Merry would have preferred to be in the second-floor bedroom at Rosie's with its rag rugs and patchwork quilts.

Every time she visited Holden, she wondered what Rosie would have said about his dream home if she'd had the opportunity to visit it. Actually, she had a pretty good idea what their foster mother would have said. "Bigger and fancier doesn't necessarily mean better." It was what Rosie had often told Holden when, as a boy, he would speak enviously of his more affluent classmates.

As Merry washed up at the sink with its gold-plated faucets she remembered how every fixture in Rosie's bathroom had been old and cracked and the linoleum floor cold. There was no brightly lit mirror or vanity, just a solitary bulb that hung over the mirrored medicine chest above the rust-stained sink. Holden often complained about how long it took for the hot water to reach the bathroom on the second floor of the farmhouse.

One thing Rosie's bathroom did have was the best-smelling hand lotion in all of Hibbing. Merry would make extra trips to the sink just so she could rub her hands with the creamy lotion, which smelled like a meadow of wildflowers.

Now she glanced around automatically for a lotion dispenser. Sure enough, sitting on top of the marble vanity, was an exquisitely crafted glass decanter with a pump. Merry removed the diamond ring from her finger and smoothed the satiny lotion on her hands. It smelled like an expensive perfume, not wildflowers.

She unpacked her suitcase, then wandered through corridors filled with contemporary art until she reached the kitchen. Theresa had left a plate of cookies out for her. She was about to make herself a cup of tea when she heard the phone ring in Holden's study. She hurried to the walnut-paneled room, but before she could reach the extension on the large oak desk, the answering machine was activated.

Holden's recorded message began. Merry intended to be out of the room with the door closed before the caller had a chance to leave a message, but before she knew it, the beep sounded, followed by a woman's voice.

"Holden, it's Shannon. If you won't take my calls at the office, I'm going to keep calling you at home until you speak to me. It can't be over between us. It just can't. Please don't let it end this way." There was a dramatic pause, then an emotional, tear-laden plea. "Call me. Please."

Merry sighed. Another one of Holden's casualties. Nothing had changed. At thirty-three, he was still playing the field, refusing to commit to anyone, breaking hearts along the way. She wondered about who he'd dismissed from his life this time, because it was obvious he had.

Seeking an answer, Merry scanned the bookshelves and walls for perhaps a framed photograph, but found none. The only ones in sight were on the desk. One was her high school graduation picture, the other a silver-framed snapshot of Rosie.

Merry lifted the silver frame and gazed at her foster mother. She remembered the day it had been taken. Holden had rented the banquet room of the largest restaurant in Hibbing and invited nearly everyone in town to celebrate Rosie's sixty-fifth birthday. It was the last time the three of them had been together. Rosie had died the following spring, just a week after Merry's graduation from college.

Merry had thought nothing would ever hurt as badly as the pain she'd suffered when, at the tender age of ten, she'd learned of her mother's death. She was wrong. Losing Rosie was just as great a loss, for that dear, loving woman, along with Holden, had been one of her anchors. With her death, there was only Holden, who was two thousand miles away in California.

To fill the void in her life, Merry had applied for a foster-care license, hoping to follow in Rosie's footsteps and give to other children some of what she had received. Only, for Merry, foster parenting had been a horrible failure. As good as her intentions were, she couldn't do what Rosie had done. She didn't have the patience or the understanding to create a haven for troubled children. Instead of finding comfort in foster parenting, she had found painful reminders of her own childhood. Yet she couldn't ignore her desire to help children.

Instead of parenting, she turned to teaching, giving piano lessons to children in her home, as well as at school. It wasn't as great a contribution as Rosie had made, but at least it provided contact with children. Merry knew Rosie would have been pleased that she was sharing her music with others.

Of course that was all going to change when she married Steve. He wanted her to focus on her recording career, not waste valuable time teaching.

The sound of the front door opening had Merry hurrying out of the study. As she passed a window she noticed a red Mercedes convertible parked in front of the garage. Holden was home.

By the time she reached the foyer, he was inside, briefcase in one hand, a stack of mail in the other. It had been a year since she'd seen him, and now his hair was longer in the back and he had grown a thick dark mustache.

Merry was immediately swamped with memories. This was Holden, the one person who'd always been there for her through all the dark days in foster care, the man who'd taught her how to kiss, the man she had at one time fantasized would be her husband. Was it any wonder she felt a little breathless upon seeing him?

"Hi," she said almost shyly.

When he saw her, his scowl changed to a look of bemusement. "What are you doing here?"

"Is that any way to greet someone who's come two thousand miles to see you?" Her chastisement was softened with a smile.

He set his briefcase down and opened his arms. She didn't hesitate to go into them. He squeezed her tightly, then said, "It's good to see you." He held her at arm's length and looked her over from head to toe. "You look great."

"Thank you. So do you." Which was true. When she was away from him she tended to forget how handsome he was. She reached up to tweak his mustache. "This is new."

"Makes me look more sinister in court," he said dryly. Merry thought it made him look more rugged and briefly wondered how he would look with a cowboy hat on his head. "You seem tired," she remarked, noticing the tiny circles under his eyes.

He loosened his Windsor-knotted tie. "I am tired. This is always a busy time of year for me. Everyone wants to start the new year with a clean slate. You know, off with the old spouse, on with the new." He hooked his arm through hers and led her to the living room.

"Is that what happened to Shannon?" she couldn't resist asking.

"How do you know about Shannon?"

"I didn't mean to eavesdrop, but I couldn't help overhearing a message that was left on your answering machine," she explained. "I'm sorry."

"There's no need to apologize."

"After you hear her message, you'll know why I feel uncomfortable. She sounded upset."

He made a sound of derision. "Before you go rushing to her defense—"

She cut him off before he could finish. "I wasn't going to rush to her defense."

"Good, because the woman knew what she was doing, believe me." He went over to the bar. "Can I get you something to drink?"

"I was going to have some tea, but I'll have a glass of white wine if you're going to have something," Merry answered, taking a seat on the leather sofa while he poured their drinks.

Out of the corner of his eye Holden saw her fold her slender legs beneath her as she sat on the couch. Her dark hair fell in gentle waves down to her shoulders, framing what he'd always thought was one of the most beautiful faces he'd ever seen. As usual, whenever he saw Merry, he had the urge to take care of her.

"Are you cold?" he asked. "I can get you one of Theresa's lap robes." He handed her a long-stemmed crystal glass half-filled with white wine.

"No, I'm fine." She took a sip of the wine, then said, "I know you don't want to hear this, but your Shannon sounded hurt."

"She's not my Shannon and you can save your sympathy," he said as he sat down beside her. "She's an actress. She's good at pretending."

"So how long did this one last?"

"I don't know. Six, maybe seven months."

"That's longer than most of them. What happened?"

"Nothing happened."

"I guess not, otherwise you wouldn't be talking about her in the past tense. Did she break cardinal rule number one?"

"Which is?"

"Never assume there's going to be a tomorrow."

He grinned. "You know me well, don't you?"

Merry did, which was why a long time ago she had given up any foolish fantasy that he would ever be anything more to her than the dear friend who'd shared her childhood.

"I wish you weren't such a cynic when it comes to marriage," she said.

"I'm not a cynic. I'm a realist. The reality of marriage is that it can get ugly. And whether or not we agree on this point, it *is* true there are women out there whose goal in life is to trap a man."

Merry practically choked on her wine. "Holden, marriage isn't some evil plot to rob men of their masculinity."

"It's not my masculinity I worry about. It's my checkbook."

She clicked her tongue. "And you wonder why I think you're a cynic. Didn't you explain the rules to Shannon before you began seeing her?"

He chuckled sardonically. "Of course I did. You know me better than to ask that."

"Maybe she thought you'd fall in love with her and ignore the rules," she proposed with a lift of one delicately arched eyebrow.

"Love will never make a fool of me," he said, raising his glass as if in a toast. There was censure in her eyes, and he reached over to squeeze her hand gently.

"You didn't come all the way out here to discuss my love life."

"No, I came to discuss mine," she said evenly, running her finger around the rim of the wineglass.

"Uh-oh. Must be serious if it couldn't wait until Christmas."

"It is." She kept her eyes on her glass, avoiding his curious gaze. "I have something important I need to tell you."

Just then the phone rang. If he hadn't been expecting the call from overseas, he would have let his answering machine pick it up. He knew that for Merry to fly out to see him meant that the relationship she was in must be serious.

"Hold the thought," he said. "I'll be right back." He hurried to his study.

He spent as little time on the phone as possible, then quickly returned to the living room. Merry wasn't curled up on the couch now, but by the window staring out at the darkness. When she caught his reflection in the glass, she turned around.

"You're scowling. It must have been bad news," she commented. As usual, whenever she spoke, the huskiness of her voice made him feel as if he were her number-one concern in life.

"A case I have is getting uglier by the minute." He scraped his fingers through his hair.

"Do you want to talk about it?"

He knew she was one woman he *could* talk to. There'd been a time when he had confided in her. She knew things about his past no one else would ever know. But with his move to California they had eventually lost the closeness and rapport they'd shared when they were young, and as much as he wanted to regain them, he was reluctant to bare his soul to her.

"No, I don't want to talk about work. I want to hear why you flew all the way out here now when you're going to be coming in a couple of weeks for Christmas."

She turned away from him and stared once more at the ocean. "I'm not coming out for Christmas."

There was a heartbeat of silence, then he said, "Why not? Are you working?"

"No. I've made other plans."

"With this new boyfriend?"

Finally she turned and looked at him. "He's not just a boyfriend, Holden. He's my fiancé. I'm getting married."

The news hit him like a ton of bricks. He could feel the muscles in his jaw tighten. "You're not wearing a ring."

She looked down at her fingers. "I must have left it in the washroom."

"Then this isn't a joke?"

"No. Why would I joke about something like marriage?"

He could see by the expression on her face that she was serious. Disappointment ricocheted through him.

He shook his head as if he could deny what he had heard. "I can't believe you want to get married."

"Why not? It's what most women want at some point in their lives."

"You're not most women, Merry. You've always said you were never going to get married. 'Never ever,' I think, were your exact words."

"I said that when I was nine years old," she protested.

"And when you were ten and eleven and twelve and I think every successive year up to and including your senior year in college. Have you forgotten saying to me, 'Holden, if I ever tell you I'm getting married, you'll know I've gone crazy, so lock me up and throw away the key.'"

She made a sound of exasperation. "I didn't mean it."

"No? You sure had me fooled."

"People change, Holden. When I was younger I didn't think I ever would get married. That was before I met Steve."

"Steve?" He raised an eyebrow.

"Steve Austin. He's a wonderful man."

"What does this wonderful man do for a living?"

"He's in television."

"He's not an *actor?*" Holden asked in horror.

"No, he works for cable TV. If you've ever watched the shopping channel, you might have seen him. He's one of their most popular hosts."

"Am I supposed to be impressed?" Holden couldn't keep the undertone of sarcasm from his voice.

"He's a good man. He's honest and compassionate and considerate of my feelings." She tucked a strand of wavy hair behind her ear. Again her vulnerability touched him. She was too trusting a person, too good-hearted. She always had been, and just as he had while they were growing up, he felt the need to make sure no one took advantage of her.

"How long have you known him?" he asked.

"Long enough to know he's the right man for me." She had folded her arms across her chest and stood facing him in a defiant stance.

"Are you sure?"

"Yes."

He had always trusted his gut reactions, and right now his gut was telling him she was making a mistake. In all his years he had yet to meet a man who was good enough for Merry. He felt certain this Austin character wasn't, either.

A shopping-channel personality? The thought made the contents of his stomach curdle. No doubt the guy was a great salesman. He must have sold her some cock and bull story that made her want to forget the reasons she should avoid marriage.

"How much do you know about this guy, anyway?" he asked.

"Enough to know he wouldn't hurt me. He's a decent, honest, hardworking man."

"Then you've had him checked out?"

"No!" she replied indignantly. "He's a well-respected member of the community. I don't need to check him out."

"Merry, I advise all my clients to investigate the backgrounds of prospective spouses."

"I'm not your client," she reminded him.

"No, you're my friend and I don't want to see you get hurt."

"I am not going to get hurt."

"Not if I can help it," he told her, then finished his drink with one gulp.

"What's that supposed to mean?"

"If you're really serious about this guy, I'll have him investigated."

"You will do no such thing!"

"Why? Are you worried I'll find something?"

"I know you won't find anything because you're not going to look. Holden, we're not kids in Rosie's care anymore. I don't need you to look out for me."

He wanted to believe her, but all he could think of was the many times she *had* needed him. On more than one occasion, he had played the big brother and chased away unwanted suitors.

"Everything's perfect with Steve. Can't you be happy for me?" Her brown eyes pleaded with his for understanding, and he felt caught in a trap.

"You know how I feel about marriage, Merry."

"Yes, and just because you're cynical about it doesn't mean I have to be."

Nothing had changed. She was just as trusting as she'd been as a child. When she looked at him with those big, brown innocent eyes, he found it difficult to argue with her. "Background searches are becoming routine."

"Maybe in California, but not in Minnesota."

"The investigation would be discreet. He wouldn't know about it."

"No," she said adamantly.

"If you're not going to listen to me when I speak as your friend, at least listen to me when I speak as your attorney."

"You're not my attorney," she reminded him. "Tom Harvey gives me more than enough advice."

Again the phone rang and Holden went to answer it. When he returned just moments later, he wore a frown. "They're holding. This call is going to take a while."

"It's just as well. I'm tired. I think I'll go to bed," she said on a weary note, setting her wineglass on the bar.

"Think about what I said. Promise me you'll do that?"

She nodded, then hurried out of the room calling over her shoulder, "I'll see you in the morning."

But Merry didn't see him in the morning. By the time she'd showered and dressed, Holden had left. Theresa told her he had an early appointment and would be home for lunch.

"He said to expect him around twelve-thirty." The housekeeper set a bowl of fresh fruit in front of Merry. "Can I get you something else to go with that?"

"No, this is fine. Why don't you join me?"

"I'd like that." Just as she was about to sit down, the doorbell rang.

"I'll be right back." Theresa wiped her hands on her apron and hurried out of the dining room. When she returned, she carried a long, oblong-shaped package.

"I usually open all Holden's deliveries, but I'm not sure about this one," she told Merry, eyeing the package suspiciously. "It has a terrible odor."

"Who's it from?"

"There's no return address."

Merry examined the box, wrinkling her nose. "You're right. It does smell." She shook the package. "You'd think that if it was an early Christmas present someone would have at least put a return address on it."

"You think I should open it?"

Merry shrugged. "It doesn't say 'personal,' does it?"

The housekeeper shook her head. "I'll get some scissors."

The longer the package sat on the dining room table, the stronger the odor became. By the time Theresa returned, the air had become quite rank.

"Do you suppose someone sent food that should have been refrigerated?" Merry asked as Theresa slit the packaging tape.

"I don't know, but I think we should be wearing gas masks," the housekeeper said with a grimace.

It was obvious that the package hadn't come from a department store or mail-order company. The box had been pieced together with masking tape. When Theresa lifted the makeshift lid, she gasped. "Ooo-eee! No wonder it smells. Look."

Merry craned her neck to peek inside. Resting in a bed of shredded newspaper was a dead mackerel. She quickly covered her nose with her hand. "That's disgusting."

Theresa scooped up the package, wrapping and all, and hurried away. She returned with a can of room deodorizer and a square of white paper.

"Here's what was inside." She handed the card to Merry, then sprayed air freshener around the room.

"'One rotten one won't spoil my life,'" Merry read aloud. "It's signed 'Shannon.'"

"She's Holden's old girlfriend. I guess some women just won't take no for an answer." Theresa clicked her tongue. "The nerve of that girl."

"Have you met her?" Merry asked.

"Oh, yes." Theresa sat down to pour a cup of tea. "She's been to the house quite a few times."

"You sound as if you didn't like her."

"You know, it's none of my business who Holden dates, but between you and me, I'm happy he broke it off. She had visions of running the place, that one."

"Then obviously she didn't know Holden very well, did she?" Merry shared a knowing grin with the housekeeper. "What did she look like?"

"She reminded me of a Barbie doll. Blond, tan, lots of accessories."

Merry shook her head. "What is it with Holden and blondes?" she mused aloud. "I can't remember him ever dating a brunette."

Theresa shrugged. "I don't know why he picks any of them. They never seem to last."

Merry stabbed a piece of melon with her fork. "I think he deliberately chooses the type he knows won't last. He doesn't want a serious relationship."

"Well, I was starting to wonder about this one. She was getting awfully comfy around here. Using his exercise room, cooking in the kitchen, playing the piano."

That had Merry's cup pausing in midair. "Holden let her play my piano?" Although Merry knew it wasn't technically her piano, Holden had told her he only bought it for Merry to play when she visited him.

"She wasn't any good." Theresa chuckled derisively. "It's no wonder she hasn't made it in show business. She can't sing worth beans." Theresa took a sip of her tea, then said, "No, it's a good thing she's gone. She was no good for Holden."

A sentiment Holden echoed when he came home for lunch and Theresa showed him the rotting mackerel.

"You have no right to question my judgment in men when you get dead fish from the women you date," Merry told him over lunch.

"I only dated her. Just think what she would have done had we been married and split up," he remarked dryly.

"I told you she sounded hurt," Merry reminded him. "You should be nicer to women, Holden."

"Just because I don't make lifelong commitments to them doesn't mean I treat them badly," he argued, taking a second helping of Theresa's chicken salad.

"You're cynical about relationships," she told him. "You have been ever since I can remember."

"There's a difference between being cynical and being cautious."

"Is that what you call your attitude?" she asked in disbelief. "Cautious?"

"I'm a realist, Merry. You're a romantic. We're never going to agree on the subject of relationships," he stated practically. He broke a whole-wheat roll in two, then spread both pieces with butter. "Why don't we change the subject? I didn't come home for lunch so that we could argue."

"Good, because I don't want to argue with you, either. I was hoping we could do something fun while I'm here."

He wiped his hands on his napkin, then pulled two tickets from his pocket and slid them in her direction. "Is this the kind of fun you're thinking of?"

She reached for the tickets. They were for a performance of *Rigoletto* that evening. The gesture tugged at her heartstrings. "The last time you took me to the opera was my twenty-first birthday."

"Then it's time I took you again."

"Since when do *you* consider the opera fun?"

"I know how much you love Verdi."

"And you approve of the message in *Rigoletto*," she stated with irony.

He grinned and Merry's pulse skittered. "There are times when women need to be protected by men."

"My engagement to Steve isn't one of those times," she told him.

He shrugged. "Maybe not."

"I wish I could believe you meant that."

"Haven't I always encouraged you to stand on your own two feet?" he asked, shooting her a look that sent a funny little quiver through her body. "So, do you want to go to the opera or don't you?"

"Yes."

She couldn't prevent the rush of warmth that spread through her as he continued to gaze into her eyes. She'd forgotten how blue his eyes were.

"Tell me how you managed to get tickets at such a late date," she said, breaking eye contact.

"I have a client involved in the production. If you tell me how long you're going to stay, I can probably rustle up a couple of tickets for one of the holiday concerts in the area, as well."

"I won't have time for anything else. I can only stay until tomorrow," Merry said regretfully. "I was lucky I managed to get time off to come at all. It *is* the Christmas season."

They talked about her career for the rest of lunch. Merry thought she was going to get a reprieve from discussing her engagement. But as Holden finished his coffee he asked, "Have you thought about what I said last night?"

"Yes, and I appreciate your concern, but it's unnecessary."

"I think my concern is justified. This all happened rather suddenly, didn't it?"

She sighed. "Not really. I've known Steve for a year, Holden, and I do know what I'm doing."

He didn't argue that point. Merry got up to retrieve a brightly wrapped package sitting on the sideboard. It was her Christmas present to him.

Holden didn't open it right away but said, "I haven't gotten anything for you yet. I wasn't expecting you—"

"I know, I know. It's okay." She gestured at the package. "Open it."

He broke the ribbon and ripped away the paper. Inside the box was a cream-colored Irish-knit sweater. "It's nice. I'll think of you whenever I wear it," he told her, giving her a look that made her insides tingle. "Christmas isn't going to be the same without you."

"I know. It's going to feel a bit strange not to be here." She tried to ignore the tug on her emotions. "You should be happy. You can work to your heart's content."

"I don't want to work."

"Since when? Every year it's the same old thing, Holden. You put in your obligatory time with me, then you retreat to your study." She reached for the discarded wrapping paper and ribbon, squeezing them into a ball.

"Did you ever think I might have something special planned for this year?"

She eyed him dubiously.

"No, why would I when for years you've complained about how commercial the holiday's become?"

He snapped open his briefcase and shuffled around a few papers. "I still think that way, but I feel the same way you do about not having you here—strange. We've celebrated every Christmas together for the past twenty years."

"All except one," she reminded him.

"Yes, and we know how *that* turned out," he said soberly.

"I wasn't the one who stayed away," she reminded him.

He held her gaze. "I couldn't come home that Christmas, Merry, and you know why."

She was the one to look away first. "I wouldn't have thrown myself at you if that's what you were worried about. All you had to do was say something to Rosie."

"Like what? Merry thinks I'm in love with her because I taught her how to kiss?"

"It would have been less embarrassing. You could have written to me and let me down gently. At least then I wouldn't have made that stupid jacket for you." She tried to treat the subject lightly, but deep down inside she knew it was a wound that would always need a dab of emotional salve now and then.

"I liked that jacket."

She gave him a look that said she didn't believe him.

"I did. I still have it."

Again she looked at him dubiously.

"Ask Theresa," he said.

Merry didn't want to think about the jacket or the Christmas he hadn't come home to Rosie's, although she knew she would never forget, either.

"I guess now that you're engaged it means our promise to Rosie's been fulfilled," he commented thoughtfully.

"I'm not married yet. We don't have to spend this Christmas apart," she told him. "You could come to Minnesota."

"No way," he answered immediately.

"Why not?"

"Because I've already made plans for Christmas," he answered. "I thought those plans included you."

The fact that he could make her feel guilty angered her. "Well, I'm sorry, but I don't want to come out here, eat a nice dinner, then watch you retreat to your study and leave me alone to work on my music. That's not in my plans."

"It won't be that way, I promise."

"I know it won't because I'm not coming," she said stubbornly.

He snapped his briefcase shut and said, "Then I guess we'll break with tradition this year." He glanced at his watch, then stood and said in a businesslike tone, "I have to get back to the office."

"Holden, wait." She followed him out to the foyer. It annoyed her that he could so easily dismiss spending the holiday with her. Now that she was here in California, she realized that unless they spent this last Christmas together, she wouldn't be able to make a clean break with the past.

"I wish you'd at least think about coming home for Christmas," she pleaded with him.

"Merry, this is my home," he reminded her.

"You know what I mean."

"All right, I'll think about it," he told her, pulling on his suit jacket. He would have left without another word, but Merry stopped him.

"What time should I be ready for the opera?"

"I'll pick you up at seven," he told her, then hurried out the door, leaving her to stew over their unresolved conflict.

All afternoon she thought of things she could say to get Holden to come spend the holidays in Minneapolis. She knew none of them would work.

Rigoletto was everything Merry expected. Yet halfway through the performance she suggested they leave, knowing perfectly well that Holden was bored. He refused her offer.

Later they dined at an elegant restaurant frequented by Hollywood celebrities. On the way to their table, Holden stopped to shake hands with more than one well-known actor. Although Merry felt a little starstruck, Holden seemed indifferent to the fact that they were surrounded by the rich and famous.

No mention was made of Merry's engagement, and she was pleasantly surprised to discover how much she enjoyed their evening together. She didn't want to see it end, but as soon as they arrived back at Holden's, he took off his suit coat and rolled up his shirtsleeves.

"Are you going to work tonight?" she asked when he opened his briefcase and pulled out several manila folders.

He wriggled his eyebrows. "No rest for the cynical. What time do you have to leave for the airport tomorrow?"

"Not until four-thirty, but I can take a taxi," she said quickly.

"You're not taking a taxi," he replied in no uncertain terms. "I have to be in court tomorrow morning, but I'll be here in time to take you."

"Holden, I'd like to go home knowing that you're happy for me," she said, broaching the subject of her engagement as carefully as she could.

"But I'm not happy, Merry. I worry that you may be making a mistake."

She threw up her hands in frustration. "I knew you'd react like this."

"Then why did you come?"

"Good question." She turned away from him, but he grabbed her by the shoulders and turned her back around to face him.

"I can't pretend I'm pleased when I'm not," he told her, his gaze pinning hers.

"You don't even know the man. Why do you think it's not going to work?"

"Because you're like me—career-minded. You need to be able to throw yourself into your work without worrying about anyone else."

"No, what I need is a chance to have a real family. It's what I've always wanted. You know that. And now I've finally met a man who's giving me that chance, and you won't even try to understand."

He sighed and raked a hand through his hair. "How much does this Steve know about your past?"

"Enough. Why?"

"Have you told him about your family?"

She lowered her eyes. "I don't have any family."

"You're not an orphan, Merry."

"As far as I'm concerned I am." She wished he wouldn't talk about the past. She'd worked hard at forgetting the ugly details of her childhood, and now here he was stirring up emotions she didn't want to feel. "He knows my mother died. He doesn't need to know she was an alcoholic who froze to death on one of her binges."

"And your father?"

"I told him he's dead, too." She couldn't meet his eyes. "It's probably true, anyway. Besides, it doesn't matter. Steve is my family now," she stated confidently.

"He isn't until you're legally married to him."

"And that will happen soon."

"We'll see," he said cryptically.

"I'm warning you, Holden. If you do anything to ruin my chance for happiness, I'll never forgive you."

He sighed. "I can't pretend that I think you're doing the right thing."

"Then don't pretend. Trust me. I *am* doing the right thing."

Her tone should have left no room for argument but Holden said, "If you can tell me that five years from now, I'll give you my blessing."

"I want your blessing now, Holden, but with or without it, I'm going to marry Steve Austin."

He didn't respond. He couldn't. How could he say he was happy for her when all he could think was, What if she was making the biggest mistake of her life?

When he didn't reply, she said, "I'm going to bed. I'm tired."

He let her go without further argument, not because he was tired of arguing, but because he was unhappy.

Merry had known him long enough to recognize what his silence meant. She only wished his unhappiness didn't trouble her so much.

As she prepared for bed she promised herself she wouldn't worry about Holden's state of mind. She was making a new life. Ever since she'd arrived here she'd been thinking he could be a part of that new life. Now she knew it wasn't possible. He would always remind her of things she wanted to forget.

That was why the following morning she decided there was no point in waiting around for him to have developed another round of reasons she shouldn't get married. She called the airlines and changed her reservation.

Then she went into his study and sat down at his desk. On the notepad she wrote him a short message. She folded the paper in half and left it standing next to the calendar.

She was about to leave when she noticed airline tickets protruding from the desk blotter. Curious, she bent back a corner and saw that the destination was London. The departure date was December twentieth. Then she realized that there were two tickets—one in Holden's name and one in hers.

He really had planned something different for this Christmas. Instead of going home angry, she was going home feeling guiltier than ever. And she didn't like it one bit.

CHAPTER THREE

STEVE WAS WAITING at the airport for Merry when she returned to Minnesota. He was the familiar face she needed to see, the strong body she needed to embrace in order to chase away the feeling of having lost her sense of direction.

She wanted to bury the nostalgic feelings her visit to Holden had evoked, to return to the everyday routine she had in Minneapolis. When she sat down at the piano the following afternoon in Braxton's, she wanted to feel the peace of mind she always felt when she played her music.

However, the first request she received was not a song that evoked serenity. "Will you play 'I'll Be Home for Christmas'?" an elderly woman asked.

As Merry's fingers automatically moved across the keys, her thoughts drifted to Holden. Ever since her visit with him she had been fighting off a feeling of melancholy.

She had hoped that this season she'd be able to avoid what Rosie had always called her holiday blues. Her foster mother knew that no matter how hard Merry wanted to be full of holiday spirit, part of her couldn't forget the feelings of loneliness, the sense of desertion by her parents, that always managed to surface at Christmas.

There was no reason for those feelings this year. She was going to be far from alone. Not only would she have Steve but a family as well, a place to really call home. As soon as the last chord of the song had been played, she launched into a jazzed-up version of "Jingle Bells."

She loved to watch the effect the music had on her audience. As her eyes scanned the crowd, she spotted a girl of maybe thirteen or fourteen standing beside the display of recordings. For several weeks Merry had noticed her loitering by the makeup counter.

She wore at least three shirts, baggy twill pants and a pair of black boots that looked as if she was ready to work on a construction site. On her hands were black gloves with the fingers cut off, and slung over her shoulder was a worn backpack.

Merry couldn't quite figure out the look the girl was trying to achieve—part grunge, part punk. Her dark hair hung straight to her shoulders with streaks of green marring its shine. Dark eyeliner rimmed her eyes, red lipstick covered her mouth and both her nose and eyebrows were pierced.

Merry watched as she wandered over to the table where the cassettes and CDs were stacked. Lillian Tremont, of the store's Loss Prevention Department, had told Merry the girl's name was Holly and said she had been caught shoplifting on more than one occasion. However, it wasn't designer jeans or expensive makeup the teenager usually slipped into her backpack, but food. Chocolate Santas, imported mints, expensive nuts.

Besides loitering in the aisles, on several occasions Holly had sat down and played one of the pianos that were strategically placed throughout the store. Each time, the department manager had had to ask her to leave.

Now, as Holly fingered the cassettes not far from where Merry sat, she aroused Merry's interest. Merry glanced around, expecting to find someone from Loss Prevention watching Holly from nearby. There was no one as far as Merry could tell.

She felt a bit relieved. Ever since she'd first set eyes on the girl, she'd found her curiosity piqued. On several occasions she'd caught the girl staring at her. When she'd smiled and acknowledged her presence, Holly had disappeared.

This time the girl didn't see Merry's eyes on her. She was too busy glancing around nervously for the security guard. Merry thought she saw a flicker of fear on her face. But just as quickly it was gone and a cockiness replaced the uncertainty. She swung her elbow and a small stack of cassettes went tumbling to the floor. When she bent to pick them up, one found its way into her pocket.

"Can you play 'Winter Wonderland'?" A voice brought Merry's eyes back to the small crowd gathered around the piano.

Temporarily distracted by the request, Merry missed what happened next. All she knew was that when she glanced back to the table of cassettes and CDs, Holly was gone. A survey of the crowd indicated no trace of her.

When Merry had dinner with Steve later that day she told him about the girl. "I've seen people slip bottles of perfume and boxes of jewelry into their pockets, but never one of my recordings."

"She probably had a whole backpack of stolen goods," Steve said soberly. "I wish you'd called security. You don't need to be hassled by some punk kid."

"She wasn't hassling me," Merry insisted. "And I don't think she's a punk kid."

"You said she had more rings in her flesh than you have on your fingers and that she looked as if she dug her clothes out of a recycling bin," he reminded her.

"She didn't look any worse than other teenagers I see in the store."

"But she's a thief."

"All she took was one of my cassettes."

"Yes, and you did nothing about it." There was no missing the censure in his voice.

"What was I supposed to do? By the time I called security, she'd have been out of the store. Why are you so upset about this?"

He reached over to squeeze her forearm. "Because you're so trusting of strangers. You only want to see the good in people, Merry. What if this girl has a record or, worse yet, is a member of some street gang?"

"The people in Loss Prevention say she's more of a nuisance than a threat to security."

"Look. I'm only concerned for your safety. Remember the time that man sat down beside you and started banging on the keys?"

"This girl doesn't even come near the piano. All she wants is my recording."

He placed his hand over hers placatingly. "Is it any wonder? You make wonderful music."

"For adults maybe, but not many kids her age want piano music. They want to hear stuff by Pearl Jam or Toad the Wet Sprocket."

He shuddered. "Whatever. I want you to promise me that if she shows up again, you'll notify security."

"I doubt she'll be back."

"Hopefully she won't." He poured Merry another glass of wine. "I say we forget about work and talk about a subject dear to both of us. Christmas."

After her visit to Holden, it was not a subject dear to Merry's heart. "What about it?" she asked.

"The girls want to know if your feelings are going to be hurt if they take charge of everything."

The "girls" were Steve's daughters, Julia and Renée. Ever since Merry had been dating Steve, they'd made no secret of the fact that they thought Merry was the perfect mate for their father. Once they'd heard about the engagement, they'd fussed over Merry as if she were already their stepmother.

The thought that anyone could be getting hurt feelings caused Merry to shift uneasily. What she didn't want to be discussing at the moment was who would do what and who would be offended if someone else did it.

"Tell them whatever they want is fine with me," she said.

He squeezed her hand. "Are you sure everything went all right in California? You seem a little blue since you've been back."

She looked at him and wanted to tell him what was really bothering her, but how could she explain to him that, even though the Christmases she'd spent with

Holden were far from ideal, she would miss being with him?

She sighed. "I guess I'm feeling a little guilty because Holden had planned a trip to London for us this year."

"Without asking you first?" There was criticism in his tone.

"It was to be a surprise."

"Still, if you only see each other once a year, he can't expect that you're automatically going to be with him. Besides, Christmas isn't a time to be traveling. It's a time to be with family."

Those were Merry's sentiments exactly, yet she couldn't help but feel badly about breaking her promise to Rosie. Nor did she like ruining Holden's surprise.

"I told Holden I couldn't go," she said, unable to keep the edge from her tone.

He eyed her suspiciously. "You didn't want to go, did you?"

"No."

"Well, then, I don't see why you should feel any sort of guilt over this holiday. You've done everything you can to be considerate of his feelings. You went to California to see him, you invited him to Minnesota for Christmas and he refused—isn't that what you told me yesterday?—so what more could he want?"

Merry found herself reluctant to discuss Holden with her fiancé. Steve couldn't relate to what she and Holden had gone through as children. Besides, she didn't want to think about the past, and inevitably she did when she talked about Holden.

"I'm sure everything will be fine," she said with a forced smile.

"It's going to be better than fine. It's going to be the best Christmas you've ever had. Holden's going to be sorry he wasn't here."

DURING MERRY'S performance at Braxton's the following afternoon, Holly showed up. She was dressed in what appeared to be the same clothing, only this time she wore a black stocking cap on her head.

At first she stood across the aisle in the purses, casting furtive glances in Merry's direction. Eventually she moved over to the display table where the cassettes and CDs were for sale.

Curious, Merry watched as she picked up a tape and read the cover information. It wasn't long before her elbow once more knocked over a stack of cassettes, sending them to the floor. As she bent to replace the scattered tapes, one ended up in the pocket of her baggy pants.

Only this time Merry wasn't the only one aware of the girl's sticky fingers. The experienced store detective, Lillian Tremont, from her position at the perfume counter, saw the whole thing. Merry had the craziest urge to send a warning to the girl. As Holly slipped away, so did Lillian. Before they were out of Merry's range of vision, Holly had been apprehended.

Merry was relieved to be at the end of her performance. As soon as she'd autographed the last of the CDs and tapes being purchased, she quickly headed for the Loss Prevention offices.

"What can I do for you, Merry?" Lillian asked when she stepped into the tiny cubicle displaying her name.

"I was wondering what happened to Holly..."

"So you saw her pocket one of your tapes, did you?" the detective asked with a knowing look in her eye.

"Did she take anything else?"

"Uh-uh. She's in with Ken now. The police haven't arrived yet."

"The police?"

"It's standard procedure."

Of course. Merry knew it didn't matter whether it was one ten-dollar tape or a thousand-dollar fur coat; shoplifting was shoplifting—a lesson she herself had learned at the tender age of ten when she'd pocketed a Milky Way candy bar and a box of Junior Mints at the corner drugstore. The police had come and threatened to take her to the station. Only Rosie's appearance had saved her from a ride in the car with the flashing red light.

"Would it be all right if I talked to her?" Merry asked. "After all, it was my tape she took."

Lillian gave Merry a look of understanding. "Come with me," she said, leading Merry to another cubicle across the aisle.

Two faces turned in Merry's direction when she stepped into the small room. One was curious, the other frightened. It was the second one that concerned Merry. Under the harsh fluorescent lights of the security guard's office, the owner of that face looked small and vulnerable.

"Merry would like to talk to this young lady for a few minutes," Lillian told the stocky man seated at the desk.

Slouched in a chair, Holly stared at the floor as the two store detectives left the room. Merry took a seat beside her.

"Hi, Holly. I'm Merry."

The girl didn't say a word and refused to meet Merry's gaze.

"You must like piano music," Merry stated evenly.

"I was going to pay for the tape," the girl insisted. "It's just that some stuff fell to the floor, and when I picked it up I put the tape I was going to buy in my pocket and forgot it was there."

"That's what happened yesterday, too, wasn't it?"

A tinge of pink stained the girl's cheeks. "You put the store detective on to me, didn't you?" she accused.

"No, I didn't," Merry answered honestly. "You managed to do that all by yourself. Not many teenagers buy my recordings. I'm surprised you wanted them."

"I don't," Holly answered stubbornly, looking out through the glass partition to where the store detectives stood.

Merry was tempted to walk out the door and not look back, but beneath the bold makeup—the heavily mascaraed eyes and too-red lips—she saw the fearful face of a child. Holly was not as old or as tough as she wanted the world to believe.

"Were you planning on giving the tapes to someone as a gift?" Merry asked.

"No."

Merry wondered if she wasn't wasting her time. "How old are you?" she asked.

"Why don't you ask them?" Holly jerked her head in the direction of the store detectives standing on the other side of the glass partition.

"I'd rather ask you."

"Why?"

It was a question Merry didn't know the answer to. This girl was a stranger, like the hundreds of other kids she saw every day in Braxton's, yet for some reason she wanted to help her.

"I'm curious to know why someone your age would risk getting arrested for one of my cassette tapes," Merry said.

"Didn't they tell you?" This time the girl met her gaze straight on and stated boldly, "I'm *bad.*"

"I don't believe that," Merry said, trusting her instincts.

"Then you're one of the few people who doesn't." She slumped down even lower in her chair in an attempt to appear bored by the conversation.

Again Merry wondered if she shouldn't leave, but there was something about the girl that made her ask, "Do you play the piano?"

"Don't make me laugh," Holly drawled sarcastically.

"Why is that a funny question?"

She shrugged. "It just is."

"Would you like to play the piano?"

"No."

Merry wondered at that, since she knew the girl had been caught playing the store pianos. She also wondered why there was so much anger in such a small person. Just then the door opened and a woman with graying, blunt-cut hair and wearing a plaid coat entered.

Holly groaned and drawled sarcastically, "Oh, terrific. I should've known they'd call you."

"I wish *you'd* called me," the woman admonished, casting a puzzled glance in Merry's direction.

"Why? So you could give me another lecture?" Holly muttered sullenly.

Seeing Merry's questioning gaze, the woman extended her hand. "I'm Bonnie Hawthorne, Holly's foster mother."

The announcement shouldn't have come as a surprise to Merry. All the signs were there—the anger, the defensiveness, the lack of self-worth. No wonder Merry felt sympathy for Holly. Looking into her eyes had been like looking into a mirror.

"How do you do." She shook the older woman's hand. "I'm Merry Mattson."

"Yes, I know. I recognized you. I'm a regular customer of Braxton's," the woman said with a smile. "I hope Holly hasn't caused a problem for you."

"Not at all, but I'm afraid she may have caused a problem for herself." That remark brought another groan from the slumping Holly.

"Would you mind if I spoke to Holly alone for a few minutes?" Bonnie Hawthorne asked.

"She might as well leave," Holly interjected, gesturing at Merry. "I don't know what she's doing here, anyway."

A sentiment Merry echoed silently. When she stepped outside, she glanced back through the glass partition at the sullen teenager and felt a surge of sympathy. Something Rosie had said one time when Holden had been in trouble played in her memory. *Kids need someone to stand up for them, to fight for them.*

Lillian had returned to her cubicle. With her now was a police officer. Merry tapped on the open door and went in. "What if I said I had given her permission to take the tape?" she asked Lillian.

The store detective and police officer exchanged glances. "Merry, this isn't the first time Holly Denton's been caught pocketing stuff that doesn't belong to her," Lillian said.

"It was only one ten-dollar tape. You said you didn't find anything else in her backpack, right?"

"You don't want her to be charged, do you?" There was compassion in the store detective's eyes.

Merry shrugged. "It *is* the Christmas season." She paused. "What if I pay for the tape. Can't you write in the report that it was a gift from me?"

Lillian sighed. "I'll be back in a minute," she said, then left Merry alone with the police officer.

"Do you think I'm making a mistake?" Merry asked him.

The officer shook his head. "Holly's had some tough luck for a thirteen-year-old. She can probably use a break."

"You talk as if you know her."

"Our paths have crossed on more than one occasion." He smiled mirthlessly.

"Then Lillian's right. She does have a record."

"Truancy, shoplifting, curfew violations—those kinds of things."

"Where are her parents?"

"I'm not sure she has any. She's been in foster care ever since I can remember."

Merry was standing by the door, which enabled her to see into the office across the hall. She glanced once more through the glass partition and and saw not a teenager, but a child. Holly deliberately looked away, but not before she'd given Merry a message. *Stay away from me.*

Merry knew that message all too well. In the short time she'd done foster care, she'd discovered that it was common for foster kids to isolate themselves from others—just as she herself had tried to do as a child. Had Rosie been here, she'd have said Holly was a child in need. It was something Merry had sensed the first time she'd seen the girl, but having already failed as a foster mother, Merry doubted anything she could say or do would make a difference to Holly.

As soon as Lillian assured her there would be no charges pressed, Merry thanked her and the policeman and left. The last image she had of Holly Denton was the girl sitting slumped with a hopeless look on her face as Bonnie Hawthorne wagged her finger at her.

Throughout the remainder of the day, Merry found she couldn't forget the shoplifting incident. She kept hearing Rosie's voice saying, *Children must discover the resources they have within themselves.*

As hard as Merry tried to put Holly from her mind, she couldn't help but wonder if music might be that resource for her.

"I DON'T BELIEVE you've heard a word I've said all night," Steve complained as he and Merry dined at

Murray's in downtown Minneapolis. "You're not still thinking about that girl they caught shoplifting, are you?"

Merry smiled apologetically. "I know I shouldn't be but . . . she just looked so vulnerable."

"Somehow I'm having trouble picturing someone with a nose ring and wearing combat boots looking vulnerable," he stated dryly.

"She's a child."

"You told me she has a criminal record already."

"Truancies, shoplifting and curfew violations. Hardly major offences."

"Maybe not, but these cases are best left to professionals who deal with such situations on a daily basis. I know it was an unsettling experience for you, but I really think you should put it out of your mind."

That was something easier said than done. Ever since Merry had learned that Holly Denton was a foster child, she'd been playing their conversation over and over in her head. *I'm bad,* the teenager had told her, but instead of discouraging her, as Holly had no doubt hoped her words would do, Merry's interest had grown.

Taking her silence for agreement, Steve said, "How about if we talk about a more pleasant subject?" He reached for her hand. "The girls want to know when the wedding's going to be."

It came as no surprise to Merry. As soon as Steve had told his daughters the date of their engagement party, Julia and Renée Austin had started to make plans for their part in the wedding—much to Merry's dismay. She was afraid that if she didn't do something soon, any control she had over her own wedding would be taken away.

"Maybe we should get through the holidays first and then decide," she suggested, suddenly feeling pressured to make a decision she wasn't ready to make.

"I thought you said we'd set a date as soon as you'd seen Holden."

"Yes, but you know how busy our schedules are from now until Christmas. I think it would be better if we waited until the holidays are over. Then we'll be able to devote the time necessary to making the arrangements."

He eyed her suspiciously. "You're sure that's all it is?"

She nodded. "What else would it be?" she asked innocently, looking down at the food on her plate.

"I guess I was worried that maybe Holden had said something to you when you were in California that would cause you to have...second thoughts about us."

Guilt kept her gaze averted. She should have told him about Holden's reaction to her engagement, but she remained reluctant to discuss him with her fiancé.

"Holden's rather cynical about marriage in general," she said. "Probably because he's a divorce attorney and sees the ones that don't work."

"Well, it's too bad he isn't coming here for Christmas, because I could show him how much I love you and assure him that he has absolutely nothing to worry about." He paused and squeezed her hand. "I'd never hurt you, Merry."

"I know that." This time she met his gaze.

Steve squeezed her hand again. "You're going to have a real family, Merry. My children will be your children, my parents your parents. I'm going to make you forget there was ever a time when you were alone."

Merry should have told him that she had never *really* been alone. It was true she had no family, but Rosie and Holden had always been there for her.

But she didn't want to think about the past. Especially not now. Her future with Steve was what mattered. Once they were married, her life would be complete. After years of feeling adrift, she'd finally put her feet on solid ground. How could she have let one visit to Holden send her emotions tumbling? Instead of dreaming about the future, she was thinking about the past.

And all because of Holden.

As HARD AS HE TRIED to focus on the work in front of him, Holden didn't see contracts and affidavits. That was because his thoughts were preoccupied with one image—that of Merry in a wedding gown, standing at the altar with some faceless man. The harder he tried not to think about it, the more agitated he became.

It hadn't come as any surprise that a man had asked her to marry him. Having known her for twenty years, he'd seen quite a few men come and go in her life. Until now, she'd sent every one of them packing. Marriage wasn't for her. She'd told him that hundreds—no thousands—of times. She had. And they both knew it.

Yet now she was engaged to be married to a man he hadn't even met! That bothered him. He hadn't heard one word about this TV-shopping host until she'd made a promise to marry the guy.

He heaved a great sigh and tossed the legal briefs aside. To Merry a promise meant it was as good as done. Even if she was to have second thoughts about this guy, he doubted she'd ever break that promise.

It was a frightening thought and one that prompted him to call her several times throughout the day, leaving messages on her answering machine. She didn't return a single call.

He finally reached her late that night. "Are you all right?" he asked anxiously as soon as he heard her voice.

"I'm fine. Why wouldn't I be?"

"I've been calling all day and you haven't returned my—"

"Yes, I know. I'm sorry, but I just got home now. It's been hectic." The apology in her tone was like that of a polite stranger.

"I've been worried about you."

"I'm okay, Holden."

She really *was* distant with him. He found himself having to work to contain his annoyance.

"You left before I could say goodbye," he said, trying not to sound critical.

"Didn't you get my note?"

"Yes, but I wanted to take you to the airport myself."

"You were busy." Her tone was still like that of a polite stranger.

"I'm never too busy for you, Merry."

There was a brief silence, then she asked, "Holden, why did you call?"

"You didn't tell me when the wedding is going to be."

"We haven't set a date yet."

"I see."

"We're having a party in a few days to announce our engagement. Would you like to come?"

It was obvious she hoped he'd say no, so he obliged, "I can't get away right now."

"I understand."

He could almost hear the relief in her voice. Frustrated, he decided to end the conversation before he said something he would regret.

By the time he finally made his way home, he was still thinking about her. As he sat down to the plate of cold cuts Theresa had prepared for him, he found that the housekeeper had also left a videotape on the counter with the message "Watch this. There's something of interest on it for you."

Holden shoved the tape into the VCR connected to the portable TV in the kitchen. Then he sat down to watch while he ate his supper.

His appetite soon deserted him, however, when he saw the content of the tape. It was a cable TV program called "Let's Shop" with "everyone's favorite host," Steve Austin. The man who would soon be Merry's husband.

Holden could only stare in disbelief as the suave, good-looking older man hawked everything from power saws to diamond rings. He was smooth, he was fast-talking, he was irritatingly glib, and he was all wrong for Merry. She was as wholesome as milk. This guy looked as if he'd have no qualms about selling mittens to Hawaiians.

"I bet you don't go to a barber but to one of those salons with a French name," he accused the image on the screen.

He shoved the plate of cold cuts aside. What was Merry thinking? Why would she want to tie herself to a man old enough to be her father?

Of one thing he was certain: he needed to find the answers to those very questions. There was only one way to do that. He reached for the phone.

"I need a ticket to Minneapolis for tomorrow morning," he told the airline reservation clerk.

CHAPTER FOUR

MERRY RECEIVED an unexpected visit from Holly Denton's foster mother during her performance the following afternoon.

"May we talk to you when you're finished here?" Bonnie Hawthorne asked discreetly.

It was then that Merry noticed Holly standing in the back of the crowd, looking as if she wanted to be anywhere but in the department store.

"How about if I meet you in the coffee shop downstairs in about forty-five minutes?"

The woman mouthed a thank-you, made her way to Holly. The two of them disappeared from view.

Merry finished her performance, then quickly changed out of her red sequined dress into a pair of black leggings and a bulky knit sweater. When she got to the coffee shop, Bonnie and Holly were seated at a table by the wall.

"Thank you for coming," Bonnie told Merry as she sat down. "Holly has something she wants to say to you."

Merry thought Holly looked as if the last thing she wanted to do was speak to her, but to her credit, the girl managed to speak politely.

"Thank you for giving me the tape."

"You're welcome," Merry said gently.

"Lillian Tremont told me what happened," Bonnie said soberly. "I appreciate what you did for Holly yesterday."

The teenager squirmed and Merry was grateful for the appearance of the waitress. She and Bonnie ordered herbal tea, while Holly asked for a soda.

"We have something for you," Bonnie said as soon as the waitress had gone.

With seeming reluctance, Holly reached into the pocket of her baggy pants and pulled out a wad of crumpled dollar bills. She set them on the table, then shoved them in Merry's direction.

"It's for the tape," Bonnie explained.

Merry's eyes met Holly's. The trouble she saw there made her shudder. Ten dollars to a thirteen-year-old in foster care was a lot of money. "It's not necessary to pay me."

"Oh, but I think it is," Bonnie stated. "She took something that didn't belong to her."

Again Holly squirmed and Merry's sympathy grew. Logically she knew Bonnie Hawthorne had a point, but emotionally all she could see was this unhappy child who wanted desperately to be anywhere but here in front of the woman who'd witnessed her humiliation.

"I'd rather Holly gave the money to one of the Christmas charities," Merry told her. "There are so many people going without this time of year."

Bonnie nodded in understanding. "Of course. That's very kind of you, Ms. Mattson."

Merry watched Holly's eyes follow the dollar bills as Bonnie gathered them up and deposited them in her purse. She wondered where the money had come from and how hard it would be for Holly to earn more. No one knew better than Merry how scarce money was to a foster child.

There was an awkward silence, then Bonnie said, "You play beautifully, Ms. Mattson. It really is nice to be able to hear such lovely music at this time of the year."

"Thank you," Merry answered, carefully watching Holly's reaction to their conversation. "Do you like Christmas music, Holly?"

Her answer was a mumbled, "Some of it."

"Actually Holly loves music," Bonnie said cheerfully. "She's seldom seen without headphones covering her ears."

"Have you ever thought about playing the piano?" Merry asked the thirteen-year-old, curious about how she would answer.

"No. I told you yesterday I don't know how."

Bonnie shot Merry a look that said the girl wasn't telling the truth.

"Would you like to learn?" Merry asked.

"No." She scraped her chair back and announced, "I'm going to the bathroom."

Bonnie offered to go with her, but the girl didn't want anyone accompanying her. Merry watched her leave the coffee shop, scuffing the heels of her heavy black boots all the way.

As soon as she was gone, Bonnie said, "She *does* like to play the piano. I found her sitting at the old upright in the church basement one Sunday after services were over. She was playing something quite pretty—until she saw me. Then she stopped and pretended she was just fooling around."

"Do you think she might have had lessons when she was younger?"

"Knowing her background, I'd say it's unlikely."

"So she could be gifted musically and no one would know." It was a statement of fact, not a criticism.

Bonnie leaned forward and said, "With so many children in the foster-care system, it's a struggle just to take care of basic needs. And then there are those kids who don't want anyone to find their strengths—not even themselves."

Merry nodded in understanding, then took a sip of her tea. "How long has Holly been in foster care?"

"I think it's been about two years."

"Then she hasn't been with you all that time?"

"No. She only came to me in September."

"Where are her parents?"

"Good question. Her father just up and left when she was a baby. Her mother—" she heaved a sigh and shook her head in regret "—well, she had a lot of problems and couldn't take care of Holly."

"Does she still see her?"

"Oh, no. Parental rights were terminated a while back."

"What about adoption?"

"A couple of families have tried, I understand, but it didn't work out. She's not an easy child to live with. She's my sixteenth foster child, and she's been the biggest challenge I've had."

"You have other children?"

"Right now my husband and I have four foster teens plus two of our own."

Merry could see the kindness and patience in the older woman's eyes.

"I just wish I could get through to her," Bonnie said. "She has so much anger inside."

"I'm sure you're doing everything you can," Mary said reassuringly.

"I'm afraid it's not enough. I'm not sure how much longer we can keep her."

The news disturbed Merry. "I hate to hear you say that."

"Me, too," Holly's foster mother confessed. "But what's important is that Merry's with a family that meets her needs."

"I can understand that, Mrs. Hawthorne."

"Please, call me Bonnie," she said with a shy smile.

Merry returned the smile and said, "And you must call me Merry, okay?" When Bonnie nodded, Merry took another sip of tea and went on, "Tell me something, Bonnie. How does Holly get along with the other teenagers? Every time I've seen her she's always alone."

"She's never really fit in with the rest of them. Most of the time when she's in the house she keeps to herself. She just goes off and listens to music on her headphones."

That didn't come as a surprise to Merry. "She must have *some* friends."

"A couple, but they're not the kind I would pick for her. You know what I mean?"

Merry nodded.

"You know, today when I saw you sitting at the piano I didn't know if I should try to speak to you or not," Bonnie said modestly. "I wasn't sure whether you'd want to talk to me. In fact, I still can't believe

I'm actually sitting here having tea with the Lady in Red.''

Merry smiled. "Actually, I'm glad you came by. I found what happened with Holly yesterday very unsettling. It's good to know she has someone who cares what happens to her."

"I do care. That's why I gathered up my courage to come today." Again there was that shy smile, but Merry sensed that beneath the soft-spoken exterior was a strong woman.

Before Merry could ask any more questions, Holly returned from the washroom and Bonnie announced they had to be going. "I didn't mean to keep you so long," she told Merry as she pushed her arms into her worn plaid coat.

"You didn't. And I enjoyed our visit," Merry said. Holly's response was to roll her eyes toward the ceiling.

Bonnie didn't catch the gesture but gave Merry a grateful smile. "I hope you and your family have a wonderful Christmas, Merry."

"The same to you, Bonnie." Then she added, "You, too, Holly."

The girl simply shrugged and turned away.

Later that day, Merry thought about their conversation and felt an odd restlessness. Hearing Bonnie Hawthorne talk about foster children touched an emotional chord Merry hadn't played in quite some time.

It had been five years since her experience as a foster parent. At the time she'd wanted to follow in Rosie's footsteps, but then she discovered that taking in foster children, instead of being rewarding, was distressing, for it brought up too many painful memories. As much as she had wanted to help children in need, she knew that for her own survival, she had to avoid situations that resurrected the past. She had to move forward and not look back.

But now, seeing Holly Denton, she was finding it increasingly difficult to do that. It wasn't simply the anger that Merry responded to in Holly, but another emotion that haunted anyone who'd been abandoned.

Despair. Holly Denton knew she was not going to return home. As good as Bonnie Hawthorne might be to Holly, she couldn't fulfill for Holly one of life's very basic human needs—a permanent home, a family of one's own.

It was a need Merry understood well. It was the reason that, at twenty-nine, she still didn't feel as if her life was complete. But that was all going to change shortly, she reminded herself. Her marriage to Steve would give her the family and home she had only dreamed about.

It would also provide her with a husband who liked to cook. Since Merry had few culinary skills and little interest in acquiring any, Steve was a godsend. And today she'd welcomed his suggestion that he have dinner ready for her that evening. True to his word, he had filled her town house with all sorts of delectable aromas by the time she arrived home.

"I expected you earlier," he called from the kitchen as she hung up her coat.

"I stopped to have a cup of tea with Bonnie Hawthorne, the foster mother of the girl who was caught shoplifting yesterday."

"I thought we agreed you weren't going to get involved in that girl's problems," he said, bringing her a glass of white wine.

His authoritative attitude irked her. "I'm hardly *involved.*" Merry accepted the wine and turned her head so that the kiss he intended for her lips landed on her cheek.

"Dinner's almost ready. It's swordfish with steamed baby carrots and asparagus—your favorite," he told her, returning to the kitchen. She followed him in.

"So what did this woman want?" he asked.

Merry could hear the disapproval in his voice and thought if she was wise she'd tell him the meeting was only so that Holly could give her the money for the tape. But something prompted her to elaborate on the details of their conversation.

"I wish you hadn't gotten involved in any of this," he said petulantly.

"I told you I'm not involved," she replied, taking a stool at the bar that separated the kitchen from the dining room.

"You got her off the hook with the police," he reminded her, although Merry thought it sounded more like a chastisement than a reminder. "That's something I still don't understand."

"I felt sorry for the girl. Do I need a reason to be kind to another human being?" she asked, feeling suddenly on the defensive,

"Of course not, but you know nothing about this girl except that she's a foster child. Darling, not all foster children are like you."

"And they're not all disturbed, as you seem to think," she said curtly.

He checked the contents of a pot on the stove, then stared at her across the bar. "You're angry with me. I shouldn't have said anything."

His penitent look made her soften. "I thought you of all people would understand. You do so much charity work."

Wearing one of her aprons and a pair of oven mitts, Steve resembled the TV chef known as the Gourmet Grandpa, an impression enhanced by the reading glasses he had perched on the end of his nose.

"I want to understand. Tell me why all this is so important to you." He turned his attention to the bowl of salad greens on the counter.

"I'm not sure I know why it is," she admitted candidly. "There's just something about this girl that won't let me forget her."

Steve shot Merry a glance as he tossed the salad with oil and vinegar. "She's a child and you've always responded to children," he said pragmatically. "It's why you're reluctant to give up teaching."

Merry knew that the feelings Holly Denton stirred in her were not like those she felt for her students. They were more than that.

"I'm wondering if she might not be gifted musically," she said. "No one's ever taken the time to find out."

"You're not thinking of tutoring this girl, are you?"

Now that it had been said aloud, Mary realized the idea had been playing at the back of her mind ever since Bonnie Hawthorne had said she'd heard Holly play the piano in the church basement.

"It *is* what I do," she reminded him.

"Yes, but we decided you weren't going to take any new students, that you were going to focus on composing and recording."

"One more wouldn't hurt," she rebuked, annoyed that he referred to her career decisions as if they were his, too. "It might be that Holly Denton wouldn't even be interested in taking lessons from me."

He made a sound of disbelief. "Are you serious? She'd jump at the chance. Anyone would."

Merry smiled indulgently. "I appreciate the flattery, but not everyone wants to take piano lessons." She watched him carry their food into the dining room. She would have offered to help, but past experience had taught her that when Steve was in his chef mode, it was best to let him take over completely.

As she sat down to a meal that was as good as any served at the best restaurants in town, she again realized how lucky she was to have a fiancé who loved to cook.

She smiled at him. "You spoil me. Dinner for me is usually something from the frozen food in my freezer."

"You're worth spoiling. Once we're married, you won't ever have to wheel the shopping cart down the frozen-food aisle again. If I don't feel in the mood to cook, we'll eat out."

"Are you sure it won't bother you that I'm not Betty Crocker?"

"Not in the least." As soon as they were seated at the table, he lifted his wineglass to hers. "To many more nights like this—the two of us ... alone."

No sooner had the toast been made when the doorbell rang. When Merry started to get up, Steve stopped her. "It's probably a salesperson of some sort. I'll take care of it."

Merry ignored his offer and rose. "You made dinner, so you sit. I can say no to a stranger just as easily as you."

Only it was no stranger standing on the other side of Merry's door. It was Holden. A black wool derby was cocked at an angle on his head, his trench coat was open despite the cold, and he had a definite five-o'clock shadow. He looked dangerously attractive with that thick, dark mustache trimming his upper lips. Once again, as it had happened in California, his appearance made her feel a bit breathless.

"Wh-what are you doing here?" she stammered.

"Is that any way to greet someone who's come two thousand miles to see you?" He used her own words on her.

She laughed, a sound that was laced with nervousness, then stepped aside, indicating he should come in. She quickly closed the door and faced him, her arms folded across her chest.

"Well?" he said.

"Well what?"

He set his luggage down. "Don't I get a hug?"

Before she could answer, Steve appeared, still wearing the bibbed apron over his shirt and tie. "Merry, is this someone you know?" he said, eyeing Holden.

"I would definitely say so," Holden replied, with a rather smug expression that would have annoyed any man interested in Merry.

It achieved the desired result. Steve's look of inquiry changed to one of suspicion as he stepped closer to Merry.

"Holden, this is Steve Austin," she said, flustered.

"Ah. The fiancé." Merry could see Holden was taking a psychological inventory of Steve.

"And Steve, this is Holden Drake."

"Ah. The childhood friend." Steve's manner was equally assessing.

The two men shook hands.

"This is a surprise," Steve said smoothly. "Merry didn't tell me you were coming." Although his tone was mild, Merry could see the tightness in his mouth. He was not pleased to see Holden.

"That's because I didn't know he was coming," she explained, then deliberately slid her arm around Steve's waist in a reassuring gesture of affection. "Holden's caught me by surprise, too."

"You invited me to your engagement party," he reminded her.

"You said you were too busy to come."

He gave a devilish grin. "I rearranged my schedule."

Her smile was not sincere. "Great. Now the two of you will be able to get to know each other a little." She glanced from Holden to Steve.

"And you and I, Merry, will be able to spend some time together," Holden added almost flirtatiously, which did little to improve Steve's disposition. "I hope I didn't come at a bad time. It looks like I'm interrupting something." A twinkle in his eye, he stared pointedly at the apron wrapped around Steve's trim midsection.

Until Holden had come, Merry had seen nothing odd about Steve's apron. Now she realized it did make him look a bit silly. She could see Holden looking at him with that same critical eye he had aimed at all of her boyfriends.

Annoyed, she wanted to tell him he was interrupting, but she knew it wouldn't bother him. He was staying. She could tell by the set of his jaw.

"We were just sitting down to dinner. Let me take your coat and you can join us," Merry suggested, even though she knew Steve would be disappointed that their dinner for two would now be for three.

"I was hoping I could take the two of you out to eat, but if you'd rather stay in..." Holden let the words trail off as he handed Merry his trench coat.

One look at her fiancé's face and Merry knew she could not let Steve's efforts go to waste.

"We'll eat here," she said firmly, then put Holden's coat in the closet and gestured for the three of them to move to the dining area.

"It's a little early for me to eat dinner," Holden said with a glance at his watch. "But you two go ahead. I have some calls to make and I'd like to wash up."

"You can use the spare bedroom. It's where I have my sewing, but there should be enough room for your things," Merry told him.

He nodded, then reached for his luggage. As he walked away, he called over his shoulder, "Enjoy your meal." Merry could have sworn there was a smirk on his face.

The food was cool if not nearly cold by the time Merry and Steve returned to the candlelit table. It was obvious from Steve's expression that he was not happy.

"Maybe we *should* go out. This doesn't look very appetizing now, does it?" He curled his lip in distaste as he stared at the food in front of them.

Merry tasted a mouthful. "It's great. It'd be a shame to let all this go to waste."

"Yes, well, I wouldn't have prepared it if I'd known we were going to have company." He was unable to keep the annoyance from his voice. "Why didn't you tell me you'd invited him to our engagement party?"

Again she felt as if she was being scolded and she didn't like it one bit. "Please keep your voice down. He's just along the hall," she reminded him in a near whisper.

"I would think a man in his position would see that an unannounced visit is an inconvenience, especially at this time of the year."

"His arrival was unexpected, but I don't think his visit will be an inconvenience," Merry contradicted. "Besides, you told me to invite him to come for Christmas."

"Christmas is more than two weeks away! Do you think he's planning to stay that long?" Steve's mouth twisted into a grimace.

"I told you I don't know," she snapped a bit impatiently. "You heard everything he said to me."

Just then Holden reappeared. "Sorry to interrupt, but I thought I'd take a quick shower. You don't mind, do you?" His appearance stunned both of them. He had loosened his tie and unbuttoned his shirt so that his skin was showing. Although it wasn't the first time Merry had seen his bare chest, for some reason she found herself averting her eyes.

"Go ahead," she mumbled, her cheeks turning a delicate pink.

"I need a towel."

"Oh—second door on your right, middle shelf," she answered.

Holden grinned, completely undaunted by her obvious discomfort.

"Your face is red," Steve said when Holden had disappeared.

"Of course it is. I think Holden overheard us arguing about him."

Steve looked as if he wasn't convinced that was the reason for her flush. "He's not going to stay here, is he?"

"Well, I'm not going to make him go to a hotel. I've always stayed at his place whenever I've gone to California." She sprinkled pepper on her salad.

"You said he has servants."

"Yes. So what?"

"If he stays here, the two of you will be alone together."

"What are you saying? That we need a chaperon?" she asked with a humorless laugh.

"You're two single adults of the opposite sex."

"Who grew up together in the same house, using the same bathroom, the same kitchen and all the other things that brothers and sisters share."

"But you're not sister and brother. That's my point."

"No, we're friends—very good friends and I trust him completely. And frankly it bothers me that you're making a fuss over all this. You aren't jealous of Holden, are you?'' she asked, trying to ignore the memory of that little rush of breathlessness Holden's appearance always generated.

Steve reached over and covered her hand with his. ''I wouldn't be honest if I said it didn't bother me that he's staying here. I can't help it if I think there's not a man alive who wouldn't be interested in you as a woman.''

''Well, Holden isn't, and I hope you're not going to suggest such a thing again,'' she said indignantly, trying to forget that there'd been a time when she'd wanted him to be interested in her as a woman.

Steve raised her fingers to his lips. ''I'm sorry. His appearance came as a shock to me, that's all.''

It had to Merry, as well, but not for the same reasons. She wished Steve would stop talking about Holden as if he were an old boyfriend. ''Holden's been like a big brother to me. I want the two of you to be friends.''

''Then I'll do my best to make that happen.'' Steve gave her an endearing smile.

''I'm sure Holden will, too.''

Merry saw how wrong she was later that evening as the three of them had coffee in front of the fire in her living room. Conversation was awkward at best, with the two men sizing each other up. Merry mostly blamed Holden. No matter how hard Steve tried, Holden refused to meet him halfway. She was relieved when Steve finally announced he was leaving.

After seeing him out, Merry returned to the living room to find Holden rattling around in her liquor cabinet. "Don't you have any Scotch? I could use a drink after all that."

"After all what?" she demanded angrily, facing him with her hands planted on her waist.

"Trying to be pleasant to Mr. Personality."

"Most people don't find it such a challenge, but then most people aren't so determined not to like someone."

"He didn't like me any better than I liked him," Holden said in his own defense.

He lifted a decanter of amber-colored liquid. "What's this?"

"Cognac."

"I should've known he'd drink cognac. It goes with the gingham apron." He set the bottle down with a thud.

"All right. Just stop." She held up her hands. "I'm sure you didn't come here to make fun of the man I love."

Holden had forgotten how incredibly dark her eyes became when she was angry. "No. I came to rescue you."

"I don't need rescuing," she told him in no uncertain terms, the message in those dark eyes changing from anger to challenge.

"I think you do."

"I can't believe you came here on the spur of the moment. You never do anything without making plans first."

His behavior had surprised Holden, too. It was one the few times he'd acted first and thought later. Now he knew it was a good move. "I had to come. Theresa made me a tape."

"A tape of what?"

"Steve in action on the shopping channel."

"And that's why you came? Because you saw him on television?"

"He's all wrong for you, Merry."

She gaped at him in astonishment. "And you can tell that by looking at a videotape?"

"That, and four hours of listening to his sales pitch here in your living room."

"The way you interrogated him I'm sure he felt like he was a guest on 'Geraldo.'"

"All I did was ask him about himself."

"And now I suppose you think you know everything there is to know about him?"

"I know enough."

"You know nothing," she contradicted him, her eyes flashing. "Steve Austin is one of the kindest, gentlest men I know. He's honest and sincere. He's sensitive—"

"He's old," Holden interrupted.

"Forty-eight is not old," she protested.

"It is. He probably has kids your age." He punctuated his statement with a laugh.

When she blushed, he said, "Oh, good grief. He does have kids your age, doesn't he?"

"No, they're younger than I am."

"How much younger?"

"Julia's twenty-one, Ryan's twenty-four and Renée's twenty-six."

"Don't tell me you're going to become a step-grandma, as well?"

"No, he doesn't have any grandchildren. Why are you cross-examining me about this? His age isn't the issue."

"It should be."

"Why? Because it's important to you?"

"Because when you're middle-aged, this guy will be drooling on his chin—if the marriage lasts that long."

"My marriage will last," she said with fervor.

"I've heard that line before," he said cynically.

"Don't be like this, Holden," she pleaded, her voice softening. "Can't you just be happy for me?"

He raked a hand through his hair. "How can I be happy when I think you're making a mistake?"

"It's *not* a mistake, and nothing you can say is going to convince me it is. If that's why you came, you've wasted your time."

"Time I spend with you is never wasted, Merry."

Gone was the courtroom tone that had been in his voice. He came toward her until he was poised only inches from her. "I'm staying for a while, Merry. Get used to it." And before she could come up with a response, he planted a kiss on her cheek and left the room.

CHAPTER FIVE

WHEN MERRY STEPPED into the bathroom the following morning, she was greeted by moist air and the scent of Holden's after-shave. It was different from the one he'd worn as a teenager, the one that used to make her almost swoon, but this one was just as potent. Automatically her senses reacted and she experienced a tiny tickle of pleasure. But then it was quickly chased away by the spurt of annoyance she felt at the sight of wet towels on the floor.

A dark green velour robe hung on the back of the door and a leather travel case with its contents spilled out over the marble top of the vanity reminded Merry she was sharing her space with a man. Not a very tidy man at that.

"What does he think this is? A hotel?" she grumbled. Not since she'd lived with Rosie had she shared a bathroom with Holden. Back then he didn't have the assortment of personal-care items that now littered her vanity. Impatiently she returned the bottles and tubes to the leather case. As she stuffed his razor inside, her fingers brushed against a foil packet.

Her face warmed. So what did she expect? Holden was a normal, healthy single man who obviously practiced safe sex. Then she noticed there wasn't one, but several foil packets. She pulled her hands away as if she'd been burned.

Steve's words echoed in her brain. *You're not brother and sister.*

"It doesn't matter. We treat each other like brother and sister," Merry said aloud as if defending herself to her traitorous senses. She draped a towel over the leather travel case so that the condoms were out of sight.

As steaming water pelted her skin in the shower, she pushed all thoughts of Holden from her mind. She needed to concentrate on the day ahead of her. With students to teach, a performance at Braxton's, and a taping to do at the recording studio, she had no time to worry about him.

Only he was hard to ignore. With no Theresa to pick up after him, there was evidence of his presence throughout the town house. In twelve short hours he had made himself at home. His toothbrush hung next to hers, his tie dangled from a doorknob, and his shoes sat in the hall.

Merry found him in the dining room, his papers and books spread across the table. He sat with his laptop computer in front of him, his fingers tapping away at the keys, the telephone receiver tucked between his ear and shoulder.

Wearing the thick Irish-knit pullover sweater Merry had given him, he looked like a model in a men's magazine. It was no wonder he turned women's heads, Merry thought, suddenly recalling the foil packets in his travel case. She was unable to stop the flush of pink on her cheeks.

It didn't matter. He didn't notice. He was in the middle of a phone call and, except for a nod in her direction, was totally focused on the conversation.

Since it was obvious he was conducting business, Merry poured herself a cup of coffee and wandered into the living room so as not to eavesdrop. It wasn't long before he was standing in the doorway saying, "Where's the closest fax machine?"

"I have one on the desk in my room."

"Good. My secretary's going to fax me some papers later this afternoon." He was about to return to his work when she stopped him.

"Holden, why did you come to Minnesota when you have so much work to do?"

"You needed me. I've always been there for you when you've needed me, haven't I?"

Again Merry felt a delicious shiver of pleasure travel through her as he gazed at her. But he was deliberately using his charm to score points in their battle, and it made her say, "Well, you can go back home. I have Steve."

He chuckled sarcastically. "I know. That's why I'm here."

Now it was Merry's turn to chuckle sarcastically. "I think we need to talk."

"Can it wait? I'm in the middle of something."

"No, it can't wait," she said firmly.

He sat down beside her on the couch. "Okay. Out with it. I'm listening."

Yes, he was, and piercing her with eyes that had always had the power to make her forget she was angry at him. It didn't help that he smelled of the woodsy scent that had permeated the bathroom, and she realized just how much broader he was than Steve. He took up much more of the couch. She shifted uncomfortably, leaning away from him.

"I don't want us to fight, Holden, especially not over my personal life."

"Then we won't," he agreed easily.

"Do you mean that?"

"Of course." He reached out and touched her cheek, sending a tiny current of pleasure through her.

"I'm glad to hear that," she said, getting to her feet. "I'm engaged to Steve. If you only came with the intention of changing that..."

"I came because you asked me to," he said, getting up to stand beside her.

"You said you were too busy to leave your work."

"I brought it with me. Besides, I have business here."

She wondered what kind of business, but didn't ask. "How long can you stay?"

"I'd like to be here for Christmas. After you left I started thinking about the promise we made to Rosie. We told her we would do whatever we could to spend Christmas together," he reminded her. "I know how important promises are to you."

"Are you serious? You really are planning on staying through Christmas?"

He nodded. "You were right. It would be strange not to be together. Besides, it wouldn't be the same without bumsteads, would it?"

Bumsteads were Rosie's idea of specialty sandwiches on Christmas Eve. Egg and tuna salad on hotdog buns with lots of melted cheese.

"I'm sure Theresa would make them for you," Merry said.

"But who would put a book on your pillow?"

Another of Rosie's traditions. Every Christmas morning she and Holden would awake to find a book had been left on their pillows while they slept. After Rosie had died, Holden had kept up the tradition, often leaving exquisite art books for her.

"Am I going to cause problems for you if I stay?" he asked, his eyes fixed on her thoughtfully.

"Not as long as you don't expect that I'll change my mind about London."

His eyes narrowed. "How do you know about London?"

"I saw the tickets on your desk," she confessed, her skin warming at the thought.

"I wanted to make this Christmas special for you."

"I know," she said, swallowing the lump in her throat. "But it *is* going to be special. After all these years, I'm finally going to be a part of a family."

"I thought we were family to each other."

The flat tone with which he delivered that sentiment eased her guilt. "You know what I mean. Every Christmas you and I wished for the same thing—a real family."

"Maybe when we were kids, but we're adults now, Merry."

"I still want that real family, Holden."

He studied her pensively for a moment, then said, "I know you don't want to hear this, but the guy's old enough to be your father. And after listening to the way he talks to you, I'm not so sure that isn't what's attracting you to him."

"You think I'm looking for a father figure?"

"Aren't you?"

"No!" She turned away from his intense scrutiny. "It wouldn't matter if the man I married was twenty-eight or forty-eight. You would still disapprove, because you're jaded when it comes to marriage."

"With good reason. If you spent a week in my office you'd know why I'm concerned," he argued.

"I told you before. I don't need your concern," she retorted.

"Do you want me to leave?"

"No." The reply came quickly. It was the only answer she could give, because for now that he was here, she realized how much she wanted him to be with her at Christmas.

"Good, then I'll stay."

"Good," she echoed. "But please don't ruin our time together by dissecting my relationship with Steve."

He sighed. "I'll try."

"Thank you. This visit could be an opportunity for you and Steve to get to know each other. Maybe if you give him a chance, you won't be so suspicious of him."

"Maybe," he said, his eyes narrowing.

"You're not going to scare him away," she cautioned him. "He's not easily intimidated."

"And when have I ever intimidated any of your boyfriends?" he asked innocently.

"Have you forgotten Richard Gant?"

Holden gave a derisive snort. "He was a creep."

"He would have taken me to the prom if you hadn't threatened to give him a knuckle sandwich."

"You didn't want to go with someone like that. The guy was sleazy. Besides, you went to the prom."

"Yeah, with the biggest nerd you could find for me."

"Eldon Zensky may not have been the best-looking guy in school, but at least he didn't try to jump your bones in the car, either."

"That's because he was a foot shorter than me and weighed less than I did. He knew he'd lose." She sighed.

"He was decent," Holden insisted.

"And so is Steve," she countered, which only elicited a groan from Holden. "You always said that someday my prince would come."

"And he will. You just have to keep looking." He gave her his roguish smile, the one that had always made her want to smile back.

"Funny, funny. Have you had breakfast?" she asked perkily, deciding it was best to change the subject.

"You know I've never been any good in the kitchen," he said, his smile sparkling in his blue eyes.

Merry's heart skipped a beat, and she felt a rush of pleasure—which she decided to ignore. "What do you feel like?"

"Oh, I don't know. Maybe some eggs, toast...a few strips of bacon."

"Then you want Millie's coffee shop. It's two blocks down, on the corner of Fifty-sixth and Boone," she told him cheekily.

His grin broadened. "Still have a dead bolt on the oven door, eh? You'd think, with Rosie for a guardian, one of us would be able to handle a frying pan."

"I can. I just don't like it."

"Okay, get your coat and I'll take you out to breakfast—or is Mr. Personality coming over to poach you an egg?"

She shot him a reproving look. "His name is Steve and he knows I seldom eat breakfast."

Holden clicked his tongue. "Rosie would be upset if she heard you say that. How about if I run to the bakery and bring back some apple-cinnamon muffins?"

Merry softened toward him. Apple-cinnamon had been her favorite when they were kids. "I have students coming this morning. Soon."

"I'll hurry," he said with a wink that sent another current of pleasure through her. "Oh, by the way." He paused on his way out the door. "Someone named Bonnie Hawthorne phoned while you were in the shower. I left her number by the phone."

Since Holden's arrival, Merry hadn't thought about Holly Denton once. Now that she had a message from the girl's foster mother, she could think of little else. As soon as Holden was out the door, she dialed Bonnie's number.

"Thanks for returning my call, Merry," the older woman said gratefully. "I just wanted you to know that Holly's money went to the Christmas food bank."

"Then it went to a good cause," Merry responded pleasantly. "Actually I'm glad you called, Bonnie. I've been thinking about our conversation yesterday." The idea that had been niggling the back of her brain took shape. "I think Holly should have piano lessons."

"She didn't sound very interested when you questioned her about it," Bonnie pointed out.

"No, but that could be because she's so down on herself right now. She might be too angry to admit she wants to learn."

"It's funny you should mention the subject. After I met with you I called her social worker. She told me that at one time Holly did have piano lessons at school, but they were discontinued because of discipline problems. None of the teachers could handle her."

"But you said you've heard her play."

"Oh, yes. In the church basement that time."

"So obviously she has an interest. It could be she just hasn't found the right teacher."

"She can be a difficult child, Merry," Bonnie said flatly.

"Maybe she wouldn't be so difficult if she had something like music in her life. Music might be a way for her to feel good about herself."

"She hasn't found that to be true so far."

"What if I was her teacher?" Merry offered, surprised at the ease with which the suggestion popped out of her mouth. If Bonnie Hawthorne hadn't called, she wouldn't have proposed the idea.

"You want to teach Holly?"

Merry heard the disbelief in her tone. "You don't think it's a good idea?"

"I do think it's a good idea, only Holly's a child with many problems. Are you sure you want to take on those problems?"

"I grew up in a foster home, Bonnie."

"Ah. Then you know what she's going through."

"Yes. And I know that music is what saved me from getting into the kind of trouble Holly's been in."

"It would be wonderful if it had that effect on Holly, but right now she needs stability in her life. If the lessons don't work out, it might cause more damage than good." Bonnie expressed her reservations honestly.

"Isn't it better to try and to fail than never to try at all?" Merry asked.

There was a pause, then Bonnie asked, "What did you have in mind?"

"I thought the two of us could get together, and Holly could make the decision for herself whether or not she wants to take lessons."

"And if she says she does," Bonnie asked, "where will she practice?"

"There must be a piano at the school she could use. Or what about the one at the church?"

"Yes, I'm sure she could practice on either of those, but—" Bonnie hesitated "—I'm afraid we don't have the finances to pay for lessons."

"I'm not asking to be paid."

Again, Bonnie hesitated. Finally she said, "Are you sure you want to get involved with something like this?"

"Yes." The reply was made with conviction, for Merry had seen in Holly's eyes, along with the despair and the anger, a cry for help and a plea for understanding. She'd also caught a glimmer of hope there, a glimmer she didn't want to see snuffed out.

She reached for her day planner. "With the holidays I'm awfully busy, but I could meet with Holly this evening," she told her, even though it meant changing her plans to attend a dinner party with Steve. "Can she be here by seven?"

"I'll make sure she is." There was excitement in the older woman's voice. "Thank you. This could make a real difference in Holly's life."

Merry got the number of Holly's social worker from Bonnie with the intention of getting in touch with one of Holly's piano teachers and learning more about the girl's potential. When she and Bonnie hung up, she thought about how music could perhaps do for Holly what it had done for her. If Rosie were still alive, she'd have been pleased to know that her foster daughter was helping another child find this inner resource.

Still, Merry couldn't help but have mixed feelings. She was making a new beginning with Steve, putting the past behind her. Teaching piano to a troubled teen might be a disaster—and not just for Holly.

Steve had advised her to give up teaching so that she could focus on recording and performing. During the past year, she had benefited from his career advice. Teaching piano to Holly Denton would not be something to which he would give his stamp of approval. Well, he'd just have to accept the fact that there were some things that were her decisions and her decisions alone.

DISASTER WAS EXACTLY what Steve thought her charitable offer was going to bring. When he called later that morning and she told him the reason she couldn't go the dinner with him, he acted more like the father figure Holden accused him of being, rather than the supportive fiancé she needed him to be.

"I can't believe you went ahead and did this without discussing it with me first," he said with barely concealed annoyance.

"We did discuss it."

"You said you were considering tutoring her. You didn't tell me you were going to go ahead and do it."

"I didn't realize I needed to consult with you every time I made a decision," she shot back. "In case you've forgotten, I check the box marked Adult when I fill out a questionnaire."

Immediately he was defensive. "I'm not treating you like a child."

"Yes, you are."

"No, I'm not."

There was a moment of silence before Merry said, "I can't believe we're arguing over this." Actually she couldn't believe they were arguing at all. It was a first for their relationship. In the past year he had never raised his voice to her, not even in fun.

"Maybe we ought to change the subject," she muttered.

"Fine. I just hope you know what you're getting yourself into."

Merry had harbored exactly that fear, but she didn't need him to remind her. She needed reassurance, not skepticism.

"Did Holden say how long he's staying?" There was an edge to Steve's voice, indicating to Merry he was still upset about Holden's presence. She decided not to tell him of Holden's intention to stay for Christmas.

"It depends on his work," she said evasively. "You don't like him, do you?"

"He's a little too combative for me, but then most lawyers are. If it's important to you, I'll make sure we get along," he said placatingly.

"I want you to like him, not tolerate him."

"That might be a little easier to do if he wasn't staying in your town house."

"Steve, he's like a brother to me," she told him for what seemed like the hundredth time, ignoring the rush of heat that flowed through her at the memory of finding condoms in Holden's travel case.

"As long as he remembers that."

The conversation was making her feel decidedly uneasy. She thought it best to end it. "Look, I have to get ready for work. Will I see you at all today?"

"Since you're not going to have dinner with me, it's unlikely."

For a grown man he sounded remarkably like a small child, Merry thought. "Well, you could always stop by later."

She expected another childish retort, but he surprised her by saying, "Or I could skip the party and come to your place, instead. While you're with your student, Holden and I could see if we could find some common ground."

"I'd like that, but I should warn you, Holden may be working. He's brought his laptop and I don't expect we'll see much of him."

"If that's the case, I'll simply sit quietly and wait for you."

Merry squirmed uncomfortably. "I'm not sure that's such a good idea."

"Are you saying you don't want me there?"

There was definitely hurt in his voice.

She chose her words carefully. "I just think it's better if I meet with Holly when no one else is around. She doesn't need an audience yet."

"What if I sit in the kitchen?"

Merry dismissed his suggestion by saying, "It would be best if I called you when we're through."

"You'd better, because I'm not leaving you alone with Holden the entire evening."

ALTHOUGH HOLDEN HAD attended Merry's recitals, he'd never seen her in Braxton's. Entering the department store, he could hear her music before he actually saw her, the warm melodies evoking the same serenity that always came over him whenever he heard her play.

When he was close enough to see her sitting elegantly yet demurely on the piano bench, he was momentarily stunned by the lovely picture she made in her red sequined dress. Her dark hair was pulled back from her fine-boned face, erupting in a riot of curls at the nape of her neck. Her Mona Lisa smile seemed to say she knew some delicious secret that no one else did. It was no wonder Steve Austin wanted her for himself. Holden imagined there were few men who wouldn't find her enchanting, and he was surprised it had taken this long for her to receive a marriage proposal.

But then, he knew that few men had been able to penetrate the reserve Merry had carefully constructed. She did not give her heart lightly or frequently—which was what bothered him about her relationship with this Austin character.

A surge of jealousy rippled through him. She was too vibrant, too young and too talented for a man close to fifty.

As Holden listened to her play, she was unaware of his presence. He saw her seduce the crowd with her charismatic performance, watched as everyone from toddler to senior citizen succumbed to her charm. He would have stayed hidden had the woman in front of him not requested a tune. When Merry looked at her, she saw Holden.

She played the request, then immediately launched into a lively rendition of "Frosty the Snowman."

Holden couldn't help but smile. When he was fifteen he had been asked to his first dance by a girl named Connie Sanders. Little did he realize when he accepted that Connie was on the entertainment committee, and his duty as her escort was to dress up as a snowman. When Holden learned of his role at the dance, he wanted to back out of the date, but Rosie had insisted he go. After all, he had accepted the invitation and Connie had spent her baby-sitting money to rent the costumes. From that day on, Merry sang "Frosty the Snowman" whenever she wanted to tease him.

When she finished her final number, he walked over to the piano and clapped enthusiastically. "Bravo, bravo—especially 'Frosty the Snowman.'" He sat down beside her on the bench.

"Whatever happened to Connie Sanders, anyway?" she asked with a grin.

"Don't know, don't care."

"That's always the way it's been for you with your women, hasn't it?" she said reflectively. "Holden

Drake, the Houdini of Heartache. Watch out or he'll escape into thin air."

"Very funny, Ms. Mattson," he said dryly.

"What are you doing here?" she asked.

"I thought I'd go with you to the recording studio. You did say you were going this afternoon, didn't you?"

"Yes, but..." She hesitated.

"I'd like to come along—if you don't mind." When she still hesitated, he said, "You do mind, don't you?"

They were interrupted by a pregnant woman with a toddler in tow who shyly pushed her way up to Merry for an autograph. Holden watched in amusement as Merry chatted with the young mother. A strange emotion stirred inside him when she bent to take the tot's fingers in hers. As the two women talked about Christmas and children, one thought ran through Holden's mind—Merry would make a good mother.

"I'm impressed," he said as soon as the woman and child had gone. "You have fans."

"Amazing, isn't it?" she said, a look of wonder on her face as if she still couldn't quite believe it herself.

"It doesn't surprise me. You've come a long way from the farmhouse in Hibbing. This is a different world from the one we left behind." He spread his arm in an all-encompassing gesture of the ornately decorated department store.

"I guess dreams can come true," she said wistfully.

"Has your dream come true?"

Again they were interrupted, this time by a store employee who had a message for Merry about her schedule for the week. As soon as the woman left,

Merry looked at her watch and said, "I'd better get changed."

"You haven't answered my question. Do I get to go with you to the recording studio?"

She smiled and said reluctantly, "Okay. Come with me." She led him through the crowded aisles, up the escalator and through a door marked Employees Only. It was a small lounge with a dressing room, a vanity, a full-length three-way mirror and a bank of lockers.

"Have you made plans for dinner?" he asked as she opened one of the lockers and pulled out a pair of jeans and a sweater.

"I'm probably going to have to grab some fast food. I have a new student coming at seven."

"I thought you weren't taking any new students."

"I'm not, but this is a special case." She disappeared into the dressing room, instructing Holden to take a seat. "It's a thirteen-year-old girl," she told him from the cubicle, then went on to explain Holly's situation, including the shoplifting incident.

By the time she was changed, she'd finished the story. "What do you think?" she asked as she opened the dressing-room door.

Holden knew she wanted his opinion on the foster child, but one look at her skintight jeans and figure-hugging red sweater sent his thoughts in one direction only, and his hormones reacted in an alarming manner. He quickly berated himself. What was wrong with him? Ever since he'd seen this Austin character, he couldn't look at Merry without thinking of her in a sexual way.

"Well?" she said. "What do you think?"

"About what?" He'd forgotten what she'd been talking about.

She made a sound of exasperation. "About giving Holly piano lessons."

"Oh, right. Well, we both know it isn't easy being a foster child. She may be difficult."

"You think God is going to get even with me?" she asked as she put the sequined dress in a garment bag.

He smiled wistfully. "Rosie never complained about you being difficult when it came to practicing the piano."

"Rosie never said any of us was difficult ever."

"She had a lot of patience."

"And you don't think I do?"

He studied her briefly, then said, "I think that if you want to tutor this girl, you should tutor her."

Merry smiled. "Thank you for saying that. I've been second-guessing myself ever since I suggested I take her as a student."

"Why is that?"

Merry leaned against one of the chairs, her hip resting on its arm. "I can't help but wonder if I'm only doing this because of some need inside me I want fulfilled."

"You probably are." When she gave him an affronted look, he added, "So what?"

"So it means I'm being selfish."

He made a sound of disgust. "There's nothing wrong with wanting to do for someone else what's already been done for you. Why should you feel guilty about wanting to emulate Rosie. That is what you're doing, isn't it?''

She nodded weakly. ''The first time I saw Holly I heard Rosie's voice in my head telling me there aren't any bad kids, just bad situations kids get caught in.''

''She would have told you to give this girl a chance.''

''I think so, too,'' Merry said, feeling that familiar sense of connection. Holden might not be her brother, but he was closer to her than any other person. It had been that way since she was nine, and it was at this minute that she realized how much she missed that closeness.

''If you tell me what time she's coming, I'll make myself scarce,'' he suggested.

His offer caught her off guard. What she hadn't expected was that Holden would be sensitive to her situation with Holly and that *Steve* would be the one giving her problems. ''Seven. It shouldn't take more than an hour.''

''That's not a problem. I'll stay in my room—plenty of work to keep me busy.'' He looked at her and saw not a helpless girl, but a very capable woman. When she was a child, she'd looked up to him for guidance, but now she no longer needed him in that role. The fact that she didn't need him to watch over her made him more aware of her as a woman. He found her independence extremely attractive.

Only, she appeared to be reluctant to assert that independence when it came to Steve Austin. As much as she professed to have left the past behind, he knew that it was *because* of the past she was marrying a man old enough to be her father.

He couldn't let that happen. Promises or no promises, he would make sure she was the strong woman Rosie had wanted her to be. He would not stand by and watch her marry the wrong man for the wrong reasons.

CHAPTER SIX

"WHY DON'T YOU show me what you can do." Merry set Holly Denton down at the shiny black piano and lifted the fallboard.

"What do you mean, *do?*" The sullen look that had been on Holly's face ever since she'd walked through the front door was firmly in place.

"Play something for me." Merry gestured to the keys.

"I told you before I don't know how to play the piano."

"Not at all?"

"No."

Merry knew she wasn't telling the truth, but she was careful not to accuse her of lying. "There must have been a mix-up, then. I was told you had lessons."

"Well, you were told wrong." Holly folded her arms across her chest, burying her fingers beneath her shirtsleeves as if to protect them from the ivory keys. "If you'd talked to any of my piano teachers, you would know the lessons didn't work."

In the short time Holly had been in her house, conversation had been a struggle. Merry had made little progress in getting the girl to talk about herself at all. She decided to change tactics.

"You don't want to be here, do you?" she said.

"Why don't you just write down that I'm hopeless and let me go?"

Merry could feel the girl's hostility and fear settle between them. "Is that what you want to be? Hopeless?" she asked gently.

"It's what I am." Holly made the statement as if it was a proven fact.

"I don't believe that." Merry knew it would take time to reach this girl. "Do you know why you're here?" she asked.

"Yeah. You want to do your good deed for the day."

Her response plucked a guilt string in Merry's heart. Not only would she need time to reach Holly, she was going to have to keep a tight rein on her emotions. She searched her memory bank for one of the many platitudes Rosie had recited when she was a child, but came up with nothing.

"Well," she ventured at last, "it won't be much of a good deed if we don't accomplish anything, will it?"

Holly shrugged. "It doesn't matter. No one's going to be surprised. They'll just say you picked the wrong charity case."

"I'm not interested in providing charity," Merry told her. "I want to help someone discover the pleasure of making music, someone with a gift that few people have."

"I don't have a gift."

"I think you do." She sat down beside Holly on the bench and played the beginning of a popular song. "I don't need music to play. In fact, when I first took lessons, I had a problem playing at all because I couldn't connect the notes on the page to the melody in my head."

"So?"

"If you've taught yourself to play by ear, chances are you'd have had difficulty learning piano the traditional way," Merry said cautiously.

Holly didn't comment.

"Not many people can play by ear. We're in a very select group."

"What makes you think I'm in that group?"

Merry lifted her fingers from the keys. "Because I've talked to one of your other piano teachers."

A rosy pink colored the teenager's cheeks.

"I also heard from several of Braxton's employees that you've made music on the store's grand pianos." Merry resumed playing softly and Holly remained silent. "I want to help you discover what a joy making music can be, but I can't do that unless you let me."

"You're wasting your time. I'm not any good."

"Why don't you let me be the judge of that? Music is powerful stuff," Merry told her, her fingers continuing to move across the upper octaves. "Whether you're listening or playing, it's an emotional experience. It can make you happy or sad, angry or calm. It can be a memory jogger, too. Don't certain songs remind you of certain times in your life?"

"I guess," Holly conceded reluctantly.

"What's your favorite kind of music?"

She shrugged. "I don't really have a favorite."

"Who do you listen to most often? What group or individual?"

"Mostly the Violent Femmes or the Cranberries."

Merry grimaced inwardly. "Is that what you'd play if you could play the piano? Rock?"

"Maybe."

Merry stopped playing. After several moments of silence, she said, "Play something."

"What?"

"Anything."

Holly hesitated, but finally the fingers came out from beneath the shirtsleeves. Merry stood up to give Holly access to the entire keyboard.

The popular song Holly played was not without mistakes, but it told Merry the girl was indeed gifted musically. For someone who didn't have a piano and who hadn't successfully completed any music lessons, she played remarkably well.

"That's very good!" Merry complimented her when she was finished.

"I made a lot of mistakes," Holly mumbled.

"They'll become fewer and fewer the more you practice. If you'll let me, I'll teach you to play both by ear and from sheet music."

"But I don't have a piano. How can I practice?"

"Bonnie told me she can arrange for you to practice at school during the week and at your church on weekends."

"Yeah, right." There was a heap of sarcasm in her response.

"Is that a problem?"

The girl rolled her eyes. "No one stays after school to practice piano."

How well Merry remembered. How many times had she heard the whispers? *Merry Mattson has to stay after school to practice because she's a foster child and doesn't have any money for her own piano.*

It was those memories that prompted her to offer, "You could practice here."

"You'd let me use this piano?" She gazed in adoration at the shiny black grand.

"My schedule's a little hectic right now, but we could probably manage to arrange a time that would be convenient for both of us."

Holly eyed her suspiciously. "Why are you doing this?"

"Because someone did it for me when I was your age. I know what it's like to be thirteen and in foster care."

"*You* were a foster child?" Holly's eyes rounded in amazement.

Merry nodded. "I lost my parents when I was nine. I didn't think I'd ever get over the pain, but then I discovered something that could make it hurt less—music."

Holly looked as though she were weighing the idea in her mind. "I'm not sure Bonnie could bring me over every day."

"Maybe you could take the bus."

Holly shrugged. "Maybe."

"Why don't you think it over while I get us something to drink?" Merry went into the kitchen and poured two glasses of soda. When she returned to the living room, Holly was admiring her collection of teddy bears stacked in the corner.

"Do you like my bears?" Merry asked, setting the silver tray on the glass-topped coffee table.

"Yeah, they're cute." Holly reached for a glass of soda. "I guess you don't let your kids play with them. They still look new."

"I don't have any kids. I'm not married."

"So? Lots of people have kids without being married. This is the nineties, you know."

"I guess I'm old-fashioned. I thought I'd wait and get a husband first."

"I'm never getting married."

Before Merry could respond, Holly exclaimed in delight, "Neat, a snow globe with bears inside! I love these things." She lifted the expensive globe and tipped it upside down then right side up to watch the white crystals drift to the bottom. "This wouldn't last long in the places I've lived."

Holly continued to wander around the room, her fingers touching the various furnishings. She paused in front of the fireplace to admire the wreath of pine-cones and red ribbons Steve had given her. It was the only Christmas decoration in the house, a fact Holly didn't miss.

"How come you don't have a Christmas tree?"

"Because I usually spend Christmas in California."

"Is that where you're going this year?"

"No, I'm staying here."

"Will you be getting a tree, then?"

"No."

"I guess you don't like all those needles getting stuck in your carpet."

"They can make a mess," Merry agreed, prefer-ring to let the girl believe she didn't have a tree for housekeeping reasons, rather than admit she wanted no reminders of a season filled with unhappy memories for her.

Holly chattered on, as if once started, she couldn't stop. "I've never been in a house with white carpet. Aren't you afraid it'll get dirty?"

Along with the soda, Merry had brought out a plate of Christmas cookies Holden had brought back from the bakery. She offered them to Holly and said, "It can be cleaned."

"How many foster homes were you in?" she asked Merry as she reached for a star-shaped sugar cookie.

"Just one. I was lucky."

"I'm on my seventh and I think Bonnie wants to get rid of me, so I'll probably be on my eighth before you know it."

Because this was all said without any emotion, Merry had no way of knowing just how deeply the moves affected Holly. She would have liked to contradict her, but she honestly didn't know if Bonnie planned to request she be moved to another home.

"So have you made a decision? Would you like to take lessons from me?" Merry asked.

Before Holly could answer, the doorbell rang. Holly set her glass down and reached for her coat. "That'll be Bonnie."

Merry went to answer the door. Out of the corner of her eye she saw Holly slip several cookies into her pocket.

"How did it go?" Bonnie asked as soon as Merry opened the door.

"Maybe you should ask Holly that," she suggested, motioning the woman inside.

"Merry says I can practice on her piano if we can figure out a way to get me here," was the first thing Holly said, a glimmer of hope in her eyes.

Bonnie looked surprised, but managed to say, "I think we can work something out."

Merry smiled gratefully. "Good, because I know Holly and I are going to get along just fine."

MERRY'S OPTIMISM was not shared by Steve. The following afternoon when he arrived and found Holly sitting at Merry's grand piano, his handsome face wrinkled in a frown.

"You didn't tell me you had another lesson today," he said in a low voice.

"I don't. Holly's going to practice here because her foster home doesn't have a piano."

He looked over her shoulder to where the thirteen-year-old sat. "Is this going to be a regular thing?"

"Until someone can find her a used piano."

He looked as if he wanted to protest against the girl's presence, but before he could say another word Merry asked, "Why are you here? I thought we weren't having dinner until seven-thirty."

The frown disappeared. "I brought you something."

Merry looked, but saw nothing in his hands.

"It's outside. I wanted to make sure you were home before I brought it in. I'll be right back."

He disappeared, and a curious Merry hurried over to the window. Spreading the blinds, she looked out to the driveway where Steve was muscling a large pine tree from the top of his car.

"That can't be for me!" she exclaimed.

"Did you say something to me, Merry?" Holly wanted to know.

"Er, no, I was just thinking out loud. Keep playing. It's all right."

Merry hurried back to the door to wait for Steve. The scent of fresh pine tickled her nostrils as he carried the tree into her house.

"Where do you want it?" he asked.

"That's the problem. I don't want it," she blurted without thinking. Seeing the hurt expression on her fiancé's face, she quickly added, "It's a lovely tree, but I don't have any room for it."

"We'll move the furniture around," Steve told her, setting the tree down in the middle of the living room.

"But I don't have any ornaments or lights or garlands..." She trailed off in a whine.

"We'll buy some," he told her.

"It hardly seems worth the effort. I'm seldom here."

He waved away her objection. "It won't feel like Christmas if you don't have a tree. I got such a good deal on it through the station I couldn't turn it down." He wore a satisfied grin.

Merry chose her words carefully. "I wish you'd asked me first."

"Then it wouldn't be much of a gift, would it?" He was making it difficult for her to not to accept it.

Merry rubbed her forehead. "Maybe you should take it to your place."

"I already have a tree," he reminded her. "Here. Hold it by the trunk while I go get the stand from the car." He motioned for her to hold the tree.

Reluctantly Merry wrapped her fingers around the cold bark, grimacing as pine needles pricked her arm. Holly had stopped practicing and sat staring at her.

"You must not have told him about the needles getting into the carpet, huh?" she said to Merry.

"No." Merry pursed her lips.

"It's really a nice tree," Holly said, getting off the piano bench to circle the pine. "It doesn't have any bare spots like lots of them do."

"Do you have a tree at home?"

"Yeah, sort of. Bonnie has one of those plastic ones." She inhaled deeply. "This tree smells good."

"Yes, it does, but I really don't have a place for it."

"You could move your bears," she suggested. "Do you want me to help?"

"No, I'd rather have you practice until Bonnie gets here."

Merry didn't mean to sound as if she didn't want Holly touching her bears, but it was obvious Holly took it that way. Dejected, she crept back to the piano.

At that moment Steve reappeared with a red-and-green metal stand he said was guaranteed to hold the tree straight. Before he could prove the box's claim, however, his pager beeped.

After a quick phone call he announced to Merry that one of the station's hosts had taken ill and he had to go on the air to cover for him.

"But what am I going to do with this?" Her eyebrows lifted as she stared at the pine tree. "I can't stand here all night holding it."

"I'm sorry, but I really don't have time to mess with it right now," Steve answered. "Maybe Holden will get it in the stand for you."

"He's not here," she said coldly.

Steve took the tree from her and shoved it into a corner. "It'll be all right for a few hours. If Holden won't do it, I'll come over tomorrow and take care of it for you. You're in luck. It's freshly cut," he said, then left in a hurry.

"Some luck," Merry muttered as she closed the door on his departing figure.

"I could help you put it in the stand," Holly offered from her position at the piano.

"I'm afraid I wouldn't even know where to begin," Merry responded unenthusiastically.

Holly shrugged and looked away. That was twice Merry had turned down her offer of help—which was not what the thirteen-year-old needed.

"Well, I guess we can try following the instructions," Merry said, surveying the tree skeptically. She picked up the box containing the stand. "Says here it's easy."

Holly was off the piano bench and down on her knees within seconds, pulling the packaging from the stand. "It says you need a screwdriver."

"I've got one somewhere, but..." Merry paused, then snapped her fingers. "I know. I'll be right back." She went to the kitchen drawer and retrieved a dinner knife. "This is what Rosie used to use when she couldn't find a screwdriver."

"Who's Rosie?"

"My foster mom."

Holly nodded in understanding, then read the printed instructions aloud while Merry attempted to follow her directions. After several unsuccessful attempts to get the tree to stand properly in the metal base, Merry sat back and declared, "Now I know why I never had one of these things."

By the time Bonnie arrived, they were no closer to getting the tree upright. Bonnie offered to help, and the three of them wrestled it into position. But when they removed the support of their hands, the pine listed noticeably. Merry gave up. She thanked Holly and Bonnie for their help, and soon after, they were on their way.

Once she was alone, she sat down and stared at the sight before her. That was how Holden found her—gazing at a crooked pine tree.

"Where did that come from?" he asked, eyeing it curiously.

"It was a present," Merry answered flatly.

"Let me guess. Mr. Personality."

"Don't start in on him, Holden. I'm not in the mood," she warned, her voice ragged with emotion. When he bent down and fiddled with the screws in the stand, she added, "You don't have to straighten it. It's not staying."

"Why not?"

"Because I have no room for it."

"Did you tell Steve that?"

"Yes, but..."

He sat back on his heels and stared at the pine. "We haven't had a real tree at Christmas since Rosie died."

"They make a mess," Merry said quietly.

"Yeah, but I like the smell of fresh-cut pine."

"It only reminds me of how unhappy we were as children."

"Not all the memories are bad." He was silent for a moment, then said, "Remember the time we carried our pillows and blankets downstairs on Christmas Eve and Rosie would let us sleep on the floor next to the tree?"

Merry smiled wistfully. "It was cold."

"That didn't send you back to your bed, though. You said you didn't care if your feet got cold because you wanted to go to sleep near all those tiny tree lights twinkling in the dark."

"We thought they were like stars," she said softly.

"We lay awake for hours talking about all the great things we were going to do someday," he mused, a far-off look in his eyes.

"We thought we could make a wish and it would come true. Only, we woke up in the morning and discovered nothing had changed. We were still two homeless foster kids."

For the first time in a long time he saw vulnerability in her face. It made him want to wrap his arms around her and hold her close. Not to comfort her, but because she looked so beautiful staring at the tree with her pale face.

"You better put some water in the base of that stand," he said a bit gruffly, rising to his feet. "The tree'll dry out quickly in here with the furnace running."

"I don't plan on keeping it."

Holden gazed at her pensively. "What do you plan to do with it?"

"I don't know, but there's no room for it in here."
She gave him the look he remembered so well from his
youth, the one that said, *Help me out of this.*

He reached for the trunk of the pine and, with a
quick jerk, lifted it, metal stand and all, and carried it
to the patio door. He slid the glass door open, then
hefted the tree out onto the wooden deck, where it
stood just as crookedly as ever.

When he was back in the living room, he asked,
"How's that?"

"Fine," she answered, then began picking up the
needles that had fallen off in the short time the tree
had been indoors. Holden hunkered down beside her
and stopped her busy fingers.

"Now that the problem with the tree is taken care
of, how about having some dinner with me? Or do you
have plans?"

"No. I was supposed to go out with Steve, but he
was called back to the station."

Holden fought the urge to say, "Good." Instead, he
reached for the phone and called a local restaurant to
have two orders of barbecued ribs delivered. Then he
poured a glass of wine for her and a Scotch for himself.

"You haven't told me how your new student is
working out," he said, sitting down beside her on the
sofa.

She took a sip of the wine before answering. "Better than I expected. Holly's quite talented."

"So you're going to work with her?"

"Uh-huh, although I'm not sure it's the smartest
thing I've ever done," she admitted.

"Why's that?"

She shrugged. "Lots of reasons. One is that I don't really have the time for a new student, not if I want to do more performing."

"But you enjoy teaching."

"I do."

"So *make* time for it."

She sighed and leaned her head back. "It's not that simple."

Holden studied her thoughtfully. "Does having Holly around remind you of the past?"

"A little." She paused. "Although her situation is quite different than mine was. She's still being bounced around. From what Bonnie Hawthorne tells me, I wouldn't be surprised if Holly has to move again. It makes me realize how lucky we were to have Rosie."

"If we'd been lucky, we wouldn't have been in foster care in the first place," he said with a trace of bitterness.

"But we were and we survived." She took another sip of wine and said, "And it's all behind us now."

Holden continued to study her. "All you've told Steve about your parents is that they're both dead, right?"

"Yes. I told him I don't have any family." As usual, whenever any mention was made of her family, a guarded look came across her face.

"As a lawyer I should tell you that it's not a good idea to start a marriage without full disclosure of each other's background," Holden said gently.

"I'm going to tell Steve about Janet and Bob."

He didn't miss the fact that she referred to her parents by their first names, not as Mom and Dad. "When?"

"When it becomes an issue."

"That's my point. You don't want to wait until there's an issue involved. Merry, the guy's not going to call off the engagement because he discovers your parents weren't Ozzie and Harriet Nelson."

"And do you tell all the women you date what happened to your parents?" she wanted to know.

"I'm not planning on marrying any of them."

"No, so your secrets are safe, aren't they?" she said almost enviously.

"Since I don't plan on marrying, I guess they are," he answered without a trace of sarcasm. No one knew the whole truth about his past, although Merry knew more than most people.

"I don't need any legal advice from you, Holden. I told you I have Tom Harvey for that."

"And I can guarantee you he's going to tell you the same thing. Don't leave any skeletons in your closet."

"All right. I hear what you're saying."

He doubted she did. Merry was a great one for placating. She would say she agreed with him, then turn around and do the opposite of what he recommended.

She leaned her head back against the cushion and closed her eyes. He could see that her fingers still clenched the stem of her wineglass. He set down his glass and reached over to place his hand on the back of her neck.

"You're so tense. Why?" he asked, rubbing the tight muscles.

She groaned as his fingers connected with taut ligaments. "This time of year I'm always tense. It's the hectic pace, I guess."

"If we were in L.A., I'd take you to see Maynard. He can work the kinks out of anyone's muscles."

She opened her eyes and twisted her head to look at him. "You have a massage therapist?" she asked on a note of disbelief.

"See? There *is* something you don't know about me," he answered. "If you've never had a full-body massage, you don't know what you're missing. Turn around and I'll try to work your shoulder muscles," he instructed. When she gave him a dubious look, he added, "I'm not going to hurt you."

Reluctantly she presented him with her back. "I think I'm too ticklish for this."

"I won't go near your feet, I promise," he told her, remembering how she used to go into a fit of giggles if he so much as touched one of them.

He didn't say another word, but worked her shoulder muscles until gradually she began to relax. As he worked, he could smell her perfume, a light floral scent that teased his senses and made him wonder how the flesh beneath her cotton-knit sweater would feel against his fingertips.

"Mmm. That does feel good," she said on a breathy sigh that produced a knee-jerk sexual reaction in Holden. Suddenly his thoughts were preoccupied with a fantasy of what it would be like to give her a full-body massage.

His fingers moved from her shoulders down her back, gently working her spine. Before he realized it, he was no longer massaging, but caressing, wanting to feel her curves.

She glanced back over her shoulder as his fingers found their way to her waist. From the look in her eye, he knew she was as aware of the sexual tension between them as he was. More than anything at that moment he wanted to kiss her, and unless he had totally missed her signals, she wanted it, too. But before he could react, the doorbell rang. Dinner had arrived.

CHAPTER SEVEN

THE FOLLOWING DAY began with Merry oversleeping. From that point on, her schedule was off. Therefore, it didn't surprise her when Holly called to say she'd be an hour late.

It was dark by the time the thirteen-year-old finally arrived. When she entered the house, Merry saw her peer into the living room and make a quick perusal.

"You must not have been able to get the tree to stand straight, huh?" she asked as she took off her jacket.

"There really wasn't much room for it in here, anyway," Merry answered.

The girl nodded, then went to sit down at the piano. "Did you make him take it back?"

Merry shook her head. "It's out on the deck."

Holly's eyes swung to the vertical blinds covering the glass patio door. Merry felt compelled to walk over and open the louvers. "See?" She gestured with her arm.

"At least you got it to stand up straight."

Merry turned to glance outside. Sure enough, the pine stood as straight as a tree in the forest. Merry knew there was only one person who could have done it—Holden.

"It's kind of neat that you put it on the deck. Now you can see it from in here and everyone outside can see it, too," Holly said pragmatically.

Merry stood for several moments staring at the tree. Why had Holden bothered?

"You sounded kind of mad when your boyfriend brought it over," Holly remarked.

"I'm not mad at him," Merry said.

"Are you going to marry him?"

"Uh-huh."

"Oh." Holly shrugged, then held up several completed work sheets Merry had given her the day before. "Do you want to see these?"

"Have you finished them already?" Merry crossed over to the piano and glanced at the papers. "This is great, Holly."

"It's not as hard as I thought it would be," the girl said with a crooked grin.

Merry returned her smile. "That's what I like to hear." She gave Holly a few reminders about the music she'd assigned for their next lesson, then left her alone to practice.

Already behind schedule, Merry needed to get ready for the Christmas party Steve was hosting to officially announce their engagement. The thought of the party created a small knot in Merry's stomach. Not only would many of Steve's relatives be there, so would Holden. Lately she'd been finding his presence more and more disturbing, and she knew Steve wasn't comfortable around him, either. She only hoped Holden would behave himself and not say anything to cause tension among the three of them.

In her room she found a note lying on her pillow. It said, "Don't worry. I'll be home in time for the party at Steve's. Hope you like your tree better today. H."

She had planned to wear a simple two-piece silk burgundy dress, but the thought of the evening ahead had her searching for a confidence booster. She found it in the form of a black sequined halter with a short black skirt.

It would be a dramatic change from her usual evening apparel. Instead of making her look elegant and sophisticated, it made her look young and sassy. To complement the sequins she added the dangling diamond earrings Steve had given her for her birthday. The final touch was a jeweled comb to hold back curls dusted with glitter.

As she surveyed herself in the mirror, she debated whether to change into the burgundy dress. A glance at her watch told her it was too late to change, and she quickly grabbed a beaded handbag and left the bedroom.

She couldn't hear any music being played on the piano and wondered why. She found Holly at the refrigerator with the door open. When she saw Merry, she quickly slammed it shut. "I'm sorry."

"If you're thirsty, you're welcome to help yourself to a can of soda," Merry told her. A glance at the girl's baggy pants told her she'd already helped herself to a couple. They bulged from her pockets.

Holly murmured, "Thanks," and slid past Merry, her eyes downcast. When she reached for her jacket, Merry asked, "Have you finished practicing?"

"Bonnie said I could only stay forty-five minutes today. And I'm supposed to ask you if it's okay if I come in the morning tomorrow since it's Saturday and there's no school.'' She buttoned her jacket and reached for her backpack.

"That's fine. How about ten?"

Holly shrugged. "Okay."

"Where are you going?" Merry asked as she headed for the door.

"I thought I'd better wait for Bonnie outside."

"Why?"

"Because...you know," she said ambiguously, her eyes still downcast.

"Because you went into my refrigerator looking for something to drink?" Merry gently probed.

She didn't look up. "I'm sorry. I should've asked first."

"It's all right. From now on I'll set refreshments out for you—some soda and maybe a snack in case you're hungry." Merry knew from past experience that some foster children hoarded food, a habit developed from going hungry once too often.

Holly finally met Merry's gaze. "You're too nice to me."

"You deserve to have people treat you nicely."

The girl quickly looked away. "I gotta go."

"You're welcome to wait in here. It's awfully cold outside."

Holly shrugged. "It's all right. Thanks for letting me practice," she said, then hurried out the door.

Merry didn't know quite what to do. Should she call the girl back inside or let her wait on the front step? She chose the latter course of action and went over to the window to peek outside.

Holly was not on the front step, but next to the garage. As if aware of Merry's watchful eyes, she turned her back to the house so Merry couldn't see her face.

A few minutes later Holden arrived. The first thing Merry asked him was if Holly was still out there waiting for her ride.

"That's your music student?" he asked with a lift of his eyebrows.

"Yes. I told her she could wait for her ride in here, but she insisted on going outside. I think she thought she was inconveniencing me."

"She wanted a smoke."

Merry groaned. "If I'd known, I wouldn't have let her go." She heaved a sigh. "Why do these kids think cigarettes are so cool?"

"Because they're kids. And if I remember correctly one summer when I was working at the bowling alley I caught a certain fourteen-year-old dropping coins in the cigarette machine so she and her friend Colleen could be cool like their peers."

"All right, so I tried it once, too, but if you remember I also got sick and never tried it again."

"Lucky for you. If I had caught you a second time I would've told Rosie where your baby-sitting money was going."

Merry's teeth tugged on her lower lip. "Do you think I should say something to Holly?"

"It's not what *I* think," he said. "It's what *you* think that matters."

She gave him a quizzical look. "Why do you always do that?"

"Do what?"

"Every time I ask for advice, you tell me it's up to me to decide what to do, but whenever I *don't* want your advice, you're there to give it to me, anyway."

"Number one, I don't think I should make decisions for you. You're a strong, competent woman who's in control of her own life—something I think you need to remind Steve of. And number two, the only time I get involved in your decisions at all is when I can see you're making a foolish one."

She held up her hand to stop him. "Don't say it. I know what's coming next and it's better left unsaid."

He looked as if he had to bite his tongue. He didn't say anything, but let his eyes rove over her figure, which only made her want to squirm.

"By the way, why did you straighten the tree?" she asked, avoiding his eyes.

"You know me. Can't stand to see anything crooked. Besides, I figured sooner or later you'd bring it back inside and I'd end up doing it, anyway."

"You're wrong. I won't."

"Why not?"

"Because I'm spending Christmas at Steve's. Why do I need a tree when he has a lovely one in his living room? You'll be able to see it this evening."

"Oh. You're talking about the party." He grimaced.

"You don't have to go if you don't want to."

"Of course I'm going. By the way, you look sexy in that dress," he said in such an offhand way Merry felt more self-conscious than if he'd been flirting with her. Now she wished she *had* chosen the burgundy silk dress.

Discomfited, she murmured, "We should get going. Are you ready?"

"Is this good enough?" he asked, gesturing at his clothes.

She nodded, thinking he looked incredibly handsome. As usual, he wore a jacket and tie, and with his hair brushing his collar and his mustache outlining his lip, he looked like a rebel in a suit. Merry felt her senses react once more.

"I told Steve we'd be there by seven," she told him as she reached for her coat.

"Don't we have time for a drink first?"

"You can get something there," she said dryly.

"Oh, what a thought. An evening of rum punch and cognac," he drawled sarcastically.

"Please don't do anything to embarrass me," she pleaded.

He looked affronted. "Don't worry. I have my social graces tucked in my pocket."

"Well, just don't forget to bring them out."

As soon as they arrived at Steve's, Merry knew the evening was going to be a long one. One of the first comments she heard was, "Oh, I didn't realize she was so *young*."

Merry stifled a sigh. With the exception of Steve's children, everyone at the party looked old.

"You didn't tell me so many people were going to be here," she whispered to Steve as he helped her off with her coat.

"It's just family. You're not nervous about meeting them, are you, darling?" Keeping his arm at her waist in a proprietary manner, he led her into the living room.

She *was* nervous. Every face that stared at her made her wonder if they were comparing her to Steve's deceased wife. Suddenly, Merry, who'd never had a family but always wanted one, felt overwhelmed. Ever since she'd been a child she had hated walking into rooms filled with strangers. The shyness she thought she'd conquered returned with a vengeance. Instinctively her eyes met Holden's.

She wanted him at her side when Steve introduced her to the unfamiliar faces. As if he could read her mind, he slid in alongside her, despite Steve's proprietary manner. However, Julia Austin took one look at Holden, and a predatory gleam lit her face.

She boldly hooked her arm through his and declared, "I'll take care of Holden, Dad. You show off your fiancée."

Merry found herself looking at Steve's daughter in a whole new light. She was no longer simply a college student, but an attractive blonde who had her size-nine body squeezed into a size-seven dress.

Steve had told Merry that his daughters would be responsible for the buffet supper, but it was Renée, the older daughter, who did all the work. The only task Julia tackled was opening the champagne, for which she shamelessly begged Holden's assistance.

Although there was no piano for Merry to play, her music softly filled the room from CDs on the sound system. For weeks Merry had looked forward to this evening, yet now that it had arrived, she found it a disappointment. Most of Steve's relatives were older than he was, and she discovered she had little in common with them. They were a quiet group, so quiet that Merry wondered if any of them knew how to have fun.

By the time she'd been introduced to all of them, she felt as if she'd been inspected and evaluated and come up short. She'd had her fill of polite small talk and was tired of forcing her smile. She'd seen little of Holden, who spent most of the evening in a quiet corner with Julia. When she finally had a chance to speak to him after dinner, she was a bit cranky. He was light-hearted.

"Nice party," he commented pleasantly.

"How would you know?"

"What's that supposed to mean?"

"You've spent the entire evening on the sofa with Julia." After checking to see that no one was watching, she slipped off her left shoe and rubbed the back of her heel.

"She's the one person in this room who's my age."

"Your age?" she repeated in disbelief. "She's twenty-one."

"I'm closer to her in years than I am to the rest of these people," he said, glancing about the room.

Merry ignored the remark. "You could at least try to be social."

"You didn't want me to make a scene. I'm not. I'm sitting quietly enjoying the company of your future stepdaughter."

She eyed him suspiciously. "I'm warning you, Holden. Don't pump her for information about Steve."

"I wouldn't do that," he said.

Merry pursed her lips. "Yeah, right."

"For your information," Holden continued, "we've been talking about the justice system. You didn't tell me Steve had a daughter interested in law school."

"She told me she was premed."

"No, she's seriously considering law."

"And that's what the two of you have been talking about all night? The law?" Merry lifted one eyebrow.

"Partly. Having just broke up with her boyfriend, she needed someone to listen to her."

"Oh, and you're a shoulder to cry on, is that it?"

"No, I'm just someone who's listening to her—something her father apparently hasn't done."

Merry rushed to her fiancé's defense. "That's not fair. Steve's been very good to her."

"Maybe, but she can't talk to him about this. He liked the ex-boyfriend."

"So did I. He was nice."

"Maybe, but it sounds as if he was all wrong for Julia. She's a smart, ambitious young woman. She needs someone who doesn't feel threatened by that." He reached for a handful of nuts and popped them in his mouth.

"And who would that be?" she asked sarcastically.

"I didn't say I want it to be me." He looked shocked at her suggestion.

"Then maybe you should make an effort to circulate, instead of isolating yourself in a corner with her. You're not doing her a favor by encouraging her attention."

"I'm only talking to her."

Merry would have debated the point, but the appearance of the two people they were discussing made them fall silent. Julia sashayed over to Holden, batting her false eyelashes shamelessly. She was followed by her father, who didn't look at all pleased that his daughter was flirting with Holden.

Merry didn't blame him. The sight of Holden with Julia was a problem for her, too. It gave her a funny kink in her stomach. That was nothing compared to the out-and-out jolt she experienced when Julia dragged Holden over to the mistletoe hanging in the archway and planted a kiss on his mouth. Pretending not to notice, Merry quickly turned to Steve and asked him to get her another glass of punch.

It turned out to be a very long night for Merry. She was in no mood to answer what seemed to be an infinite number of questions about the wedding and listen to anecdotes about married life. And she was tired of overhearing comments about what a wonderful hostess Steve's wife had been. Tongues had wagged as word spread that Merry hadn't provided a single item on the buffet table.

It was obvious that Holden was enjoying himself much more than she was. Eventually her head was throbbing and she'd had enough of the endless small talk and the toasts to her future. She wanted to leave.

When Julia offered to act as hostess so that her father could drive Merry home, Holden protested. "There's no reason for your father to leave his party," he said with the smile that had been turning female heads all night, including Steve's ninety-year-old aunt. Merry had to give him credit. When he wanted, Holden could be very charming.

While Julia retrieved their coats, Steve stood with a protective arm around Merry's shoulders, a forced smile on his face. "I hate to send you home alone," he said to Merry, his fingers smoothing back a stray curl.

His comment brought a frown to Holden's face. "She's not alone. She's with me."

Steve's grip tightened on Merry. Uncomfortable with the tension between the two of them, she moved away. "Excuse me."

She stepped between them and across the tiled entryway to a small alcove where framed portraits of Austin family members filled the walls. As she studied the photographs she heard Julia come up behind her.

"You'd better be careful, Merry. You're standing under the mistletoe," the younger woman said.

Merry was about to glance back at her fiancé when Holden crept up behind her and planted a kiss on her mouth. It was a chaste kiss, a brief meeting of warm lips that meant no more than the kisses he usually planted on her cheeks.

Only this time Merry's senses didn't respond as if it was a chaste kiss from an old friend. She wanted to wrap her arms around him and hold that warm, moist mouth against hers. It shocked her, the unexpected reaction she had to him, and she pushed him away.

"Dad, shame on you! You weren't fast enough," Julia scolded good-naturedly. "Don't move, Merry. My father needs a chance."

In a flash Steve was in front of her. His kiss was everything Holden's wasn't. Hard. Possessive. Demanding.

Only Merry's senses didn't react to her fiancé's kiss the way they had to Holden's. Partly because she knew that the only reason Steve was making such a passionate demonstration was he was angry that Holden had kissed her. Annoyed, she pushed him away, too.

"It's late. Thanks for a lovely party," she said politely.

She watched Holden give Julia a kiss on her cheek and Steve a handshake, then allowed him to escort her to the car. As soon as they were inside, she let him have it.

"You deliberately did that to annoy Steve," she accused.

"Did what?" he asked innocently, turning on the ignition.

"Kiss me under that stupid mistletoe."

He backed out of the drive and turned down the street. "It's Christmas. I always kiss you at Christmastime," he said innocently.

"Oh, pig's ass!"

He chuckled. "I haven't heard you say that since we were kids. Rosie would turn over in her grave if she knew you still used that expression."

"I don't think she'd have been exactly thrilled with your behavior this evening, either."

"I was the perfect gentleman."

"Pig's ass."

"I was."

"You did everything in your power to irritate my fiancé. I watched you all evening. I wouldn't be a bit surprised if that wasn't the reason you were hanging around Julia. Just to get back at Steve."

"I hung around her because she was the only one with any life in her. I can't believe you think that getting that bunch for a family is the pot of gold at the end of the rainbow."

"There's nothing wrong with his family," she defended her future in-laws, forgetting that earlier in the evening she'd been thinking similar thoughts.

"Not if you happen to like stodgy old farts. 'Fun' must not be in the Austin dictionary."

"You could have tried a little harder to fit in," she admonished him. "And you could have been friendlier toward Steve."

"I was friendly."

"I'm sure Julia thought so," she said petulantly. She sighed and bit her lip. "I should have known you'd try to ruin it for me."

"I didn't ruin it for you!" he denied hotly. "I want you to answer me one question. Who made you unhappy this evening? Me or Steve?"

"You both did," she blurted. "It was my engagement party and you didn't offer a single toast to my happiness." Very seldom did she cry, but suddenly she felt weepy.

"I'm sorry," he said tenderly, reaching over to cover her hand with his. "I should have, but there seemed to be enough Austins to do that. Besides, I wasn't in a festive mood, especially not after I heard you give Steve credit for your success as a musician."

"He *is* the reason I'm a success."

"No, he's not," Holden stated firmly. "You're a success because you're you. You have the talent, Merry, not Steve. You're the one with the recording contract, not Steve. He may be a slick salesman, but he's done nothing that any other smart salesman wouldn't have done. He's promoted you."

"Why are you so critical of him? Everybody else I know thinks we're a perfect match."

Holden snorted. "Perfect for him maybe. In you, he's gaining a great product to market."

She sighed again. "What's the point in arguing? We're never going to agree on the subject, and it's only creating tension between us."

"We're not arguing. We're discussing your relationship with your fiancé," Holden said smoothly, pulling into the driveway of her building.

"Discussing? Steve is right. You *are* confrontational," she threw at him before getting out of the car.

"Just because I examine both sides of an issue doesn't mean I'm confrontational," he said, following her up the steps to the front door.

"That's my point. I don't want you examining *any* sides of my issues." She inserted the key and opened the door.

"I have to. I care about you."

"I'm not going to enjoy your visit if you keep harping on Steve's unsuitability, Holden." She turned to face him, a plea in her eyes. "I do want to enjoy your visit."

Holden closed the door behind him. "You will, I promise. Tomorrow night I'm going to take you someplace special for dinner."

She shrugged out of her coat. "Steve, too?"

He took the coat from her and hung it in the closet. "Julia told me Steve's working tomorrow night."

"So you *did* pump her for information."

He ignored the reprimand. "Just be ready tomorrow night at six."

"Where are we going?"

"I ran into an old friend who invited me to his house in the country. It's a casual Christmas party, only a handful of people, so you don't need to worry about glitter—although on you, it looks good."

His eyes moved over her appreciatively, and Merry felt her stomach do the flip-flop that was becoming more and more frequent now that Holden was her house guest.

"The only requirement," he added, "is that you dress in warm clothes. We're going to be outdoors part of the time."

"You hate the cold," she reminded him.

"I can take it if you can," he said. "Of course if your fiancé won't let you go…" He let the words hang there in the air, a challenge in his tone.

"He doesn't control me," she said stiffly. "I'll go. Now, if you're through cross-examining me, I'm going to bed."

She started to leave, but he stopped her with a gentle tug on her arm. "Wait." He reached into his pocket and pulled out a wilted piece of mistletoe. "I stole this from the Austins so I wouldn't have to feel guilty about kissing another man's fiancée good-night."

He dangled it over her glittery curls and gave her a kiss that was as fluttery and soft as a feather. Then he vanished down the hall.

Merry didn't move for several seconds, not because she was stunned by the kiss, but because she was left thinking of how much she wished he'd kissed her the way Steve had, as if he wanted to possess her.

As she prepared for bed, she heard Holden moving about in his room. Unbidden came thoughts of *him* preparing for bed—how he looked without his shirt, his hair rumpled, his five-o'clock shadow and how it would feel against her skin.

Again Steve's words echoed in her memory. *You're not brother and sister.*

No, they weren't, and in the few days he'd been staying with her there'd been too many reminders of that. Steve was probably right about one thing—it wasn't a good idea for any man and woman to be living in such close confines when they weren't related.

As she lay in bed she tried to convince herself that was all it was—the normal reaction any woman would feel sharing her home with a man. The intimacy of the arrangement made her conscious that he was an attractive, virile man.

Not only that, his presence reminded her of things she preferred to forget—such as the time she'd acted just like Julia. Rosie had called her feelings for Holden hero worship. But what Rosie hadn't known was that those feelings had been triggered one night when Holden was home from college for Thanksgiving weekend.

She'd had a crush on a boy in her school, and had just suffered great humiliation at his hands. It had been too much to bear, and she'd been sobbing into her pillow in the middle of the night when Holden walked in.

Wearing only a pair of jeans, he'd come right to her bedside. When she realized he was standing over her, she told him to leave. He didn't. He turned on the small lamp on the nightstand and sat on the edge of the mattress, urging her to stop crying.

"I can't," she told him on a sob. "My life is ruined forever."

"No, it's not," he said.

"It is, it is," she kept repeating between her sobs.

"Merry, what happened?" he asked. "Did some boy hurt you?"

"It doesn't matter," she wailed. "But I'll never let another boy near me. I don't want to. I hate them! All of them!"

Holden didn't say anything for a moment, just listened to her cry. Then he said in a near whisper, "You don't hate me, do you?"

"No." It was a muffled sound.

"Merry, listen to me. Just because one boy is too stupid to recognize a special girl when he sees one doesn't mean you're not special."

"It's so embarrassing. He...he told everyone at school that I didn't know how to kiss, and now all the guys snicker when I walk down the halls."

"He only said that because he's angry you didn't give him what he wanted, Merry."

"You mean...sex?"

"Yeah. Some guys are real jerks about it. If they don't get what they want, they make up lies about the girl."

"But it's not a lie," she told him. "I...I don't know how to kiss."

"Sure you do. All girls do. It comes naturally."

"Not for me. I can't kiss and I don't like it when boys touch me." She paused, then said dramatically, "I think I'm frigid."

"No, you're not. Look at me."

She refused, burying her face in her pillow, her body curled in a ball. "Go away...please."

"I'm not going away. I want to help you."

"You can't."

"Yes, I can."

He began touching her as if she were a small child needing comfort, smoothing her hair away from her brow. Gradually the sobbing diminished. He slid onto the bed, propping himself against the headboard and stretching his legs in front of him.

"Come on. Sit beside me like we always do when we talk."

Reluctant at first, she finally sat up and moved closer to him. He switched off the small lamp and looped his arm around her, gently pulling her to his side.

"The reason you don't want any of those guys touching you is because you don't have real feelings for them. You're not frigid, Merry."

As he talked, his thumb made a tiny circle on the hand he held. "Do you want me to prove it to you?" he asked.

She looked up at him, knowing full well what the proof would be. She nodded, looking to him for reassurance.

Then he lifted her chin and outlined her mouth with his fingertips. "You're very beautiful, Merry. It's no wonder guys want to touch you," he said in a hoarse voice.

Then his mouth covered hers in a soft kiss. It was a mere brushing of lips, yet for Merry it was as if she'd finally reached the end of a very long road. He kissed her again, this time his lips lingering a second longer until finally his mouth clung to hers, molding and shaping until it was no longer a question of whether it felt good, but how much better it made her feel.

Passion stirred in Merry, creating sensations she'd never experienced before. She wanted the kiss to go on forever. She wanted to make Holden part of her skin, part of her nerve endings, part of her very soul.

Her lips parted and the kiss deepened. She heard Holden groan, then shift so that her head was now on the pillow and he was over her. Her fingers wound themselves into his hair, then moved down his neck, reveling in the feel of his broad, naked back. His skin was hot to the touch, matching the heat that seared her insides.

This was Holden. Her Holden. The only man who would never hurt her. The only man she would ever love.

But he hadn't loved her. The reason he'd kissed her and caressed her had just been to show her that she did know how to kiss, that she was not frigid.

That night their relationship had changed. If she'd had any illusions that it had been anything more than a kissing lesson, they'd soon been shattered. Holden had gone back to college as if nothing had happened between them. When he hadn't come home for Christmas, Merry had known she was harboring false hopes to think he felt the same way about her as she did about him.

The problem was that to this day she hadn't met a man who could kiss as well as he did. Not even Steve. And it was that thought that kept her awake into the wee hours of the morning.

CHAPTER EIGHT

IT WAS SNOWING when Merry awoke the following morning. As she got out of bed and glanced out the window at the delicate flakes drifting to the ground, she could hear the shower running. Her thoughts turned to the man standing beneath the spray of water and her body warmed.

"Stop it!" she chastised herself aloud. "It's not like you're a teenager anymore."

With impatient movements, she straightened the covers and fluffed the pillows. She started for the door, then stopped. Ever since Holden had arrived she hadn't ventured out of her room without getting dressed first.

She looked forward to the day when he'd return to California and she'd have her cozy, comfortable home all to herself. Only she wouldn't be alone for long, she realized as her diamond twinkled up at her from her finger. Soon she would be married and living with Steve.

Merry suddenly realized that not once since he'd proposed had they discussed living arrangements. Obviously Steve assumed she would want to move into his house. He took a lot for granted. She hadn't realized just how much until Holden had arrived.

A restlessness filled her and had her pacing the floor until finally she did what she always did when she needed to relax. Forgetting that all she was wearing were her pajamas, she went into the living room and sat down at the piano. Playing never failed to make her feel in control and confident.

Instead of the holiday tunes she played so frequently at this time of year, she played a Beethoven sonata that she'd performed at one of her recitals when she'd been in college. When she finished the emotional piece, a solitary round of applause echoed in the silence. She turned to see Holden sitting on the sofa, an appreciative gleam in his eye.

"You should be performing with a symphony orchestra," he said.

His praise warmed her. "Being a concert pianist is a lonely job, and it wouldn't pay me what playing my pop tunes does."

"Are you saying John Q. Public isn't as discerning a listener?"

"I guess I am."

"And what about you? What music do you prefer?"

"Well, I like to play by ear. I couldn't do that if I played in an orchestra. Besides, I like to create music. I'm working on a new recording. Want to hear one of my new songs?"

"You need to ask?"

Again his appreciative smile warmed her and she was eager to please him, just as she'd always been as a child. Then she forgot everything but the music as her fingers created their magic.

"Seems like old times, doesn't it?" he remarked when she lifted her hands from the keys and turned to face him. "The first thing you used to do on Saturday mornings when we were kids was rush downstairs and play the piano."

"Yes, and Rosie would scold me for not taking the time to change out of my pajamas first," Merry reflected wistfully.

"You'll get no scolding from me," he said with a slow grin that made Merry's heart thump a little out of rhythm. "I like the way you look in pajamas."

Merry glanced down at herself, suddenly self-conscious. Why hadn't she at least put a robe on? Although her satin pajamas covered her from neck to ankle, they were still rather intimate apparel.

"I'd better get dressed," she told him, hoping he hadn't noticed the rush of heat to her cheeks. "Holly will be here in a few minutes." She was about to slip by him when the doorbell rang.

Her eyes met his. "That's probably her now. Will you let her in?" Fearing her pajamas revealed more than she wanted Holden to see, she quickly headed for her bedroom, saying as she went, "Tell her I'll be out in a few minutes."

She could hear amusement in Holden's voice as he asked, "Does she know what to do on her own?"

"Yes. She'll be fine."

Although "fine" was hardly how Merry would have classified the music she heard as she showered and dressed. Discordance filled the air until finally there was no sound at all.

Merry wondered if the girl was in the kitchen looking for something to eat. She realized that in her hurry to get away from Holden, she'd forgotten to set refreshments out for her.

However, she found Holly not at the piano or in the kitchen but standing by the patio door looking out at the pine tree, which was now frosted with snow.

Merry crossed to her and said softly, "Hi. Are you having problems with the music?"

"It's not going to work out," Holly replied disconsolately.

"Don't get discouraged." Merry touched the girl's arm. "It takes time to learn to do anything well."

"Well, I don't have any time."

"Why? What's the problem?"

"I . . . I'm not going to be around for a while."

"Are you going away?"

She looked at Merry, her eyes cloudy. "Bonnie hasn't told you?"

"Told me what?"

"I'm leaving the Hawthornes."

Merry felt a great wave of empathy. "I'm sorry. No, Bonnie didn't tell me. Do you know where you're going?"

"It depends on what happens in juvenile court," she admitted solemnly.

"Juvenile court?" Merry's heart sank. "What kind of trouble are you in, Holly?"

The girl chewed on her lip before saying, "You don't want to know."

"Yes, I do." Merry reached for Holly's hand. "Maybe I can help."

Holly pulled her hand out of Merry's grasp, saying, "Not if I'm sent to a group home you can't."

Merry knew that being sent to a group home was a disciplinary action. It was a place where Holly would encounter other troubled teenagers. It would mean a temporary loss of freedom and yet another transition for a child who needed permanence in her life.

"That doesn't mean the lessons have to stop," Merry told her with an optimism she wasn't feeling. "We can probably figure out some way for you to continue. You do want to continue, don't you?"

"No."

Her answer caught Merry totally off guard. "I'm sorry. I thought you wanted to play."

"I do, but it isn't going to work out," she repeated. "Besides, I shouldn't come here."

"Why do you say that?"

"Because I'm just in the way. You have other stuff to do. You don't need me making noise." She kept her eyes downcast as she spoke.

"I have other students, Holly."

"You're a music teacher?"

Merry nodded. "I used to teach at Emerson Elementary, but now I only have a few students here in my home."

"How come you quit?"

"I wanted to perform more than I wanted to teach—or at least I thought I did. Lately I've been thinking that I shouldn't give up my students, because I really like teaching piano. It gives me great pleasure." She paused. "I want to teach you, Holly."

The girl shrugged. "You can get other students."

"Not any as gifted as you."

"I didn't sound gifted today."

"That's because your heart wasn't in your playing. You're worried about what's going to happen in juvenile court next week."

"Every time something good happens to me it doesn't last," Holly said on a note of self-pity that struck a familiar chord in Merry. How many times as a child had she thought the same thing?

"This time it might be different."

The look Holly gave Merry said she didn't believe her.

"You know what you need?" Merry said. "You need to play." She led her back to the piano and sat her down. "Instead of thinking all those bad thoughts, let the keys express your emotions for you. I don't care how dissonant it sounds."

"What's dissonant?"

Merry played several atonal chords. "Stuff that sounds like that—out of tune, not in harmony."

"But I want my playing to sound like your music."

Merry was genuinely touched. "It will eventually. But for now it has to sound a little dissonant. If you don't want to practice the music I assigned you, play anything you like."

Holly did as Merry instructed, making at times what Merry would have classified as noise, not music, but Merry pretended not to notice. While Holly played, Merry thought about the thirteen-year-old's predicament. In the short while she'd known Holly, a slender thread had been woven between them. She wished she could give Holly what Rosie had given her—hope. As she listened, an idea formed in her mind.

"Holly, how would you like to come with me to the recording studio?" she asked when the playing stopped.

"Would they let me in?"

"If you're with me, they will. We're doing a session for my next CD, and I thought you might like to see the difference between playing live and in a studio."

"But Bonnie's going to be here soon," Holly said on an unhappy note.

"I can tell her I'll bring you home when we're finished. That is, if you want to go..."

"Won't I be in the way?"

"No, of course not. If we phone Bonnie now we might be able to catch her before she leaves."

Holly agreed, and from that point on she was like a different child. On their way to the studio, they stopped for a pizza, despite Holly's protests that she wasn't hungry.

From the look on Holly's face as they entered the studio, Merry could see that few experiences in the girl's life could compare with this one. With pupils as round and big as glass marbles, she watched and listened attentively to every explanation and demonstration.

It was an afternoon well spent, for not only did the session go smoothly but it seemed to Merry she'd broken through the wall of reserve Holly had erected. The thirteen-year-old returned to her foster home with a satisfied grin.

Merry, however, didn't return to her own home smiling. As much as she wanted to help Holly, being with the girl left her with a strange, almost empty feeling inside. As Holden drove her to their dinner party, he noticed she was not herself.

He commented on that, then asked, "Did you have a fight with Steve?"

"Sorry to disappoint you, but no," she lied, not wanting to admit that she and Steve had quarreled when she'd told him she couldn't see him after work because she was having dinner with Holden.

"Then what is it?"

"Spending the day with Holly can be a sobering experience." She told him what had happened and why she'd taken her to the recording studio.

"Do you know what kind of trouble she's in?"

"She wouldn't tell me. I was hoping you might be able to find out." She cast him an appealing glance.

"Sorry. They're not going to let me anywhere near juvenile court, not when I practice family law in California. Why don't you talk to her foster mother?"

"I'm going to. Holly thinks that even if she doesn't get sent to the group home, she's going to be moved."

"I'm not surprised. If she's been in a lot of trouble, it can be disruptive to the foster home, especially if there are other kids around."

"Rosie never would've sent any of us away," Merry said quietly.

"No, but there aren't many Rosies in this world, are there?"

They rode in silence, then Merry said, "It bothers me to think of Holly being shuffled from home to home. It's too bad someone doesn't adopt her."

"Having a criminal record doesn't make her an attractive candidate for adoption," he pointed out.

"She's not a criminal." Merry was quick to rush to her defense. "The reason she's been in trouble is the situation she's in. She needs a stable environment."

"Every child does," he agreed. "There are no bad kids..."

"...only bad situations," she finished for him.

"And then there are those kids with no parents." She sighed. "Isn't there some way we can find a foster family that'd be right for her?"

"That's the job of the Department of Human Services, remember?"

"But it's not working."

"You don't know that. Maybe the next family she meets will be the right one."

"And if it's not?"

He shrugged. "Then she continues to have problems." He glanced at Merry. "This is really bothering you, isn't it?"

"Holden, there's something about this girl that gets to me. I want to tell her she can be anything she wants to be, that she'll survive all the lousy hands life's dealt her, but I'm not sure she'd believe me."

"Probably not yet, anyway."

Merry sighed. "I just wish there was more I could do to help her."

"Have you thought about taking her in yourself? You still have your foster-care license, don't you?"

"Yes, but you know what a disaster I was as a foster mother." It still wasn't a time in her life she cared to think about.

"You were not a disaster."

"It didn't work, Holden."

"That's because you were only twenty-four. Besides, your motivation was different back then. You took in foster children as a way for you to deal with Rosie's death. The situation is totally different today. *You're* different."

She shook her head. "It wouldn't work."

He didn't argue with her, but let the subject drop as he drove the dark country roads. Merry was relieved he didn't push the issue. She was having enough trouble dealing with the emotions being Holly's piano teacher had stirred. She didn't want to think of what would happen if she was to play an even bigger role in the girl's life.

When Holden maneuvered the car down a long, snow-packed winding driveway that wound up in front of an old two-story farmhouse, Merry said, "This looks like a painting on a Christmas card."

Several cars were parked between the house and the barn. Holden pulled up beside a silver Mercedes. "Doug said he made sure when the renovations were done that the house's country charm was maintained."

As he helped Merry from the car, the sound of bells jingled through the crisp winter air. Merry turned toward the stable and saw a horse-drawn sleigh coming toward them. At the reins was a man wearing a ski jacket and a cowboy hat.

"Hey! How's it going, Holden?" He stopped the sleigh in front of the house, then jumped down and gave Holden a bear hug. He turned to Merry and said, "Hi, Remember me? Doug Jarvis."

Doug Jarvis. Merry tossed the name around in her mind but drew a blank until Holden said, "She doesn't remember you, despite your incredible popularity, because she was four years behind us in school."

Suddenly the square jaw and crooked smile clicked with Merry. Doug had only been at Hibbing High for one year, yet he and Holden had become good friends.

At that moment the front door opened and two women wearing fur-trimmed parkas came out followed by another man in a leather bomber jacket. "Doug, you did promise us warm food sometime this evening, didn't you?" one of the women asked.

"It's why the sleigh's out here, madam." He gestured like a nineteenth-century footman. "But first you have to meet Holden and Merry."

Smoothly he made the introductions. Merry learned that the well-dressed women were Jeannie and Caroline, and the third man was Rick. Jeannie was Doug's date and Caroline had come with Rick, although Merry couldn't help but notice how both women eyed Holden as if he had a For Sale sign on his back.

Doug shook the bell-trimmed reins and said, "Sleigh bells are ringing," indicating they should get on board. Holden cheerfully played the gentleman, gallantly helping each of the women into the sleigh, then snuggling in beside Merry. Doug sat up front on the driver's seat and Jeannie didn't look the least bit disappointed. She was perfectly willing to squeeze in on Holden's other side, leaving Caroline and Rick to share the seat across from them.

"Hey, Doug, where are the lap robes?" Jeannie called out to him.

"You won't need them. It's a perfect night for a sleigh ride."

"But what if we get cold?"

"Hey, guys, make sure those women stay warm back there, will you?" Doug's command was delivered lightly.

"I don't think it'll be a problem, do you, Rick?" Holden asked, draping his arms around the back of the seat so that he could pull both Merry and Jeannie closer to him.

"No problem whatsoever," Rick agreed. "We have this." He reached beneath his coat and brought out a bottle of champagne. "Who brought the glasses?"

Caroline reached into a purse the size of an overnight bag and pulled out half-a-dozen plastic flutes. Before long they were all toasting the holiday season as the sleigh glided over the snow-covered fields.

Conversation was lively as Jeannie and Caroline regaled everyone with stories of the condition of the farm when Doug had first purchased it. Somehow Merry had trouble picturing either of them with a mop and bucket in hand, but she nodded in sympathy as they recounted the horror of helping Doug clean up the place.

If their tales were for Holden's benefit, Merry could have told them he found nothing inspirational about scrubbing floors. The first thing he'd done when he'd landed a job after law school was to hire a housekeeper.

When the conversation turned to outdoor winter sports, Merry tuned out. She'd never been enthusiastic about skiing or snowmobiling. As if sensing her withdrawal, Holden tightened his arm, pulling her closer to him.

"Are you having fun?" he said close to her ear.

"It's nice," she replied, trying to straighten away from him, but he was not about to release his hold on her.

"What do you think, Holden?" Doug asked, twisting in his seat. "Does this bring back memories of Snow Days at Hibbing High?"

While Holden answered Caroline's and Jeannie's questions about Hibbing's annual winter celebration, Merry's thoughts turned to her own memories. The last time she'd been on a sleigh ride with Holden she'd been fourteen. And it hadn't actually been a sleigh but an old hay wagon that had wheels, instead of metal runners, and kept getting stuck in the snow. Everyone who was anyone at the high school was at the Benson-farm sleigh ride and barn dance.

The only reason Merry went was that Colleen Benson was her best friend and they had convinced her parents that two junior-high students wouldn't get in the way of the older teens.

Merry had thought it would be so neat to be the only junior-high kids at the sleigh ride. What she hadn't expected was that Holden would ignore her and spend all his time flirting with Colleen's older sister, Nancy.

Just when Merry had thought the night couldn't get much worse, she'd been pushed off the hay wagon by a scrawny tenth grader. Expecting Holden to come to her rescue, she discovered that there was only one thing he was going to do that night—look out for Nancy Benson.

Disgusted, Merry had walked all the way back to the barn by herself only to find the dance had already started and Holden was cheek to cheek with Nancy.

Her lipstick was smudged and Merry knew they'd been kissing.

"Are you cold?" Holden's question brought her back to the present.

She shook her head. With his big warm body pressed against hers she definitely wasn't cold. If anything, she was *too* comfortable cuddled next to him. She was relieved to see the sleigh pull up in front of a log cabin with lights shining through its windows.

"This is where we're having dinner," Doug announced when the sleigh stopped. "It's an old hunting lodge. I discovered it when I was out kicking around one day."

"It looks charming," Jeannie cooed, allowing Holden to help her down from the sleigh.

"I promised you a real country Christmas dinner," Doug said.

Holden helped Merry climb down. He didn't release her once she had both feet on the ground, but steered her toward the cabin.

"Well, what do you think?" he asked her as they stepped inside the rustic cabin with its rough-hewn furnishings, plank flooring and walls covered with antlers and trophy heads.

"It's, uh, interesting," she said, unable to think of any other suitable adjective.

Dinner was served by a woman in a black uniform and white apron. They ate by candlelight, which gave the room an intimate, romantic glow. Merry was seated across from Holden and between the other two men. That left Caroline and Jeannie on either side of Holden.

Once again, as had happened at Steve's party, Merry got to watch Holden charm women. He had a manner about him that few women could resist.

Jeannie's and Caroline's efforts to get his undivided attention were futile, for conversation traveled between all six of them. After a dinner of roasted pheasant, Doug suggested they gather around the fireplace. This time Holden positioned himself so that Merry was the only woman close to him. When he wound his fingers through hers, she didn't pull her hand away.

"Holden tells me you're getting married," Doug said to Merry.

That caused both Jeannie's and Caroline's eyes to widen.

"We haven't set a date yet, but the engagement is official," Merry answered, enjoying the look on the women's faces. She saw Holden's eyes twinkle in amusement and didn't feel the least bit guilty about allowing the women to believe it was Holden she was engaged to.

"I'm just glad it happened, otherwise Holden probably wouldn't have come back to Minnesota and we never would've run into each other again," Doug commented.

Talk turned to the past and further reminiscence about high school life. Doug had a way of telling stories that had everyone laughing.

When Holden said it was time they leave, Merry was surprised to learn it was past midnight. When they returned to the main house by the horse-drawn sleigh, Doug insisted they come inside to see the results of the renovation. Consequently it was nearly one by the time they headed back to the city.

"You're awfully quiet," Holden remarked as the car rolled over the snow-packed roads.

"I'm tired."

"Oh. Worn out from all the activity?"

"What activity? All we did was sit and visit."

He chuckled. "Well, it took a little bit of energy for you to play your charade."

"I didn't play any charade."

"No? What do you call letting Jeannie and Caroline think you and I are engaged?"

"Oh, that." Now it was her turn to chuckle. "They deserved it. I mean, there they were with dates, but they would've gobbled you up if you'd let them. I can't believe Rick and Doug didn't mind."

"Jeannie and Caroline are the fun type. Rick and Doug know that. That's why they feel safe with them."

"Safe from what? Marriage?"

"You weren't worried about me getting trapped by one of them, were you?" he asked with an affectionate tone.

She made a sound of disbelief. "I know better than to worry about that."

A smile tugged at his lips. "How come you didn't tell Doug about Steve?"

"Because I thought it would've looked rather odd to have to defend him when you attacked him," she retorted.

"I wouldn't have said anything against him."

"Ha!"

"I wouldn't. Besides, even if I had, Doug would've understood. He remembers how I always looked out for you in high school."

"Except that night of the Bensons' barn party."

"What are you talking about?"

"I'm talking about me getting shoved off the hay wagon and you not even noticing I was missing because you were playing kissy-face with Nancy Benson."

"Nancy who?"

She groaned. "I know, you don't remember any Nancy Benson. Gosh, it's a good thing I was never one of your girlfriends or you would have forgotten me, too."

Yawning, she said, "I really am tired. Wake me when we're there, okay?"

As she had so many times in the past, she used his shoulder for a pillow. Holden glanced down at her, noting her perfectly smooth complexion and the way her dark eyelashes fanned her cheek like threads of silk. He smiled, remembering all the times she'd fallen asleep on him before. Of all the women he'd ever known, she was the only one who could fall asleep sitting up.

He was glad he'd taken Doug up on his invitation. It had been a relaxing evening and a pleasure to watch Merry try to foil the flirtatious attempts of Jeannie and Caroline.

When he reached her house, he was tempted not to wake her and simply carry her inside. But as soon as he switched off the ignition, her eyes flew open.

"Are we home already?" she asked, looking about in confusion.

"It's after two," he told her, offering her a hand.

"You're kidding. I didn't realize it was so late when we left Doug's."

"Does that mean you enjoyed this evening?"

"Uh-huh."

"Good. Quite a contrast from last night, wasn't it?" he said as he led her to the front door.

She eyed him suspiciously. "So that's what tonight was all about."

"What?" he asked innocently, pushing the door open for her to enter.

"You wanted to show me what it's like to be with the singles crowd." She kicked off her boots in the entryway.

"You have to admit tonight's company was a lot more fun than last night's group of stuffed shirts," he answered, helping her out of her coat.

"Steve's friends and relatives are not stuffed shirts," she argued.

"He's too old for you, Merry. You should be out having fun with people your own age, not providing gossip for the gray-haired ladies in Steve's family." He brushed an errant strand of hair back from her cheek with his finger.

"You never give up, do you?"

"I can't help it. It bugs the hell out of me to think of you married to him." He held her eyes with his. Her hair was tousled from wearing a stocking hat, her makeup had faded, but never, he thought, had she looked more beautiful.

He wanted to kiss her, to kiss her until she admitted that Steve Austin was the wrong man for her. What he was feeling must have shown in his face, for she quickly lowered her gaze and turned away from him.

"I'm too tired to argue with you," she said. "I'll see you in the morning."

And before he could reach out and pull her into his arms, she was on her way to her bedroom.

CHAPTER NINE

"DO YOU THINK we could change our dinner reservation to three?" Merry asked Steve the following afternoon as they relaxed in her living room in front of the fire.

He frowned. "I thought you said Holden had plans for this evening."

"He does. I'm not talking about Holden. I'd like to take Holly with us."

"You want to bring your music student with us on a date?"

"Yes. I don't think she's ever seen the Hollidazzle Parade." When Steve didn't comment, Merry said, "You don't like the idea, do you."

He'd been reading the Sunday paper, but put it aside with a sigh. "I was looking forward to an evening alone with you. Ever since Holden's been here, I feel as if we haven't had any privacy."

"It hasn't been that bad," she said, but she knew what he was talking about. Holden had disrupted their lives. She was spending more time alone with him than she was with her fiancé and in a much more intimate setting.

Steve folded his arms across his chest and asked, "What is it about this girl that has you so interested in her?"

Merry shrugged. "I don't know. Maybe I see
something of me in her. Our pasts are quite similar."

"You were hardly a criminal," he said with a shake
of his head.

"I was no angel, either." She got up from the sofa
to put another log on the fire.

"What are you saying? That you were in trouble as
a child?"

"No, but I could have been. If I hadn't ended up
with somebody like Rosie for a foster mom," she told
him, poking at the burning logs with an andiron.

Steve got up and came to stand beside her. "Doesn't
this Holly have a foster mother she can turn to for
guidance?"

"She's had several foster mothers, and she's about
to be moved again. That's what concerns me. What
she needs more than anything is a stable environment. Unfortunately kids like her often get lost in the
system."

"And I suppose you want to find her." He didn't
sound very happy.

She gave him a puzzled look. "I want to help her
find herself."

"By becoming her mentor?"

"Is there anything wrong with that?"

"No, it's just..." He let his words trail off.

"It's just what?"

"You're getting awfully involved with someone you
hardly know."

Merry glared at him. "Seems to me we had this discussion of my 'involvement' before."

"Yes, and at that time you were only going to give
her piano lessons. Next thing I know she's practicing

on your piano every day. *Now* you want to entertain her."

"And that bothers you?"

"Yes, it does. Just how much help are you planning on giving this girl?"

Becoming increasingly uneasy with his attitude, Merry answered, "I'm not sure. All I know is that she's a gifted child who may get lost in the system. I can't let that happen."

"How do you propose to stop it?"

"I don't know," she answered honestly, although she had considered one possibility. She could be Holly's foster mother. But she didn't want to express that idea just now.

Steve took Merry by the shoulders and looked into her eyes. "You're a brilliant musician. You're also a warm and caring woman, which is why you're responding to this girl."

"Look. I'd just like her to come along with us tonight."

"Fine, we'll take her," he said graciously, although Merry doubted he was feeling charitable toward Holly at the moment.

To her surprise, however, Steve was very kind, almost fatherly, to the thirteen-year-old. As Merry suspected, it was the first time Holly had seen the annual Hollidazzle Parade, featuring fairy-tale characters illuminated by thousands of lights. As band members marched past with their instruments aglow, she clapped her mittened hands to the rhythm of the drummers. Delighted by the procession of floats, she forgot all about the frigid temperatures.

It was with flushed cheeks and sparkling eyes that Holly took her seat in the Italian restaurant Steve had chosen. Any misgivings Merry had about the evening were gone. Steve and Holly both seemed to be having a good time.

At least they were until Holly said to Merry, "Isn't that your brother over there?"

Merry glanced toward the entrance and saw Holden talking to the hostess. Julia was clinging to his arm.

"Why didn't you tell me Holden's plans included Julia?" Steve admonished her as he caught sight of his daughter.

"I didn't know," she replied, feeling a spurt of irritation that Holden hadn't told her, either.

"And he's not Merry's brother, Holly," Steve said.

Holly looked at Merry. "I thought he must be 'cause why else would he be living with you when you're engaged to Steve?"

Merry could see Steve squirm. "He's like a brother to me, Holly, but he's really just an old friend."

"And he doesn't live with Merry," Steve added with obvious annoyance. "He's just visiting." His brusque tone seemed to have a dampening effect on Holly.

"Sorry," she said sulkily.

"It's all right," Merry assured her, although judging by the look on Steve's face he didn't think it was all right. "Maybe we should ask the waitress to slide another table over so they can join us."

Sharing a table was not in Julia's plans, as they soon found out. She quickly rejected the invitation and asked the hostess to take them to a small table for two in the darkest corner of the restaurant so that Holden could tell her all about the law profession—or so she claimed.

From that point on, nothing was quite the same. Merry knew that Steve was not happy to see his daughter with Holden. The sight of Julia's blond head close to Holden's dark one made Merry uneasy, as well.

Holden could think what he liked, but any woman could see that Julia was attracted to him. It was another reason Merry wished they were finished eating. As soon as Holly indicated she was done, Merry suggested they have dessert at the ice-cream shop on the way home.

Later that evening, as she waited up for Holden, all sorts of images filled her imagination. Julia putting her hands on Holden's broad shoulders, Julia rubbing against him provocatively, Julia kissing him. It was the last thought that bothered Merry the most.

By the time Holden finally came through the front door, she had imagined all sorts of things, every one of them causing her great anxiety. Her first words to him were, "Why didn't you tell me you were taking Julia to dinner?"

"I thought you knew. Didn't Steve tell you?"

"No, because Julia didn't tell him."

"So what's the problem?" he asked, tossing his keys on the glass-topped table.

"Julia's young, Holden. She's not like the women you usually see."

"She's not that young. Her father's almost fifty." He emphasized "fifty."

Merry's shoulders stiffened. "Are you doing this to get back at me?"

"Doing what?"

"Dating Julia."

"I'm not dating Julia," he denied. "You told me Steve wanted to take you to dinner. I figured you didn't need me tagging along, so when Julia suggested I join her, I accepted. That's all there was to it."

"Pig's ass."

He clicked his tongue. "I hope you don't say that in front of Steve. He doesn't look the type to condone women using profanity."

"We're not talking about my fiancé, we're talking about you." She jabbed his chest with her finger.

"Then there's not a problem. I kind of like it when you lose control and cuss at me." He was flirting with her, which only added to her anger. "Just why are you cussing at me?"

"Because you're trying to cause trouble!"

"How is my having dinner with your future step-daughter causing trouble?"

"Because you only did it to annoy Steve."

He clicked his tongue again. "I don't think that statement would earn you any brownie points with your stepdaughter-to-be. I'm sure she thinks I went because I enjoy her company."

As much as Merry hated to admit it, that thought bothered her more than if he *was* simply trying to annoy Steve.

"Is she right? Do you enjoy her company?" Merry hated to ask the question, but she had to know the answer.

"More than I do her father's," he said dryly. "At least she has a sense of humor."

"If you're having such an unpleasant time, why don't you go back to California?" As soon as the words left her tongue, however, she wished she could retract them.

There was no amusement in his eyes now. "Is that what you want? For me to leave?"

Merry closed her eyes briefly. How had she gotten so out of control? What was it she really wanted? "No. I'm sorry I snapped at you." She extended a hand to him and he took it without hesitation.

"I'm sorry, too. This visit isn't going as I planned," he admitted, then he sank onto the couch, pulling her down beside him. "What's wrong between us, Merry? We've never had trouble talking in the past."

She relaxed. "I feel like I don't know who you are anymore, Holden."

"I'm the same person I've always been."

"No, you're not. You've changed."

"Are you sure it's me who's changed and not you?"

She shrugged. "All I know is ever since you arrived there's been this . . . tension between us."

"I know. I feel it, too."

"I want it to be the way it was when we were kids. We could talk about anything back then," she said on a sigh.

"You mean when we used to climb into the attic?"

She smiled. "My favorite spot."

"Not mine."

"You were too worried a big black spider might crawl on you," she teased affectionately.

"I still hate those things," he said, suppressing a shiver. "But as much as I hated them, I never left you alone up there."

"No, you were always willing to listen to me," she said softly. "I miss those talks."

He reached over to turn off the lamp.

"What are you doing?"

"Maybe we need to pretend like it's old times." He pulled her into the crook of his arm and held her protectively. The blinds on the patio weren't fully closed, allowing slivers of moonlight to shine through. "See? It's just like Rosie's attic. A little moonlight peeking through the cracks, not a sound to be heard . . . What more could you ask for?"

Merry didn't reply. She couldn't. She was too aware of the man beside her. It felt right being in his arms, sharing his warmth, his strength. Only her body wasn't responding to his as if it was seeking comfort. It wanted something more, and the thought frightened her.

"We're not kids any longer, Holden," she said at last.

"No, we're not," he agreed. She could feel his breath gently rustling her hair as he spoke. "The woman I saw sitting on that piano bench in Braxton's looked nothing like the scrawny kid who used to follow me around. She was full of confidence and poise. Full of beauty."

"It's the makeup." She tried to make light of his compliments. "Anyone can look glamorous with the right stuff."

"It has nothing to do with your makeup or your clothes. It's you," he said, his voice husky. "It's the woman you've become. You're a savvy business person, you're a warm entertainer the crowds respond to, and you're compassionate. I've seen you with Holly."

Merry's heart was racing, her skin tingling. Instead of seeing his face, she saw only lips, lips that were full and warm. Lips she wanted to feel pressed against hers. The thought made her stiffen; she knew she shouldn't be thinking along those lines.

"It's late. We should probably get to bed." She attempted to rise, but he stopped her.

"I thought you wanted to talk." His body leaned closer to hers and Merry panicked.

"This isn't going to work."

"Why? What's wrong?"

"I'm not sure," she lied. "It's probably because it's the holiday season. I'm never in a good mood this time of year."

"You should be happy, Merry." His voice had that reassuring, steady tone that was so familiar and dear to her. "You're getting what you've always wanted for Christmas—a family."

"I know."

"But?"

Several moments of silence ticked away before she said, "I'm afraid."

He squeezed her in a comforting manner, just as he'd always done when they were kids. "Afraid of what?"

"That no matter how old I get or how many children I have of my own, there's always going to be this wound inside me that opens up during the holiday season to remind me of that little girl who wanted her mom and dad to come take her home for Christmas." Her voice cracked with emotion.

"You don't need those people, Merry," he said, also just as he'd always done. "I thought you'd accepted that."

"Intellectually I have, but emotionally..." She trailed off uncertainly. "Holden, don't you ever feel something's missing?"

"Let me tell you something, Merry. There once was a little boy in me who used to fantasize that his dad would return and take him fishing and play football with him and do all the things normal dads do."

"I didn't know. You never said anything."

"It's not the kind of thing I tell anyone."

She reached for his hand. "You're telling me now."

"Because it doesn't matter anymore."

"Doesn't it?"

"No. That little boy is gone."

Merry's heart ached for that little boy. She'd never seen him, for when she met Holden he was already trying hard to act like an adult.

"Don't you ever wonder what your father's doing?" she asked. "Where he's living?"

"I know where he is."

"You do?"

"I had him traced. He's in Las Vegas. On wife number four, I believe." There was bitterness in his voice.

"Why didn't you tell me?"

"Because it doesn't matter."

"Of course it does. Have you've seen him?"

"I sent him a round-trip plane ticket to L.A." Holden paused, then said, "He never came."

Merry knew how troubled Holden's relationship with his father had been. When he was eight his father had stolen money from his boss and been fired. To put food on the table, his mother had sold Holden's most prized possession—his bike. From an early age Holden had peddled newspapers and shoveled walks to earn money to help out with expenses. When he was ten, his father had finally run off with some woman and ended up in jail after stealing a car. A year later his mother had died of a brain aneurysm, and Holden had never forgiven his father for running out on them.

Merry wanted to hold him and stroke his hair, and tell him everything would be all right, but she didn't. She knew he wouldn't appreciate her sympathy. So all she did was squeeze his hand and say, "I'm sorry."

"Don't be."

"Why? It must have hurt to be rejected by him again."

"He didn't reject me. I rejected him—twenty-three years ago when he ran out on me and my mother. The only reason I sent him that ticket was so he could see that no matter how miserable he'd tried to make my life, I'd made a success of myself."

"Are you angry that he didn't see that?"

"No. It doesn't matter. There's no place for him in my life."

Merry studied Holden silently for a moment, then said, "Is there a place for me?"

"Maybe I should be asking *you* that question."

"My marriage isn't going to mean the end of our friendship, Holden."

"Isn't it?"

"No. You're too important to me."

"Merry, Steve isn't going to let me be a part of your life."

"Of course he will. Why wouldn't he?"

"Because of this." He lowered his head and kissed her.

It was a warm, seductive kiss that caught Merry totally off guard. At first she was too stunned to react, but then her body melted into his and her lips responded to the intimate caress. It bore no resemblance to the light, friendly kisses they usually shared.

No. This kiss was long and hard and deep. When he finally pulled away, she had to bite her lower lip to keep it from trembling.

"Wh-why did you do that?" she asked.

"Because I wanted to."

She got to her feet and moved away from the couch—and him. "Well, I didn't want you to," she said, ignoring the tremors of pleasure that still rippled through her. "I'm engaged to be married."

"You shouldn't be—not if you can kiss me like that."

He rose from the couch, too, and came toward her, but she quickly stepped back, bumping into the piano bench in the darkness. "Ouch! Now see what you've made me do. I've hurt myself."

"I'm sorry. Here, come sit down and I'll make your hurt better."

From his tone she knew he found the whole situation amusing, and it annoyed her. "I don't need you to make anything better, Holden."

"I think you do," he said softly. Just then the telephone rang. She reached for the lamp switch, then the phone.

It was for Holden. "It's some woman," she said coolly, then left the room, despite his pleas that she wait. The last thing he needed to see in her eyes was jealousy.

MERRY HAD TROUBLE falling asleep that night. She could feel Holden's mouth on hers, his hands on her skin, the hardness of his body as he held her.

She'd be a liar if she said she hadn't wanted him to kiss her; she'd wanted it as much tonight as she had when she was fifteen. Only, when she was a teenager he'd kissed her to prove she wasn't frigid. Tonight he'd kissed her to prove that she wasn't in love with Steve Austin.

Why was it Holden only ever kissed her when he was trying to prove something to her? She knew the answer to that question, and it didn't please her.

The following morning, she didn't need to worry about seeing him. He was gone by the time she got up. She found a note from him on the kitchen counter saying he would be out most of the day.

Merry had planned to work on her music at home, since she wasn't scheduled to play at Braxton's. She had barely sat down at the piano when the doorbell rang.

"Julia! This is a surprise," Merry exclaimed as she opened the door and found Steve's daughter on her step.

"Hi. I hope I'm not intruding. I was going to call, but then I thought as long as I'm in the area—I'm busy running errands today—I'd take the chance you're home."

"I have today off," Merry told her, taking her coat from her. She noticed that Julia's eyes took a quick inventory as she stepped inside.

"Oh, great!" Julia said with a false brightness, and Merry had a pretty good idea she wasn't the person Julia had come to see.

"Can I get you a cup of tea?"

"Do you have any soda?"

"Sure. Have a seat and I'll be right back," Merry said, then disappeared into the kitchen, leaving a wide-eyed Julia still looking around curiously.

When Merry returned to the living room, she asked, "Was there anything in particular you wanted to see me about?"

"Yes, there was," she said, accepting the glass of soda. "Renée and I want to give you a shower. You know, for the wedding."

Merry had a queer sensation in her stomach. "Julia, your father and I haven't even set a date yet."

"I know, but Dad says it's going to be soon, and Renée and I want to start planning right away. I can't tell you how happy we both are that you're going to be our mom."

Merry stared at the young woman, trying to imagine being her mother. All she could think of was how Julia looked in Holden's arms. It was not a pleasant thought.

While Julia rambled on about how happy her father was now that Merry was in his life, Merry listened halfheartedly. No matter how hard she tried to concentrate on what the young woman was saying, she couldn't stop wondering what had happened between

Holden and Julia after they'd left the restaurant last night. Jealousy tightened her smile.

"What do you think?" Julia's question startled Merry out of her musings.

"I'd rather you waited with the shower plans until your father and I have a definite date on the calendar," Merry told her.

"Okay," Julia said with a toss of her ponytail. "But you have to promise to let us know the minute you decide. We want everything to be just perfect for you and Dad." She drained the remains of her soda and said, "I should probably get going."

"I'll get your coat."

When Merry returned, she found Julia looking out the patio door at the snow-covered Christmas pine. "Is that the tree my dad got for you from the station?"

"Yes."

"He was a little worried you didn't want it." Julia's tone held accusation.

"This place really isn't big enough for a tree, but it looks nice out there, don't you think?"

"Oh, yeah, it's fine. I guess it really doesn't matter, since you're going to have Christmas at our house."

"Yes, that's what I thought, too," Merry said pleasantly.

Julia had put on her coat, but still she lingered. Finally she asked, "Is Holden here?"

"No, he's not," Merry answered, her suspicions confirmed. The wedding shower had just been an excuse.

A note of alarm crossed Julia's face. "He didn't go back to California, did he?"

"No. Did he say he was going to leave?"

"Uh-uh. He said he'd be here for Christmas, but he has all those important cases in Hollywood. I thought maybe he *had* to go back."

"There's always that possibility," Merry answered, although she didn't want to consider it herself.

"It'd be a shame if he had to spend Christmas all by himself, even if it is in sunny California."

"I don't think he'd be alone," Merry told her. "He has lots of friends."

"But at Christmas you should be with family. Which reminds me—do you want to take over Christmas-dinner preparations? Normally Renée and I do everything, but if you want to be in charge, we'll understand."

"No, you and Renée stay in charge," Merry said. "It's fine with me."

"You have to ignore Aunt Charlotte if she calls. She's having a hard time accepting the fact that Dad's replacing Mom. Mom was her younger sister, you know," Julia told her.

Julia rambled on about the food they needed to cook and what each relative would be bringing. When she mentioned that two of Steve's three sisters were feuding and she hoped they wouldn't make a scene at dinner, Merry began to feel uneasy. If Christmas Day turned out to be anything like the party the other evening, she wasn't looking forward to the gathering.

By the time Julia left, the holiday melancholy she'd thought she wouldn't experience this year was back with a vengeance. When Steve had told her she'd have

an old-fashioned Christmas with his family, she'd
thought he meant just with his children. She didn't
realize that the entire Austin clan was going to put in
an appearance or that she'd feel as if she was trying to
take someone's place.

Julia's visit made Merry examine the realities of
marriage. She was engaged to a man with three grown
children, two still living at home with him. It was obvious that Julia and her brother, Ryan, weren't planning on moving out simply because Merry moved in.

She glanced about her living room. It was quiet. She
was accustomed to living alone. The more she thought
about marriage, the more uneasy she became. What
she needed was to see Steve, to talk to him, be reas-
sured. So when he dropped in unexpectedly, she
greeted him with a warm smile.

"I thought you had to work today," she said as he
stepped inside.

"I do. Where's Holden?"

By the look on her fiancé's face, something was
wrong. Very wrong. Merry's stomach plunged. "He's
not here. Why?"

"He's done something I think you should know
about."

Her apprehension swelled. "What is it?"

"Did you know that he hired a private investigator
to dig into my past?"

Merry's face paled. "No. Holden wouldn't do
that."

"It's true. Someone's done a credit check, talked to
my employers, even followed me around." He pulled
a business card out of his pocket. "Here's the name of

the agency he hired.'' He chuckled mirthlessly. ''They weren't very discreet.''

Merry didn't want to look at the business card. When Holden had suggested she have her fiancé investigated, she'd told him in no uncertain terms she wouldn't do such a thing. How could he have gone ahead and done it when he knew how she felt?

''Are you sure it was Holden?''

''Of course it was him,'' Steve snapped impatiently. ''Who else would have bothered?''

Merry knew he had a point. Holden was the only one interested in discrediting Steve. ''I'm sorry. I don't know what to say.''

''What was he hoping to find? That I'm some kind of crook?'' he demanded angrily. ''Do you realize how humiliating this is?''

''I don't think he was deliberately trying to embarrass you,'' she said, trying to smooth things over. ''He's a divorce lawyer, so he who works with people who do this kind of thing on a regular basis and—''

''Don't defend him.'' It was the sternest voice she'd ever heard him use.

''I'm not,'' she protested. ''I'm angry about this, too.'' But more than angry, she felt betrayed. ''I told him that I didn't want him interfering in our lives.''

''This ought to prove to you how little regard he has for your feelings. You can't possibly want him to stay for Christmas now, do you?''

''No, I don't want him to be a part of our celebration,'' she said shakily.

''I don't want him to be a part of our lives at all. He makes you unhappy, Merry. Ever since he's been here you haven't been yourself. There's no use denying it. He's not good for you.''

Steve wrapped her in his arms and cuddled her as if she were a child who needed consoling. The truth was, she did need consoling. What Steve had said was true. Ever since Holden had returned, nothing had gone smoothly. She felt confused and disoriented, unsure of what she wanted. Her sleep was disturbed, her head often ached, and her stomach churned. She felt as if she was in a continual state of PMS.

"What am I going to do?" she asked in a small voice.

"You let me handle Holden. I'll take care of things for you," Steve said in a soothing voice. "That's what a husband is for."

Merry wanted to say, *You're not my husband yet.* But she was tired and hurt and at this moment in need of someone to make a decision for her. "It's not going to be easy," she warned him.

Steve kissed her forehead and gave her shoulder a tender squeeze. "Don't you worry about it. I'm not going to let him hurt you."

Merry didn't want to tell him he was too late. The hurt had already been done.

CHAPTER TEN

WHEN HOLDEN DIDN'T RETURN before Steve had to leave for the television studio, Merry had no choice but to wait for him alone. She found herself peeking out the window blinds nervously and listening for sounds of his car in the drive the rest of the afternoon.

The person who finally showed up wasn't Holden, but Holly.

"I wasn't expecting you," Merry said to her as the girl hurried in out of the cold. "Where's Bonnie?" she asked, looking out at the drive and seeing no car.

"She couldn't bring me so I took the bus. It's okay that I came over today, isn't it?"

"Yes. Come on in." Merry welcomed the diversion. Sooner or later Holden would return, and she didn't need to spend the time till then agonizing over it.

When he did finally arrive, she was in the middle of a lesson with Holly. She ignored his greeting, determined not to acknowledge his presence until Holly was gone, but all she could think about was what she was going to say to him.

If there was one thing Merry hated, it was unresolved conflict. Unable to sit still while he rattled around in the kitchen, she left Holly at the piano and went in to confront him.

He was seated at the counter with his laptop computer in front of him. He looked so handsome, it annoyed her.

"Where have you been all day?" She tried to keep her voice even, but her anger at his betrayal put an edge on her words.

"What's wrong? Did I miss an appointment or something?"

Merry glanced toward the living room, debating whether she should even start a discussion with Holly in the other room. "You and I need to talk," she said in a low voice.

"I'm listening."

"Not now. Not with Holly here," she told him, her fingers curling into her palm.

He reached out and grabbed her by the wrist. "Why are you so angry?"

She looked down at the fingers wrapped around her wrist. "Let go of me."

"Not until you tell me why you look like you want to tear a strip off my hide," he answered. "Is it because of last night?"

Her skin warmed at the memory of his mouth on hers. She quickly looked away. "I meant what I said. Let go of me."

He released her, his eyes never leaving her face.

"Why don't you just tell me what it is I've done, and we'll settle what's eating you?"

"I don't want it settled," she hissed. "What you did was inexcusable."

"A kiss between friends is hardly cause for corporal punishment," he said with a sexy glint in his eye.

"I'm not talking about the kiss. I'm talking about you hiring a private investigator to spy on my fiancé." She could barely control her anger.

"Ah. So you know." His voice was infuriatingly calm.

"How could you do that after I specifically asked you not to interfere in my life?"

"Obviously your definition of interference and mine differ."

"You were looking to dig up some dirt on the man I love so I wouldn't marry him," she fired back.

"I wasn't trying to dig up dirt. I'm in the divorce business, Merry. In this day and age, it makes sense to investigate the person you're planning to marry. It was a professional decision, not a personal vendetta against the man."

"Steve's an honest man!" she declared passionately.

"You think so? He's making money off you, Merry."

"He's promoting me. He's going to have me appear on 'Let's Shop' to help sell my CDs."

"He's signing contracts he has no business signing."

Merry was in no mood to hear any criticism of the man she'd promised to marry. "We're going to be partners," she stated defiantly.

Holden gave a snort of disgust. "He's going to come out smelling like a rose. Then he'll be able to make all sorts of deals with your money."

"It doesn't matter whose money we use. We're going to be husband and wife! What's mine will be his!"

Intense emotion did not allow logic to play a part in what she uttered.

"That would not be wise," Holden warned. "Look, if you won't listen to me on this, talk to Tom Harvey. He knows your situation and he's impartial. He'll advise you to get a prenuptial agreement—in your situation it's definitely what you need."

"What I need is for you to get out of my life!" she snapped.

"You don't mean that," he said quietly.

"Oh, yes, I do," she insisted. "I don't need someone who is so jaded and cynical about marriage he'll do anything to ruin my chance at happiness."

"I'm not trying to ruin your chance at happiness," he denied.

"Yes, you are, and I'm sick and tired of you telling me what to do."

"I don't tell you what to do," he said. "Steve is the one doing that. He treats you like a child, Merry. Can't you see that?"

"*Stop.* I don't want to hear any more of this." She covered her ears with her hands.

She turned to leave, but he caught her by the shoulder and pulled her hands down. "You're letting this guy tell you what to do as if he's your father. You don't need a father, Merry." He took her in his arms and held her close. "You need a man. Someone who can let you be the capable woman you are."

Then he kissed her. It was a kiss like no other Merry had ever received. It plundered her very soul, telling her how much of a woman she was, urging her to trust him, to give in to the current of attraction that crackled between them.

Merry didn't want to respond, but her body wouldn't listen to the message her brain sent. Gone was all the anger, the frustration, the hurt. All that mattered was that Holden's mouth was making her feel so wonderful, so alive.

How far the kiss would have gone, Merry never found out, for Holly came around the corner, saying, "Merry, there's someone at—" She stopped, embarrassed at finding them in a clinch. Then she cleared her throat and said, "Uh, there's someone at the door."

Flustered, Merry pushed out of Holden's arms and tried to act as if the girl hadn't caught her kissing the man she'd said was like a brother to her.

When Merry didn't start for the door, Holden murmured, "I'll get it."

"I'm sorry. I didn't mean to butt in," Holly said to Merry when they were alone.

"It's all right. Have you finished practicing?"

There was an awkward silence as Holly, clearly still perplexed by what she'd witnessed, shoved her hands in her pockets and looked at Merry. "Uh, yeah. Anyway, I should probably pack up my stuff. It's after six."

"Do you need a ride home?"

"I can take the bus," Holly answered.

"No, it's dark outside. I'll give you a ride."

The girl shrugged, then went to retrieve her things, passing Holden who carried an envelope in his hand.

"It's an overnight letter—for me," he said, waving the padded mailer before setting it down next to his computer.

There was only one thought going through Merry's head. She needed to get away from Holden. "I'm going to give Holly a ride home," she told him, then hurried out to the hallway closet.

He followed her. "I'll come with you."

"No, you can't. I—I'm meeting someone," she said, even though she knew he suspected it wasn't the truth.

"Merry, let me come along," he pleaded. "You were right. We *do* need to talk."

She ignored his plea, refusing to look at him. "Are you ready, Holly?" she called into the living room.

To her relief, Holly appeared instantly, her worn-out backpack slung over her shoulder. With a "Don't wait up for me" to Holden, Merry ushered Holly out the door, not once looking back at Holden.

In the car, there was silence except for the sound of Holly's stomach growling.

"Are you hungry?" Merry asked, glancing at the girl.

"Yeah. The Hawthornes eat at five-thirty."

"So you've missed dinner," Merry said.

"It's all right. I can have a sandwich when I get home."

"Would you like to stop for a hamburger and fries?"

"You don't have to do that."

"I know I don't have to, but I want to," Merry said.

"Well, okay, but..."

"But what?"

"I don't want to mess up your plans with your fiancé."

"We don't have any plans. He's working tonight."

"Well...what about Holden?"

At the mention of his name, Merry's skin tingled. "What about him?"

"Maybe he wants to have dinner with you."

"I don't think we need to worry about Holden. Right now I feel like having a hamburger at the Malt Shop. What do you say?"

The girl gave her a rather skeptical look but finally said, "All right. I'll have a hamburger."

Merry knew it was a good decision when they sat down in the booth and she heard Holly say, "I always wanted to eat in a place like this." Wide-eyed, she looked at the restaurant decorated with fifties memorabilia. "They have neat soda glasses here," she commented as a waitress walked by carrying a tray of beverages.

"Well, you can choose whatever you want on the menu," Merry told her with a smile.

They placed their order with the waitress, then flipped through the selections on the miniature jukebox attached to the wall beside their table. "These are all oldies," Holly commented.

Merry dug several quarters out of her wallet and slid them in her direction. "Well, why don't you pick a few? Some of the old Elvis Presley tunes are great. I'm going to call Mrs. Hawthorne and let her know where we are."

She found the public phone in the lobby. After calling Holly's foster mother, she inserted another quarter and dialed her own number. When there was no answer, she absolved herself of any guilt regarding not letting Holden accompany her. For all she knew, he could be with Julia, a thought that made her feel ill.

When she returned to the booth, Holly asked, "Was Bonnie upset that I didn't come home?"

Merry shook her head. "No. It's a good thing I called, though. She was a bit worried about your skipping dinner."

"She worries a lot. Probably when I get home there'll be a snack in the refrigerator for me. Bonnie's always trying to feed people."

"So you get plenty of food to eat at her house?"

"Oh, yeah." Holly stared at Merry for a moment, then asked, "I suppose you wonder why I went in your refrigerator last week?"

"Well...yes, a little," Merry admitted. "I was concerned you might not be getting enough to eat."

"We don't get soda at Bonnie's," Holly confessed.

"Well, you're welcome to it at my place."

They listened to the opening bars of "Heartbreak Hotel" before Holly said, "Can I ask you something?"

"Sure. What is it?"

"Why do you keep nail polish in the refrigerator?"

"It's less likely to clump," Merry answered. "Sometimes in the summer I keep my eyebrow pencil and my lipstick in there, too, so they don't get soft."

Holly grinned. "It seems a little strange to find that stuff in your fridge."

Merry chuckled. "You're not the only one who thinks so. Holden said the same thing."

"Were you mad at him when we left?"

Merry knew there was no point in denying it. "Yes, I was. Holly, about what you saw..."

"You mean the two of you kissing?"

Merry nodded. "It wasn't what it looked like." She debated how she should handle the subject. At thirteen, Holly certainly knew that what she saw wasn't a brotherly kiss. "What I'm trying to say is—"

She didn't get to finish, because Holly interrupted her by saying, "You don't have tell me about it. He's so cute I bet lots of girls would like to kiss him."

"Yes, well, I don't make it a habit of kissing men just because they're cute. But Holden and I... have a special relationship."

"I know. He told me."

"He did? When?"

"The other day when he let me in. You were in the shower, and he was talking to me before I started to practice. That's why I thought he was your brother, because he told me about how when you were kids you used to wake everybody up with your practicing."

"I did. Holden and I lived in the same foster home, but he's not my brother," she explained. "I don't have any brothers or sisters."

"You're lucky."

"Why do you say that?"

Holly shrugged. "It's easier if you don't have to worry about anyone but yourself."

"Do you have brothers and sisters?"

"Yeah, but I never get to see them. My two brothers were adopted, and my sister lives with another foster family."

That led to talk about their experiences in foster care. When their hamburgers arrived, Merry watched in amusement as Holly's eyes widened at the sight of the chocolate malt the waitress also set before her. She scooped up the thick liquid with the long-handled spoon, obviously savoring the taste.

"Yum. This is good," she said. "We never get malts at the Hawthornes, either."

They talked about school and what classes Holly was taking and what subjects she liked and disliked. Merry realized that Holly Denton wasn't any different from most kids her age; she just had more obstacles to overcome.

"Can I ask *you* something now?" Merry said. She was taking the chance that the reserve between the two of them was gone.

"Okay."

"Do those rings hurt?" She eyed the gold hoops in her nose and her eyebrows.

"Only when I had them put in. You don't like them, do you."

Merry shrugged. "I'm not the one wearing them. You are. If you like them, that's what counts."

They were getting along just fine when suddenly, Holly's young face paled. Merry twisted around in her seat. Coming through the door was a group of kids who looked to be about the same age as Holly.

"Can we leave?" Holly asked. "I'm done," she said, shoving her half-finished burger aside.

"Is something wrong?"

"No. I just want to leave." She turned away from the approaching teenagers and pretended to be bending down to pick up her napkin from the floor. When they'd passed, she sat back up.

"Was there someone in that group of kids you didn't want to see?" Merry asked.

"I hate all of them. They're stuck up."

Merry didn't say anything, but glanced over to where the group of five adolescents sat. They were rather boisterous, but they weren't paying any attention to Holly.

"I don't think they can see you from where they're sitting," Merry said reassuringly.

"They saw me when they came in."

"So?"

"So tomorrow at school they're going to diss me."

"Diss you?"

"Yeah, you know. Make fun of me."

"For just sitting in the Malt Shop eating a hamburger?"

"It's more than that." She picked up her long-handled malt spoon, clanging it against the glass. "Just forget it. You wouldn't understand."

"Holly, I *want* to understand. Tell me," Merry urged, leaning closer to her.

The sullen look was back on the girl's face. Merry waited while Holly seemed to debate whether or not she could trust Merry.

Finally Holly said, "The reason I'm in juvenile court is I got in a fight with that girl with the black hair. Her name's Chelsea."

Merry again glanced toward the noisy group of kids. "Does she have to go to court, too?"

"Get real," Holly drawled sarcastically. "She's one of the *popular* kids."

"Why should that exempt her from punishment?"

"Chelsea told the principal I attacked her, and then she got a couple of her friends to back up the story."

"Weren't there any of *your* friends who could back *you* up?"

"I don't have any friends at that school."

Merry didn't comment on that. She knew that many foster children felt uncomfortable around their peers. It wasn't easy forming friendships when you moved around as frequently as foster children often did.

Holly glanced uneasily in the teens' direction. "Can we leave? Please?"

Merry didn't have the heart to make her stay.

"I'm sorry this didn't work out better," she told her as they left the restaurant.

"It doesn't matter. I ate most of my hamburger and malt." Holly paused. "It's a good thing Chelsea's mother isn't here. She'd probably call the cops just because I'm sitting in the same room as her precious daughter."

"Why don't you tell me what happened?" Merry suggested when they were seated in her car.

"Why? So you can feel sorry for poor little Chelsea, too, because she ended up with a broken finger?"

"Maybe she deserved to have her finger broken," Merry said with a hint of mischief in her eyes.

Holly stared at her several moments before speaking. She was sizing her up, and Merry knew she must have passed the test when the girl said, "You're the first grown-up I've talked to who thinks that might be true."

"I've run into a few Chelsea types in my lifetime," Merry told her. Which was true. She knew how difficult it was to be on the outside looking in and to run into someone who wanted to make sure you stayed in your place.

As Merry stopped the car in front of the Haw-thornes', Holly had her hand on the door, ready to flee. "Thanks for everything," she said in a rush and scrambled to get out of the car.

"Holly, wait. I need to know if you plan on com-ing tomorrow."

"I don't know. I have to talk to Bonnie."

Merry sighed inwardly. Just when she thought they'd made progress, Holly's wall of reserve went up again. Her trust did not come easily.

"Okay. You can call me either later tonight or first thing in the morning," Merry told her. Before Holly slammed the door shut, she added, "Anytime you feel you need someone to talk to, I'm here."

Her only response was a shrug and a nonchalant "okay."

Merry watched her walk up the steps to the house, head bent, shoulders hunched. A feeling of melan-choly swept over Merry. It had been an emotional day for her. First Steve had told her about the private in-vestigator, then she'd argued with Holden, been thor-oughly *kissed* by Holden, and now she'd become emotionally involved with Holly.

When she got home, she was relieved to see that Holden still hadn't returned from wherever he'd gone. She sat down at the piano and began to play, which was where Steve found her an hour or so later.

"Merry," he said the moment he entered the living room, "Holden paid me a little visit at the television studio a while ago."

Merry's stomach fluttered uneasily. "He did? Wh-what did he say?"

"That the two of you had had an argument. He also threatened me with legal action if I so much as laid a hand on you or your assets. It was rather ugly. Good thing you weren't there."

"I'm sorry."

"You don't need to apologize for him, Merry. But I really don't want you spending the night in this house with him. I know he's not here now—I don't see his car—and I'd like you out of here before he arrives." His hand covered hers in a comforting gesture. "Why don't you spend the night at my place?"

The offer was tempting, but Merry was strangely reluctant to accept. "I'll be all right," she said.

"I don't know about that. Holden's in a foul mood."

"It won't be the first time I've seen him in a foul mood."

"I don't want him taking it out on you. Besides, he'll be gone tomorrow, and then everything will be as it was before he came."

Merry felt as if a bird started flapping its wings in her chest. "He's leaving tomorrow?"

"I told him I expect him to be on the first plane out of here," Steve boasted.

"And you think he'll go?"

"He doesn't have much choice."

Merry doubted that Holden would be intimidated by Steve, but she didn't contradict her fiancé.

"Come on, Merry. Stay with me tonight," he pleaded.

She really didn't want to face Holden. She was afraid—not of what he would do, but of the way her emotions would betray her. As much as she hated to admit it, this wasn't about his investigating Steve's background. It was about kisses and the feelings that Holden had aroused. Confused, she needed some time to think.

"Merry?" Steve still awaited her answer.

Merry looked at him and knew he was the safer option. Because he'd declared his intention of waiting until their wedding night to consummate their relationship, she knew there would be no questions about where she'd sleep. She wasn't sure that would be the case with Holden.

"All right," she said. "I'll follow you there in my car."

IT TOOK all of Holden's willpower not to go over to Steve Austin's and bring Merry back home. The only thing that stopped him was the possibility that she wouldn't return with him, and then he'd just be playing into Austin's hand.

The digital clock beside his bed said two-fifty-seven and he was still awake. He had worked until he thought his eyes would cross if he looked at another brief. Then he'd climbed into bed hoping sleep would erase the agonizing thoughts racing through his head.

He realized that if he was truly honest with himself, it wouldn't be thoughts of the argument he'd had with Merry keeping him awake. What bothered him was where she'd gone tonight. The thought of her in bed with Austin at this very minute was enough to twist his gut into a hundred knots. Until tonight, he hadn't wanted to analyze why he objected so strongly to her relationship with the man.

Now he knew he could no longer deny the reason for his objection. He was jealous. Out and out jealous. Steve was doing for Merry what *he* wanted to be doing for her. Advising her on her business, making sure she was taken care of, making love to her....

It was that last part that bothered him the most. Until Holden had kissed her, he hadn't realized how much it bothered him. The thought of a passionate woman like Merry spending the rest of her life with a pompous creep like Austin was enough to make him sick.

Granted, *he* wasn't the right man for Merry, either, but at least he was more her age. Trouble was, she wanted him out of her life. Gone. Never to return.

Okay. She would have it her way. He'd only come because of the promise to Rosie. He'd had this Austin fellow investigated and, despite what he'd told Merry, had come up with nothing that indicated he was a con man ready to make a quick buck. He'd done everything he could to persuade Merry that Austin was the wrong man. He'd done his duty. He could leave.

And tomorrow he *would* leave. He would go back to California, listen to the whining of disgruntled wives and the grousing of angry husbands. Merry had made it perfectly clear. She neither needed nor wanted him in her life.

He punched the pillow, then pulled it over his head, hoping to shut out the image of her lying in bed with Austin.

When he finally did fall asleep, he dreamed about Merry. They were erotic dreams that caused him to wake up, aroused.

He headed for the shower. He noticed a pair of
panty hose dangling from the towel bar. How could he
forget about her when he was staying in her house,
seeing reminders of her everywhere he looked?

By the time he'd showered and shaved, he'd made
up his mind. He wasn't going to leave without saying
goodbye to her. He pulled on his clothes, jumped in
his rental car and headed for Steve Austin's.

His knock was answered by Julia. His heartbeat in-
creased as he thought about Steve and Merry lying in
each other's arms. He could feel his blood pressure
rise, but he tried to act as if nothing was wrong.

"Is Merry up yet?" he asked.

"I didn't realize she was here."

"She left me a note last night saying she was spending the night."

"I didn't know. I must have been asleep when they
came in. I'll go check and see if she's awake." Julia
disappeared up the stairs for what seemed to Holden
an eternity.

When she finally bounced back down the stairs and
said, "Are you sure she's here? She's not in the guest
room," he felt as if someone had punched him in the
stomach.

Holden couldn't bring himself to ask, *Did you
check your father's room?* As it turned out he didn't
need to say anything, for Julia bounced past him saying, "Unless she's in Renée's room."

Holden didn't wait in the entryway, but followed
Julia down the hallway. He felt as if a great weight was
lifted from his shoulders when he saw Merry asleep in
the pink bedroom, her dark hair tousled about her
head. She was safe—and she was alone.

At the sound of their voices she stirred. Recognizing Holden, she pulled the sheet up to her chin.

"Holden! What are you doing here?" she asked in a sleepy voice.

"I came over to say goodbye," he answered, which brought a gasp from Julia.

"You're not leaving! What about Christmas?" Her pretty face was crestfallen.

Holden gently steered Julia toward the door. "Would you mind if I talked to Merry alone for a few minutes?"

"Of course not, but don't leave before I get a chance to talk to you," she begged, batting her eyelashes at him.

Merry had moved so that she was propped up against the headboard, her hands still holding the covers to her chin.

"Why did you do that?" she asked when he closed the door.

"Because I want to talk to you without any members of the Austin family listening in."

"I wish you hadn't come over here." She shifted uncomfortably.

"Would you rather have me leave without saying goodbye?" He sat down on the edge of the double bed, only inches from her.

"Then it's true? You're leaving?"

"I have a ticket for the eleven-fifteen flight."

"Good."

"Good? What happened to 'Holden, it won't be Christmas without you'?"

"After everything that's happened, you can't honestly expect me to want you to stay."

"I'm not sure you know what it is you do want, Merry." He studied her briefly, then said, "Why are you hanging on to that blanket for dear life? Don't you have anything on underneath?"

She blushed and his body reacted instinctively to the thought of her naked body beneath the covers. "Didn't you bring a nightgown?"

"I . . . I forgot." She quickly changed the subject. "I'm sorry about Christmas. I'm sure you'll find someone to keep you company."

"I don't want someone. I want you," he said affectionately, unable to stop his brain from fantasizing what she must look like under the sheets.

That brought another blush to her cheeks. "But that's not what I want."

"Are you sure?"

"Yes," she insisted with a defiant lift of her chin. "Ever since you've been here I've been trying to explain to you what I want, but you refuse to listen."

"What about our promise to Rosie? She wanted us to be together." He reached for her hand, but she hid it beneath the covers.

"This isn't about Rosie."

"No, it's about us."

Again she blushed, a reaction that sent a funny little tremor through Holden's body. She looked down as she said, "There is no 'us.'"

"Don't say that," he pleaded. "We go back too far for that to happen."

"I'm sorry things turned out this way. I know Rosie wanted us to always be close, but you've forced me to choose between you and my fiancé."

"And he won. Is that what you're telling me?"

"There doesn't have to be a winner and a loser, Holden. Why can't you just be happy that I've found someone who makes me happy?"

"Do you really believe you have?"

"Yes, I do."

He stared at her for several moments and at last got to his feet. "Then there's nothing else I can say. If you need me, you know where to find me." He bent down and kissed her on the cheek, the way he always had in the past. "Goodbye, Merry."

She looked so forlorn sitting there on the bed Holden had to use every ounce of his willpower to refrain from rushing to her side and kissing her senseless.

Before he left the room, he said one last thing. "By the way, you may think your boyfriend is honest, but he lies about his age. He's fifty-four."

Before she could comment, he left the room, pulling the door shut behind him. He came face-to-face with Steve in the hallway.

"What are you doing here?" the older man demanded, unconsciously flexing his muscles.

"Saying goodbye to Merry."

"You better not have hurt her."

"See for yourself. She's in there. But you might want to knock first. She sleeps in the raw, you know." And with a cocky grin he strode to the front door and left.

CHAPTER ELEVEN

MERRY WAS ABOUT to get up and get dressed when the door flew open. Startled, she clutched the sheet to her breasts, her eyes wide as she stared at her fiancé.

"What was Holden doing in here?" Steve demanded in an angry jealous voice she'd never heard before.

"He came to say goodbye."

"So he just came barging in here? My God, Merry, you're not even dressed."

Merry didn't appreciate the censure in his tone. "That didn't stop *you*. Why should it stop Holden?"

"I happen to be your fiancé, in case you've forgotten."

"I think you're the one who's forgotten to tell something—like your real age?"

His face reddened. Without another word, he turned and left the room, slamming the door behind him. Merry called out to him, but he didn't return.

She scrambled off the bed and quickly dressed, intending to find him and apologize. But by the time she'd tugged on her panty hose she'd changed her mind.

She'd done nothing wrong. Holden and Steve were the ones who'd invaded her privacy, not the other way around. And Steve had lied about his age, too. If he had a problem with Holden's being in the room with her, he'd have to work through it by himself. Right now she needed to take care of her own emotions—which felt as discordant as the music Holly had played during that practice session.

So instead of going to find Steve, Merry headed for the door. On her way out she met Julia, who wanted to know why she was leaving without having any breakfast. Merry told a puzzled Julia to ask her father.

All the way home she took comfort in the fact that for the first time since Holden's arrival she would be alone in the peace and quiet of her house. She could soak in a tub of bubbles as long as she liked, run around in her underwear should she choose and play music any time of day or night. She would be blissfully alone.

Only, she soon discovered she wasn't going to be alone. When she arrived she found Holly sitting on the front doorstep with what looked like all her worldly possessions. How long she'd been there in the cold, Merry had no way of knowing, but judging from her red cheeks it was longer than she should have been. Merry herded her inside before asking any questions.

"Why aren't you in school?" she asked as she led her to the kitchen.

"I'm suspended."

"For what?"

"Smoking in the girls' washroom. I can't go back until Monday."

Merry bit back the reprimand that sprang to her lips. "You look cold. Would you like some hot chocolate and cinnamon toast?"

Holly nodded, and Merry quietly went about heating milk and putting bread in the toaster. She was using the time to gather her thoughts, to figure out the best approach to the girl's predicament.

Holly was the one to break the silence. "Aren't you going to lecture me about smoking at my age?"

"I'm sure Bonnie's already done that," Merry answered, setting a steaming mug and a plate of toast in front of her.

"Yeah, well, she's not going to do it anymore," Holly said, then took a bite of toast. As usual she attacked the food as if she hadn't eaten in days.

"Are you being moved to another home?" Merry asked.

"No." Holly didn't elaborate, just sipped her hot chocolate. After a while, she said, "I suppose you're wondering why I'm here."

Merry attempted to keep the conversation on a light level. "It's not just to practice, right?"

Holly shook her head. "I came to say goodbye."

Merry's heart sank. "I thought you said you weren't moving yet."

"I'm not going to another foster home," she said quietly, avoiding Merry's eyes.

Merry looked at the duffel bag on the floor. "Then where are you going?"

"I haven't made definite plans yet, but I can't stay at the Hawthornes'. They don't want me there. I thought I'd hang out with some kids I met."

"Oh, Holly." Merry looked helplessly at the girl.

"You don't have to worry about me," Holly said. "I can take care of myself."

"You're only thirteen."

"I took care of my brothers and sister when I was only ten. My mom was an alcoholic, so I learned how to do things for myself when I was a kid."

Merry wanted to remind her that she was *still* a kid, but she understood Holly's sentiments all too well. At one time she'd felt the same way—that she would rather be out on her own and taking care of herself than forced to live with a family she didn't know.

"Where will you go?"

"There's . . . places on the streets. You learn about them from other kids."

The very thought of Holly's living on the streets sent chills up and down Merry's spine. "It's not a very good life, Holly."

She shrugged. "It'll be better than what I have now."

Merry sat down beside her. "I know it's hard being moved around. When I was put in foster care I felt lost. I was angry and scared and lonely. Worst of all, I felt trapped. All I wanted was to get out, to run away."

"Did you?"

She nodded. "Twice. The first time I was only nine. I went back to the house where I'd lived with my parents, but the windows were boarded over, the doors all locked. I wanted to find my mother, but she was gone."

"What happened to her?"

She shrugged. "No one knows. At the time, everyone in town thought she'd run off with someone passing through town."

"Didn't she come and say goodbye?"

Merry shook her head. "That's why I knew she hadn't left of her own free will. About a year later the police found her body in the woods about fifty miles from where we lived."

"Was she murdered?" Holly's voice was barely above a whisper.

"No. She died from exposure," Merry answered, swallowing back the lump that rose in her throat at the painful memory.

"Exposure. Is that when it's cold and you don't have enough clothes on?"

Merry nodded. "Apparently her car broke down, and when she went to get help, she got lost." She didn't add that her mother had been drinking and had she not been so inebriated, she wouldn't have passed out in a snowbank. "What happened to your dad?"

"He left when I was nine and never came back."

"You don't know where he is?"

Merry shook her head.

"I don't know who my dad is," Holly said without any emotion in her voice.

"And your mother?" Merry probed gently.

"I want to see my mom, but they won't let me."

"Do you know where she is?"

Holly shook her head. "I think she's out of state somewhere. Maybe New York. She always said there was stuff happening in New York."

Merry knew that parental rights had been terminated in Holly's case, so she didn't suggest that her mother might return. "It isn't easy not knowing where she is, is it?" Merry said softy.

Holly shrugged. "Everyone says my mom is no good, but she was nice to me."

This was said in such a pathetic little voice Merry had to fight back the tears that clogged her throat. Like many foster kids, Holly still felt loyal to her mother. It was a sentiment Merry understood well. She'd always hated it whenever anyone in town talked as if her mother was just another drunk who didn't deserve to have a daughter.

Merry reached out to cover Holly's hand with hers. "I'm sure she thinks about you. You're such a sweet, pretty girl."

Uncomfortable with the compliment and display of affection, Holly pulled her hand out from beneath Merry's. "Where did you run to the second time? How old were you?"

"Fourteen. I went to see Holden—he was in college. He let me stay for a few days before he took me back to my foster mother's house." She paused. "He really was like a big brother to me," she told Holly, wondering what had happened to those fraternal feelings. "It could be that your next foster home will have someone like Holden for you, someone who'll look out for you, someone you can trust."

"There isn't anybody like that out there for me," Holly said with heartbreaking hopelessness.

"You won't know if you run away," Merry said gently. "I think the chances of finding someone like that are better if you're living in a foster home, rather than on the streets."

"I heard some kids say that being on the streets can be like having a family, that kids on the street watch out for each other."

Merry studied the girl for a moment. "But it's not a good kind of watching out for each other, Holly."

Abruptly the teenager rose to her feet. "I've got to go. I only came to say goodbye because you've been so nice to me."

"Holly, wait!" Merry searched for the right words, but everything that came to mind sounded like a cliché.

"I have to go," Holly said in a pained voice.

"No! No, you don't," Merry said. "You can stay and be my music student."

"I can't. It won't work out," Yet Holly's voice begged Merry to convince her otherwise.

"It *can* work, Holly. Listen to me. I know it's hard to be moved around from one home to another, but you won't be any happier on the streets. Trust me, Holly. Let me call Bonnie and tell her you're here," she begged.

"No, don't call Bonnie!" she exclaimed in near terror. "If I go back there, I'll have to go back to juvenile court, and then I'll end up in a group home!"

Merry didn't know what to do. She wished there was someone she could turn to for advice. Automatically she thought of Holden. It wasn't yet eleven o'clock. Could she still reach him at the airport?

"Holden's a lawyer. He might be able to help you," she said, even though Holden had already told her he wouldn't be able to help Holly because her case was in juvenile court. "Will you stay until I talk to him?"

Holly was reluctant to agree, but finally she mumbled an okay, which Merry quickly acted upon.

She dialed information to get the number of the airport, then waited while Holden was paged. Eventually, his voice came over the wire. When it did she could have wept with relief.

"Thank goodness you haven't gone!" she cried.

"Merry, they're boarding my flight. Why are you calling me?"

"Don't get on, Holden! Please don't get on. I need you."

"We must have a bad connection. I thought I heard you say you needed me." His tone was dry.

"Holden, this is no time to be funny," she said. "Please don't leave yet. I really do need you. Now. Will you come?"

There was no hesitancy in his response. "I'll be there as soon as I can get a cab."

"Thank you." As she replaced the receiver she turned to Holly. "He'll figure something out."

"Like what? My social worker said the only thing that's left for me is a group home."

"There might be other options," Merry told her, knowing perfectly well she was in no position to be making such a statement. "Maybe you could stay here for a few days."

Holly's eyes widened. "You'd let me stay with you in your house?"

"I have two bedrooms." She knew she shouldn't have issued the invitation without talking to the proper authorities, but right now she was probably the only person Holly trusted. If she didn't keep her, she'd be out on the streets. "Would you like to spend Christmas with me?"

"You want me to?"

Merry nodded. "Why don't I call Bonnie and talk to her about it?"

Holly looked as if she wanted to say yes, yet still she hesitated. "I wish you didn't have to call her."

"I can't let you stay here without someone's permission, Holly." She could see the anxiety on the girl's
face. "I'll tell you what. We won't make any phone
calls until Holden gets here, okay?"

"Okay. Uh, I need to use the bathroom."

While Holly was in the bathroom, Merry changed
the linens on the bed Holden had slept in. As she
pulled back the covers, the faint scent of his after-
shave teased her nostrils. She quickly removed the
sheets and replaced them with fresh ones, trying to
block out the memory of their passionate kisses.

By the time he walked through the door, Merry
nearly threw herself into his arms. "Am I glad to see
you!" she exclaimed.

"That's the first nice thing you've said to me all
week." He shrugged out of his overcoat. "So my instincts were right."

"What's that supposed to mean?"

"When I saw your sleeping arrangements at Austin's, I knew that any man who has a fiancé who looks
like you do and still puts her in a spare bedroom, instead of in his own bed, doesn't deserve you, Merry.
I'm glad you finally realized that."

He blew on his hands to warm them up. Merry knew
Holden assumed the reason she'd called was that she'd
broken up with Steve.

Before she could correct him, however, he headed
for the kitchen. "I could use a cup of coffee," he said.
As he walked past the living room, he saw Holly and
stopped in his tracks.

"I didn't call you because I broke up with Steve,"
she told him when his gaze took in Holly's things piled
on the floor. Merry gestured for him to step into the

kitchen. "She's run away from her foster home and doesn't want to go back," she said in a low voice.

He stared at Merry for several moments before saying, "Have you notified anyone she's here?"

"Not yet. I wanted to talk to you first."

He sighed and rubbed the back of his neck. "You should call her foster mother. If she's not in school, she's probably been reported truant."

Merry explained about Holly's suspension, then asked, "Can you find out about the charges against her? I know it involves an assault. She told me that much."

"I'll see what I can do, but it's not going to be easy. What are you planning to do with her?"

"I told her she could spend Christmas with me."

"And after Christmas?"

"I haven't thought that far ahead. All I know is I couldn't let her go live on the streets. She'd end up begging for food money, maybe getting into drugs and . . . Oh, Holden, you have to help me." She clung to his sleeve.

"You don't need my help, Merry. You have the solution."

"I do? What?" She gave him a puzzled look.

"You told me you've kept your foster-care license current. Call the Department of Human Services and offer to take her in."

Merry moistened her lips with her tongue. "Do you think I should?"

"Is it what you want to do?"

She ran her fingers across her forehead. "I don't know. I hoped I'd have a little more time to think this through."

Holden took a breath and released it on a sigh. "Look, Merry, someone needs to call her foster mother and tell her where she is."

"You're right. I'll take care of it now." She started to head for the phone, but then turned to him and said, "I know you can't do anything in juvenile court, but there must be someone you can talk to and find out how serious the charges are against her."

"I'll see what I can do," he told her, giving her shoulder a squeeze.

"Thank you."

"Does this mean I get to stay for Christmas?" he asked.

"I gave Holly your room," she said with an apologetic smile.

"I guess that means I go to a hotel."

Merry knew it would be best. After all the trouble his presence had caused, she didn't need him living with her. Yet she found herself saying, "You can have the sofa."

MERRY TOOK the matter of Holly's care into her own hands, first calling Bonnie Hawthorne and then contacting the Department of Human Services. Because she'd kept her foster-care license current, there were no obstacles to Holly staying with her. By the time Merry went to work at Braxton's that afternoon, Bonnie had called to arrange to bring the rest of Holly's things over the following morning. Since Holly wasn't in school, Holden offered to keep an eye on her until Merry returned.

As Merry played holiday tunes for the Christmas shoppers, she watched for the two of them, expecting

Holden would bring Holly along when he came to pick her up from work.

However, it wasn't Holden who showed up during her performance, but Steve. He came bearing flowers and a big apology for losing his temper. He stayed until she finished, then accompanied her to the employee lounge.

"You haven't told me whether or not you forgive me," he said when they were alone in the lounge. "Please tell me you're not still angry with me." He gave her a boyishly charming grin.

"I'm not angry," she answered, sniffing the roses appreciatively. "I think we should talk about this morning, though."

He took the roses from her hands and set them on the vanity, then pulled her into his arms. "When I saw Holden coming out of the bedroom, I guess I saw red. Of course it didn't help that he made some crack about you being undressed."

"I didn't know he was coming over," she said.

"I realize that," Steve said repentantly, lifting her knuckles to his lips. "I should have known the guy would come looking for you."

"He didn't do anything to me."

"Merry, he doesn't have to do anything. Just his being here is stressful for you. I can see it every time the two of you are together. He wants to control you."

"He does not," Merry protested, pulling away. "He's not the one who lied to me about his age."

"I'm sorry about that—truly, I am," Steve apologized effusively.

"What I don't understand is why you pretended to be forty-eight when you're really fifty-four. Did you think it would make a difference in my feelings for you?"

"I didn't lie because I wanted you to think I was younger. It's because of my contract with the studio. You know that this business doesn't treat aging performers well. If 'Let's Shop' finds out I'm fifty-four and not forty-eight, my career could be considerably shorter."

"Steve, that's age discrimination. They can't fire you. It's against the law."

He laughed sardonically. "You want me to rattle off a list of former TV personalities who are gone for that very reason? I only hope Holden doesn't tell anybody else what he and his little spy found out."

"I think we should leave Holden out of this discussion," she said stiffly.

He reached for her again. "You're right. There's no point in talking about him. He's gone back to California and won't be here to interfere with our lives. And I have to tell you, I feel relieved about that."

An uneasy feeling swept over Merry. She knew she had to tell Steve that Holden wasn't gone, that he would, in fact, be camping out on her sofa.

"Where do you want to have dinner?" Steve asked, acting as if all their problems had been resolved.

"I can't have dinner with you."

His shoulders sagged. "So you haven't forgiven me."

"It's not that. It's just that...something's come up."

"What is it? You look so serious. What's wrong?"

She proceeded to tell him about finding Holly on her doorstep that morning. When she came to the part about calling Holden at the airport, he reacted just as she suspected he would—in anger.

"Why didn't you call *me?*" he demanded.

"I wanted Holden's advice. He is an attorney, after all."

"Then you should've called Tom Harvey."

"Well, I didn't. I called Holden," she stated obstinately. She glanced at her watch and knew Holden would be arriving any moment. "Look, I really don't want to argue about this. Holly's going to stay with me until after Christmas."

"Merry, you're not thinking about applying for a foster-care license, are you?"

"I already have one."

His brow furrowed. "How come you never mentioned it to me?"

She shrugged. "The subject never came up. Foster parenting is something I tried almost five years ago."

He jammed his hands on his hips. "And you didn't think to tell me about it?"

"Until now, I didn't think I would ever do foster care again."

"So now you've taken this girl into your home without asking me?"

"It *is* my home," she pointed out.

"Merry, you're going to be my wife, for crying out loud." He began to pace, something she'd never seen him do before. "You go and make arrangements to take in a foster child without telling me about it, and you act as if you're the only person involved here."

"It's only a temporary arrangement."

"It doesn't matter." He stopped pacing and stared at her. "You're my fiancée. You should have discussed this with me." He resumed his pacing. "How long will she be staying?"

"I don't know."

He ran a hand through his hair. "I can't believe you did this."

"I had to," she said.

"Had to?" he repeated. He stopped again and shoved his hands into his pockets. "You chose to do it without my permission."

"Permission? Steve, I don't need your permission to do anything," she said, bristling. "And if you think I do, then we have a definite communication problem here."

Sensing he'd gone too far, he apologized and lowered his voice. "Look, give me some time to think about this, okay? I don't know this girl the way you do."

"She's not a bad kid," Merry told him. When he didn't say anything but simply raised an eyebrow, she added, "She isn't."

Further discussion was prevented by the appearance of Holly and Holden. To Merry's relief, the two men behaved civilly to each other. Steve even went so far as to offer Holden a place to stay. Merry waited for Holden to tell him he had a place—on her couch—but to her surprise he passed up the chance to taunt her fiancé. Instead, he let him think he was staying at a hotel.

For once he behaved exactly as Merry hoped he would, so why did she feel so...disappointed?

"I'M GLAD you're here," Merry said to Holly as they stood in the guest bedroom. They had just gotten home, and while Holden relaxed in the living room, Merry was helping Holly get settled. "Should we put your things in the dresser?"

"What's the point? It's not like I'll be staying." Holly sank onto the mattress dejectedly.

"Let's not think about what's going to happen next. You're here now." Merry tried to sound optimistic.

"I don't think Holden wants me here."

"Did he say he didn't?"

"No, but now I'm here he has to go to a hotel."

"No, he doesn't. He can sleep on the couch. It pulls out into a bed." Merry sat down beside her. "Is that why you were so quiet all the way home? Because you thought you'd taken Holden's bed?"

"Didn't I?"

"No. He wouldn't even be here if it wasn't for you." A thought that made Merry feel a bit unsettled. She got up and spread her arms in an encompassing gesture. "For however long you're here, this room is yours. Of course, you have to share it with these girls." Merry poked her head between two of Rosie's old dress forms and made a face.

That made Holly smile. She got up off the bed and walked around the room, eyeing Merry's sewing notions. "Do you sew?"

"Uh-huh. I make the dresses I wear for performing."

"Really?"

Merry nodded. "Most of them are in here." She opened the closet doors to reveal a rack of evening gowns.

Holly admired the glittering array. "Wow. You're good," she said in awe.

"I know the tricks of the trade. Would you like me to teach them to you?"

"I couldn't make a dress."

"Sure you could. You have long, graceful fingers—perfect for sewing."

Holly looked down at her hands and her expression turned sullen. "I didn't do very well in living skills at school. Actually I flunked. We had to sew this pillow that was supposed to look like a big light bulb. The kids in class said mine looked like a mashed potato."

"Pillows aren't quite the same thing as clothing," Merry said casually, straightening the bodice of one of the dresses. "I think you could make lots of nice things."

Holly shrugged. "Maybe."

"Okay, you think about it. In the meantime, how about dinner?"

The sullen look was replaced with a ghost of a grin. "I am hungry."

Merry smiled. "I figured as much. What's your favorite?" She rattled off a list of take-out foods.

"Aren't you going to cook?"

"I'm not very good at it," Merry confessed.

"I could make something for you. Bonnie says I make tacos better than anyone she knows."

Merry didn't want to admit that she seldom ate Mexican food. "Okay, tacos, it is."

After a quick trip to the grocery store, Merry put Holly to work in the kitchen. She was surprised to see the change that came over the girl as she took charge of the food preparation, confidently shredding lettuce and chopping up tomatoes.

"Maybe music isn't her vocation," Holden whispered in Merry's ear as he passed through the kitchen.

Merry's only answer was a lift of her shoulders.

As the three of them ate the tacos, Merry sensed a guardedness in Holly. It happened, she noticed, whenever the girl was around Holden. And despite Holden's attempts to ease the tension, Holly appeared determined to cling to her reserve.

After dinner Merry decided to take Holly shopping. Having seen the few pieces of clothing she'd unpacked, she knew Holly didn't have a dress for the holidays.

Instead of buying something off the rack, Merry decided to take her to a nearby fabric store where they browsed through pattern books in search of the right look for the holidays.

"This is a waste of time. We'll never get done by Christmas," Holly argued when Merry suggested she make a decision on a style.

"If we work together, we can do it," Merry said confidently. "The key is to find something simple. What about this one?" She pointed to a dress with an empire waist and a swing skirt. "This would look nice in that dark green velvet we saw when we came in."

"I've never had a velvet dress before," Holly told her. Standing in front of the plush fabrics, she reminded Merry of a small child in front of a candy counter.

"Do you like the look of this one?"

"Well, yeah, but—"

Merry didn't let her finish. "Then we'll get it." Ignoring Holly's protests, she asked the clerk for the pattern, then had a length of the green velvet cut from the bolt. "We'll need a few more things," she told Holly, gathering the necessary notions.

All the way home, Holly grumbled about the purchase. "You shouldn't have wasted your money like that. I might not even be here at Christmas."

"Well, I hope you will be, but you'll want to look nice no matter where you are."

"I haven't worn a dress at Christmas since I was, like, two or something."

"No? Then you'll be surprised at how special a pretty dress can make you feel," Merry said cheerfully. "When we get home we'll do all the measurements, then tomorrow we'll cut out the pieces."

"Well, don't expect me to be any good at it. I told you I screwed up in sewing in school."

"And you also told me you didn't do well in piano lessons at school, either, and look at how well you're doing now," Merry reminded her.

That silenced the teenager.

"This dress is a simple style. You're going to be surprised at how fast we put it together," Merry told her.

"If you say so," Holly mumbled.

Merry glanced over and saw that Holly's sullen look was back in place. Her fingers, however, were inside the brown paper bag, fondling the green velvet.

CHAPTER TWELVE

MERRY KNEW that she hadn't taken Holly shopping simply because the teenager needed a dress for Christmas. The awkwardness and tension between Holly and Holden made Merry decidedly uneasy, and it seemed a good idea to give everyone a break. But sooner or later, she knew, they were going to have to confront the problem.

Later that evening when they returned to the house, it was clear that Merry's other problem—Holden's opposition to her fiancé—was still in the forefront.

"Your boyfriend called," Holden announced before she'd even taken off her coat. "Three times."

"Thank you. Were there any other messages?" she asked, avoiding his eyes.

"No, just him. I think he thought I was lying when I said you weren't here."

Merry could see that Holly was glancing curiously at the two of them. "Holly, why don't you go put the new fabric in your room?"

As soon as she was gone, Merry said, "I'd appreciate your not talking about my personal life in front of Holly."

"All I did was say your boyfriend had called."

"You were ready to launch into an attack on him," she accused, unable to conceal her irritation.

"The man doesn't deserve your loyalty, Merry."

Holden would've said more, but Holly returned. Merry ushered her into the kitchen where they made a big bowl of popcorn. When Merry asked Holden if he wanted to watch television with them, he declined, taking his laptop into the dining room where he worked the rest of the evening. He didn't speak to Merry until she made up the sofa bed.

Holly had already turned in for the evening. Merry wished that she could disappear as easily as the teenager had, but Holden wouldn't let her.

"I want to talk to you," he said, coming over to help her remove the cushions from the sofa.

"Can't this wait until morning?" she pleaded, keeping her eyes on the task at hand.

"Do you want it to wait until tomorrow?"

Reluctantly she straightened to face him. The only light in the room came from a small brass table lamp with a three-way bulb on the lowest setting. It made her face look almost ethereal.

"Did you forget to call your boyfriend back?" he asked.

"What's your point, Holden?"

"Why didn't you call him back?"

"Maybe because my house guest makes my life miserable every time I try to talk to my fiancé," she retorted.

"I don't think that's the reason at all."

"No?"

"Uh-uh. I think you didn't *want* to talk to him."

She punched down the pillow she had just covered. "Well, you're wrong. I did want to talk to him. I love talking to him. I love him," she said in a challenging voice.

"You sound awfully sure of yourself."

"I *am* sure, and if you plan on staying through Christmas, you're going to have to stop this, Holden. Accept the fact that I'm engaged and that I don't want to discuss my fiancé with you."

"Okay, fine. Let's talk about you and me."

"What about you and me?" Her voice was wary.

"You have to ask that after everything's that's happened?"

"I don't know what you're talking about."

"Need me to show you?"

"Please don't," she drawled sarcastically. "If anyone's going to kiss me, it's going to be my fiancé."

He clicked his tongue. "Another challenging remark. Are you trying to be provocative, or are you just testing my willpower?"

"Neither," she said. She shook a sheet open and spread it over the bed. "Lots of men have kissed me and it's meant nothing. So what?"

"Do you want me to show you so what right here, right now, with Holly in the other room?"

As she looked at him, her lips quivered. "No."

"Why are you suddenly afraid of me, Merry?" he asked, moving around to her side of the sofa bed. "I'd never do anything to hurt you."

"No, you just want to spoil my chance at marital happiness."

"Marital happiness?" He scoffed at the words. "I'm trying to save you from heartache."

"Steve's not the one causing my heartache," she said quietly.

He heaved a sigh. "What have I done to hurt you?"

"You mean besides hiring a private investigator to follow my fiancé around?"

"Merry, I'm a lawyer. I do what's necessary to protect people's rights."

"It's pointless to argue about this," she said for what seemed like the thousandth time in the past week. "We're never going to see eye to eye on the subject. Why can't you just accept my decision and be happy for me?"

"Because I'm not happy you want to marry the guy. He's twice your age, he treats you as if you can't think for yourself, and the thought of his wrinkled flesh next to yours drives me crazy," he blurted passionately.

She squeezed her eyes shut and threw up her hands. "Stop right there. You're overstepping the boundaries of our friendship."

"Merry, we have more than friendship between us," he said, moving closer to her.

When she opened her eyes, her confusion showed in their depths. She stepped away from him. "I should never have called you at the airport today."

"It wouldn't have mattered. I still would've been here tonight."

She gave him a puzzled look.

"When you paged me at the airport today, I wasn't waiting to board my flight. I was on my way to get a taxi. I'd already decided I couldn't leave."

She dropped onto the side of the mattress and stared up at him. "But you told me you were leaving."

She looked so charming he couldn't resist the urge to sit down beside her. "I couldn't just walk away and let you marry the guy. He's not good enough for you,

Merry.'' Holden's arm found its way around her shoulder, and his fingers lifted her chin.

"You need someone who knows how to do this," he whispered, then covered her mouth with his, kissing her with an urgency he'd never felt before.

"Holden, don't," she protested, although the heat of her flesh and the softness of her lips told him she wanted it as much as he did.

He pushed her back against the pillows and covered her body with his. "Does he do this, Merry?" Holden asked moments before his tongue plunged into her mouth. Her struggle was only momentary, then her fingers were weaving through his hair, her body arching beneath his as the kiss became a fire that threatened to consume them both.

When he finally lifted his mouth from hers, she breathed, "This can't be."

"It's not going to go away," he said, slipping his fingers inside her blouse. They found the satiny smooth fabric of her bra and traced the outline of her breasts. "*I'm* not going to go away."

Her moans were not of protest but pleading. When his hand slid beneath the satin and cupped a breast, a tiny sound of ecstasy escaped her mouth. He would have replaced his hand with his lips had the ringing of the phone not interrupted them. He rolled away from her, his breathing ragged. Automatically he reached for the receiver.

"Yes?"

"I want to speak to my fiancée," the voice on the other end said coldly.

"It's for you," Holden said, extending the phone in her direction.

Merry clasped the edges of her blouse in one hand, the phone in the other, her eyes never leaving Holden's face as she said hello.

"Do you realize what time it is?" she asked Steve, then as if she could no longer stand Holden's gaze on her, she rolled over so that her back was to him and murmured, "I was going to call you, but..."

She was silent for long moments, then said, "I'm tired, Steve. We'll talk in the morning."

Another silence and then she said impatiently, "I have to go."

She slammed the receiver down on the cradle and scrambled off the mattress, buttoning her blouse. "If you need another pillow during the night, Holden, there's one in the linen closet." She set a folded blanket on the edge of the bed.

As she walked from the room, he called out, "Merry, wait."

"Please, Holden, just let me go to bed," she said without turning around.

"All right, but answer me one question."

She still didn't turn around. "What?"

"Why didn't you correct Steve when he assumed I was staying at a hotel?"

She sighed and said, "Go to bed, Holden," and disappeared.

MERRY DIDN'T WANT to think about facing Holden in the morning. She'd spent most of the night tossing and turning and wondering how her body could have betrayed her so.

She supposed she shouldn't be surprised. Holden was an attractive, experienced man who knew exactly what to do to turn on a woman. Was it any wonder her body had responded to his caresses?

He was a wonderful kisser—always had been, always would be. Unlike Steve, who... She quickly scolded herself for even comparing the two men.

Steve had always been the perfect gentleman, and she admired him for his self-control. It was an aspect of their relationship she took for granted—the fact that sex wasn't foremost on his mind. Holden, on the other hand, carried condoms in his travel case. Like before, the thought brought heat to her cheeks.

If she expected him to behave any differently when she sat down for breakfast with him and Holly, she was mistaken. He treated her as he always did. There were no furtive glances, no twinkle in his eye of a secret shared. Just the same old down-to-business Holden.

"Bonnie called while you were in the shower. She wanted to remind you that Holly has a dentist appointment at nine-thirty this morning. She said if you'll drop her off, she'll pick her up and then take her back to her place so she can pick up the rest of her things."

Merry glanced at her watch. "That'll work out great. I have to stop by the studio and pick up some music I left there."

"She also wanted to remind you about some youth program at church Holly is supposed to attend," Holden continued. His words brought a frown to Holly's face.

"It's confirmation classes," the girl said. "Do I have to go?"

Merry could see her first test as a foster parent was at hand. "Bonnie said this is the last one until after Christmas."

"But I thought we were going to work on my dress," Holly complained.

"We have plenty of time for that today," Merry assured her. "As soon as you get back from Bonnie's, we'll get started."

"We should probably leave," Holden suggested, slipping his arms into his suit jacket.

"We?" She gave him a quizzical look. "Are you coming along?"

"I'm going to have you drop me off at the car-rental agency."

Merry thought it was his way of getting her alone in the car so they could talk. She was wrong. He had her drop him off before she took Holly to the dentist.

After stopping at the studio, Merry headed for home. As she drove, her thoughts automatically drifted to everything that had taken place in the past few weeks. From the moment she'd put Steve's engagement ring on her finger, her life had become filled with stress. Normally she was confident in her decisions, but ever since Holden's arrival she'd been second-guessing herself.

Unbidden came the memory of what had happened between Holden and her last night. She'd wanted him to make love to her—something she hadn't wanted with Steve. When she was in Steve's arms, she felt comfortable. In Holden's arms, she felt like a volcano ready to erupt. He touched a part of her no other man ever had.

She shoved all thoughts of comparison between the two men out of her mind. Just because Holden was a more experienced lover didn't mean Steve was inept.

Inept. Where had that word come from? she asked herself. Her fiancé was not inept at anything. He was a wonderful man, a terrific father, a charismatic television personality millions of women adored.

He was also sitting in his car in her driveway waiting for her. He did not look happy.

Merry led him inside and offered to make coffee, but he told her not to bother. "I can only stay a few minutes, but I needed to see you." He pulled her into his arms and kissed her hard on the mouth.

Merry wanted to respond, but all she could think was that his mouth was nothing like Holden's. It didn't stir her at all. No nerve endings stood at attention, no warmth spread through her. It was, she imagined, like kissing an uncle.

Startled by her thoughts, she pulled back. He didn't want to release her, but stared into her eyes and said, "I had to see you. I hate it when we argue. You know, we never used to argue until Holden showed up."

"Holden isn't the problem between us," she told him, although deep down she knew that he was definitely a part of it.

Steve hugged her again and said, "I'm glad you said that. Ever since I saw him kiss you under the mistletoe, I've had this gut feeling that he wants to be more than your brother."

A tidal wave of guilt washed over her. She couldn't meet his eyes as she said, "I really would like to leave Holden out of this conversation."

"All right. Done," he said quickly. "As long as I know he's not trying to steal my woman from me, I can live with that."

Just then Bonnie and Holly arrived, carrying several boxes and suitcases. Steve's eyes narrowed suspiciously.

"Here she is," the older woman said cheerfully, giving Merry a grateful smile of understanding as she led Holly into the living room. "I think we have the lot, but if anything was left behind, I'll bring it over."

Steve watched the proceedings, his expression growing darker by the minute. Merry ignored him, because right now she needed to make Holly feel welcome.

"Holly, you know where you can put your stuff, so why don't you go and unpack?" She took the girl's coat, then said to Bonnie, "Would you like a cup of tea?"

"Oh, no, I can't stay. I just wanted to come in with Holly and let you know that if you have any concerns, you can call me anytime day or night." She smiled warmly at Merry. "I'm sure you'll make a good home for Holly. She needs someone special right now, and I think you're it."

As soon as Bonnie was gone, Steve's anger broke loose.

"I thought you said she was only staying for a few days. Obviously you've made a decision about having this juvenile delinquent *live* in your home without telling me," he said through tight lips.

Merry glanced uneasily toward Holly's bedroom. "She's in the other room. Try to keep your voice down."

"Merry, this isn't going to work out. How are you going to take care of a thirteen-year-old?"

"The same way any other woman takes care of a thirteen-year-old," she retorted.

"But what about your career? You're on the brink of hitting it big."

"I can be a musician and a parent at the same time, Steve," she said. "What, you think there aren't any celebrities who have children?"

"This is not your child. She's a juvenile delinquent. This isn't any ordinary situation. You're talking about special needs, problems..." His voice trailed off.

Again Merry's eyes flew in the direction of Holly's bedroom. Worried the girl might overhear their conversation, she pulled him into the front hallway, as far away as possible.

"She has a name, Steve. It's Holly. She's a child that needs help and I'm going to give it."

"Merry, you can't. I won't let you. I've worked too hard this past year to get you that record deal. I'm not going to let you throw it all away over some kid."

Now it was Merry who was angry. "You're not going to let me? You have no say in whether or not I care for this girl. It isn't your decision. It's mine."

"Of course it's my decision. I'm your fiancé."

"No, you're not." She twisted the diamond solitaire from her finger and handed it to him. "Here. I can't marry you, Steve."

All the color drained from his face. "Merry, don't say that," he pleaded.

"I have to say it," she said quietly.

"No. No, you don't. We can—"

"Steve, it's not going to work out."

"It will if we want it to. If you really want to make a home for Holly, I can live with that."

"No."

"I admit I didn't really want any more children, but if it's important to you, it's okay with me." He sounded as if he was trying to convince himself more than her. "I'll do anything for you, Merry. You must know that by now."

He tried to take her in his arms, but she eluded his grasp. "It's not going to work out, Steve," she repeated.

"It can," he insisted. "Come on, Merry. Just give it a chance. Put the ring back on your finger." He tried to give her the diamond, but she kept her hands balled into fists.

"Merry, don't do this. Not right before Christmas," he begged. "Look at all the plans we've made. My family's expecting you to be there."

"I'm sorry."

"You can bring Holly. She can be a part of the celebration."

She shook her head. "It's not a good idea."

"Merry, you've told me over and over how important family is to you. This was going to be your first Christmas with a real family. Do you really want to throw it all away because of this kid?"

"I'm not throwing anything away," she answered. "I'm ending a relationship that I've finally realized didn't have the right ingredients to make it last."

He was silent for several moments before he said, "I see. Then I guess there's nothing more to be said, is there."

He retrieved his coat from the back of the sofa where he'd flung it when he'd first come in. "You're going to regret this someday," he said. Then he turned and stalked out the door.

MERRY PHONED IN SICK. There was no way she could handle playing the piano at Braxton's today. And she really did feel sick. She hated confrontation, and the one with Steve had been particularly devastating. Even though she'd said what needed to be said, she knew she'd hurt him.

She wished Holden was here right now. She needed his presence, needed his reassurance that she would be all right. But he wasn't here, and she had to pull herself together for Holly's sake.

"I'm all done putting my stuff away," the girl announced when she came into the kitchen and found Merry sitting at the table staring off into space. "Is everything okay? You look kinda weird."

Merry forced a smile to her face. "I'm fine," she lied. "I think I might be getting a cold. My nose has been runny today."

"Are we going to be able to work on the dress, or do you have to go to work?"

"I called in sick. I don't feel too bad, though and I would like to get started on your dress—as soon as I finished my tea. Would you like something to eat?"

Holly's tense features relaxed into a smile. "Uh, what have you got?"

Merry opened the refrigerator and grimaced. "Not a whole lot, I'm afraid. Maybe we ought to go to the grocery store first."

"It's all right. I'm not very hungry. Bonnie bought me lunch. I'd rather we started on my dress, if that's all right with you."

It was more than all right with Merry. Sewing was just the therapy she needed to chase away the blues. She and Holly spent the afternoon in Holly's bedroom working on the velvet dress, a project that kept both of them busy. Merry was grateful for the diversion; she didn't want to think about Steve or Holden.

When Holly's stomach growled, Merry knew it was time to stop. "Should we break for dinner?" she asked, even though food was far from her thoughts.

"I'd rather not, but I guess we have to, huh?"

"Why don't I order a pizza? That way we can keep working until it arrives," Merry answered.

Holly agreed.

It was while they were eating pizza that Holden came home.

"Hi. You're just in time for Domino's Supreme Classic," Merry told him as he entered the kitchen.

"I've already eaten," he told her. "I only stopped by to get my things."

Merry's stomach dropped. "You're leaving?" She got up from the table.

"No. I'm not going back to California. I'm checking into a hotel."

"I see," she said, although she really didn't see at all. "If that's what you want."

He sighed. "It's not what I want, but it's what's best for right now. Besides, you and Holly don't need me underfoot."

Merry wanted to tell him that she did need him. That she had grown accustomed to having him around. She wanted to tell him about her broken engagement, to talk to him about her anxieties concerning Holly. She needed him to be the friend who'd always been there for her whenever she had her holiday melancholy. But it was clear he didn't want to be there with her, and the thought sent a stab of pain through her.

"Which hotel?" she asked, following him out to the entry.

"The Radisson, downtown. How did everything go this morning?"

"Fine."

"Have you talked to the social worker on Holly's case?"

"Yes. She's going to stop by tomorrow."

"Another reason I shouldn't be camped out on your couch." He hoisted his bags under his arms. "I'll talk to you tomorrow," he said as he left.

"But I need you," Merry muttered under her breath. He didn't hear her. She pushed the door shut with more effort than necessary and returned to the kitchen.

As soon as she and Holly had finished eating, Merry suggested that the girl put away the sewing and get ready for her confirmation class. Merry drove Holly to the church, then returned home to an empty house.

She tried not to think about Holden the rest of the evening, yet continually found her thoughts coming back to what had happened on the sofa bed the night before. Obviously it had meant nothing to Holden, for he hadn't even mentioned it today. She scolded herself for hoping it *had* meant something to him. After all these years, she knew Holden well enough to know that to him a kiss was just a kiss.

For her it had been more than a kiss, just as it had been fourteen years ago when he proved to her she wasn't frigid. Holden had always affected her like no other man, only she hadn't wanted to admit it. Now he was acting as if nothing had happened between the two of them last night!

When she went to sit down at the piano, she noticed his daily planner under the end table. She didn't hesitate a moment. She picked it up and went out to the hallway to get her coat.

CHAPTER THIRTEEN

HOLDEN SAT in front of the television, a glass of Scotch in one hand, the remote control in the other, cursing his good sense. For it was because of his good sense that he was sitting alone in a hotel room, instead of at Merry's place asleep on her sofa.

Liar, a little voice inside his head cried. *You don't want to be asleep on her sofa. You want to be in her bed and not sleeping.*

In fact, he'd wanted that for as long as he could remember. But until recently he'd been able to accept that sleeping with Merry was not going to happen. He shared something with her he'd never found with any other woman—friendship—and he vowed he wouldn't screw it up by bringing sex into the equation. There were boundaries one didn't cross, but ever since he'd felt the fullness of her breasts and kissed the sweetness of her mouth, the boundary lines had become increasingly fuzzy.

He took another swig of Scotch. All these years he had controlled his desire for her. Now it seemed uncontrollable. Maybe it was bound to happen. After all, she was beautiful, sexy, alluring. He shut his eyes in an effort to blot out the tantalizing image. He didn't want to have sexual feelings for someone he'd always treated like a sister.

Only she wasn't his sister. Never had been, never would be. She was Merry, the closest friend he'd ever had, the only woman who understood him. At least she used to understand him.

She used to share his views on marriage, too. She'd always been as wary as he was of the "happy ever after" myth. Now she was looking for a fairy-tale ending to her relationship with Steve Austin and ignoring everything experience had taught her. Briefly he'd considered taking her to bed simply to prove to her that what she felt for Austin wasn't love. He'd quickly cast that idea aside, however. If he had sex with her, it wouldn't be to teach her a lesson. Oh, no. It would be for the pure pleasure of it.

He finished the Scotch and set the glass down with a thud. He should have gotten on the plane heading back to L.A. And he would have had it not been for the discovery that Merry and her Prince Charming slept in separate beds.

He groaned. Anyone with half a brain could see that the old coot was all wrong for her. The problem was how to convince Merry there was more to life then playing house with a man old enough to be her father. Every time he mentioned the guy's name she defended him more passionately. Maybe he needed to try some reverse psychology—act as if he approved of the marriage.

It'd be hard. He'd have to stifle the urge to gag every time she sung Austin's praises, but he'd tolerated unpleasant situations before. He could do it. He *would* do it.

He got up to pour himself another Scotch, then stopped by the window. As he stared out at the downtown skyline, he wondered what Merry was doing at that very moment. Was she with Austin? Was his wrinkled flesh rubbing against her smooth skin? The thought was enough to make him down the shot of whiskey in one gulp.

Only, his fears turned out to be unfounded. There was a knock on his door, and when he opened it Merry was standing there.

"Oh! You *are* here," she said, looking a bit surprised when he answered.

He stepped aside, indicating she should come in. "Is this a social visit or am I again being summoned to come to your aid?" He didn't intend for his voice to be laced with sarcasm, but she looked so damned sexy in her red coat that it was an automatic defense mechanism.

"You left this at my place." She pulled the daily planner from her purse and handed it to him. "I thought you might need it."

He took the planner from her and tossed it onto the mahogany desk against the wall. "You could've called. I would've come for it tomorrow."

"I didn't just come here because of that," she admitted, unbuttoning her coat. It slid from her shoulders and landed on the king-size bed.

Holden's heartbeat accelerated. "And what would be the other reason you wanted to see me?"

She wore a pair of faded jeans and a baggy sweatshirt that hid her curves. Yet Holden doubted she could have looked sexier had she worn something tight and slinky. He averted his eyes from her figure.

"I wanted to thank you. I didn't get a chance to tell you how much I appreciated everything you did to help me with Holly's situation." He could hear a nervousness in her voice.

"You're welcome. Can I get you something to drink?" he asked, crossing to the bar in the corner.

She shook her head. "I can't stay long. I have to pick up Holly by nine."

"Everything going okay?"

"Yes, fine. We spent most of the day sewing a dress for her for Christmas. It's green velvet with puffy sleeves. It should look nice on her. It's quite festive actually." She was rambling. He wondered why.

"I'm sure it is." He poured himself another Scotch. "I take it that means you'll be including Holly in your plans with the Austins."

"Actually there's been a change in my Christmas plans. I'm not going to Steve's," she blurted, as if she were telling him she'd canceled a magazine subscription.

He glanced over his shoulder to ask, "Is he coming to your place?"

"No."

"You're not spending Christmas with him?"

"No."

Merry was standing on the opposite side of the bed. He wanted to leap across it and hug her. He didn't. He simply said, "Good." He didn't look at her, but at the amber liquid he was swirling in his glass.

"Is that all you have to say?" Merry stood with her hands on her hips.

He glanced at her and shrugged. "I'm happy we don't have to spend the holidays with the senior citizens," he said evenly.

"Don't you even want to know why?"

"Ethel and Margie couldn't decide who would bring the spinach dip?" he asked flippantly.

Holden loved the way her eyes flashed with indignation. Ever since they'd been kids, she'd always acted the same way when she was upset.

"Steve doesn't think Holly should be..." She trailed off in disgust, saying, "Oh, I don't know why I bother. It's obvious you don't care."

"I do care." He set his glass down on the nightstand and walked around the bed toward her. "But I don't think you came all the way over here to tell me you're not spending Christmas with Steve-o. You're avoiding the real reason."

"What other reason would there be?" The air crackled with tension.

"Why don't you tell me."

She reached for her coat. "I think I'd better go." Her voice was barely above a whisper.

He covered the short distance between them in a flash, taking the coat from her hands and tossing it aside. "Merry, tell me why you came."

"I wanted..." She hesitated.

"You wanted what, Merry?"

She didn't answer.

"You know what I think? I think you came because the same thoughts that have been going through my head all day have been going through yours."

"I can't read your mind," she said, turning her back to him.

He leaned over and said close to her ear, "Oh, yes, you can."

When she started to step away, he caught her by the shoulders and turned her around to face him. Then he lifted her chin with one finger and studied her.

"You can pretend that you don't feel the same thing I'm feeling and that you're not thinking the same thing I'm thinking, but we both know what's happening between us."

"It shouldn't be happening." The look in her eyes contradicted her words and sent desire swelling inside him. "Holden, don't do this."

"I'm not doing anything except looking at you," he told her, although he knew the message in his eyes was telling her more than any words could.

"Then why does it feel like you're touching me?"

He didn't answer, but traced the delicate line of her cheekbone and the sensitive curve of her upper lip. His mouth replaced his fingers, placing kisses across her cheeks until they found her lips. He moved his mouth slowly over hers, searching for the response that would confirm what her eyes had already told him.

Her response didn't take long to occur and its intensity caught him off guard. The same longing that made his body ache made her cling to him, instinctively seeking greater intimacy.

The touch of her hands on his body made him weak, tempting him to forget everything but the passion that had burst to life between them. In a matter of seconds they were stretched out on the bed and she was moving sensuously against him.

Holden slid a hand under her sweatshirt. The warmth and smoothness of her flesh sent him reeling, and in one swift motion, he lifted the fleecy fabric over her head. She didn't object, but looked at him with eyes smoky with desire.

"You're so beautiful, Merry," he murmured thickly as he stared at the flesh bulging from the satiny bra. "I tried to keep this from happening, but..." He couldn't finish his explanation for she was pulling him to her and kissing him hungrily.

Holden pressed his mouth into her scented flesh as pent-up desire tightened his body. "I'm tired of pretending I don't want you, Merry..."

"Then stop pretending." She unbuttoned his shirt and put her hands inside, moving across tense muscles in an exploring caress. The leash he had on his self-control was growing looser by the minute.

"I know what I want, but are you sure you know what you want?" He gave her one last chance to put out the fire they'd ignited.

"This...this physical thing between us isn't going to go away simply by ignoring it." Her voice had a breathless quality.

"So we should get it out of our systems. Is that what you're saying?"

For an answer she kissed him again, a long, slow invasion of his senses that rocked Holden to his very soul. She left him with no doubt that she was willing, that she, too, was ready to stop fighting their need for each other.

Clothes vanished beneath fingers and all talking ceased as they explored each other intimately, exalting in the uninhibited physical discovery of each other. She was everything he'd fantasized she'd be, making him aware of sensations he'd never experienced before. They let their passion take them to a world where nothing mattered but the ecstasy they shared.

When it was over, he felt as if his life would never be the same. It frightened him, this feeling that he had given something of himself he wouldn't be able to recover. Never before had that happened to him when he'd been with a woman.

He'd always prided himself on being in control of his passion, yet it was Merry who had to remind him to use protection. It was a scary thought, that he had wanted her so badly he could forget to use common sense.

Consequently, as they held each other, letting the echoes of passion shiver through their bodies, he couldn't say a word. It had been a profound experience he wasn't ready to talk about.

When she finally lifted her head, there was satisfaction in her eyes and something else—something he didn't want to see. Possessiveness. And it was all his fault. He'd given her every reason to have that glimmer in her eye. Before she could make any declaration of her feelings, he kissed her.

When he finally released her mouth, she laughed. "Give me time to catch my breath." She rolled away from him. "I can't believe we did that. It was good, wasn't it."

He stole a sideways glance at her and saw the dreamy look in her eyes. Guilt started to edge out the afterglow of passion. "It was good," he agreed softly, closing his eyes as if he could blot out the truth. Yes, it was good. Too good.

She sighed. "I never thought it would be like this. I feel like there's a sunrise taking place inside me."

Holden made the mistake of looking at her again. With the flush on her cheeks and the glisten of moisture on her skin, she was more beautiful than any sunrise he'd ever seen. He couldn't keep from touching her.

"Maybe this is the dawn of a new beginning for us," he told her as his fingers lazily stroked her body.

She shuddered as he found the moist flesh between her thighs. "You'd better not do that or else I'm going to have trouble leaving."

"You don't want to leave, do you?" he asked, enjoying the path his hand was taking.

She stilled his fingers. "I have to. I have to pick up Holly."

He rolled onto his back and groaned. Merry scrambled off the bed, scooped up her clothes and headed for the bathroom.

"You don't need to go in there. I've seen it all," he called out to her, but she ignored him.

A few minutes later she came out fully dressed. "I knew the only way these clothes would get back on my body was if I was alone," she said.

"If you wait a couple of minutes I'll get dressed and walk you to your car," he told her when she reached for her coat.

"You don't have to do that."

"I want to do that."

Unlike her, he didn't go into the bathroom to get dressed, but pulled on his clothes right in front of her. He found it amusing that she averted her gaze. She hadn't so much as blinked an eye when he'd peeled off his clothes.

All the way down the hall to the elevator she was quiet. Normally he didn't want to talk after having sex, but this time he found the silence disturbing.

"Sleepy?" he asked.

"Not really."

"You're awfully quiet."

"I'm thinking."

"About what?"

"Us, of course. Look what just happened."

"I thought we both agreed it was good," he commented, holding the elevator door open for her.

"It was, but it changes everything." The doors slid shut and the elevator descended.

"Nothing has to change."

She sighed. "I knew you'd say that."

He was sorry he'd broken the silence. "Look. It's late. This isn't the kind of conversation I want to have in an elevator."

"You wanted to know what I was thinking," she reminded him.

"So now I know." He didn't mean to sound so short, but he didn't want to analyze what had happened between them.

They were both silent until they reached the parking garage. He walked her to her car and waited until she had the key in the lock before asking, "What's your schedule like tomorrow?"

"I'm working at Braxton's from twelve till four."

"I'll be over in the morning."

"I have to take Holly to school at eight. It's her first day back after her suspension."

"I can drive you."

She nodded, then opened the door and climbed inside. She was about to close it when he leaned into the car. In one swift movement his mouth was on hers, kissing her as if they were back in his bed and about to make love.

When the kiss ended, they were both breathing heavily. He looked into her eyes and said, "It was good," then closed the door.

With trembling hands, Merry started the car. Holden didn't move from where he was standing until she'd driven out of sight.

LONG AFTER SHE LEFT, Merry kept hearing those words. *It was good.* They brought a smile to her face, even though she knew that as good as it had been between her and Holden, it wasn't necessarily going to happen again.

From the way he'd kissed her when she was seated in the car, she wanted to believe there would be many more nights like tonight, but she'd known Holden long enough to know better. Tonight was a "get it out of our systems" night. He himself had said it.

She supposed she should feel remorse over giving in to the temptation to make love with him. The truth was, however, she had no regrets. For years she'd wanted to know what going to bed with him would be like. Now she knew. It was like having the sun rise inside of her.

He'd said it could be the dawn of a new beginning for them. She hadn't wanted to press him as to what he meant by that statement, preferring to think that he welcomed the new intimacy of their relationship, that now they were more than friends. But what did he see for them in the future?

She knew one thing for sure. She loved him. She always had, always would. It was the reason she'd disapproved of his love life. She didn't want there to be other women in his life. Not while they were growing up, certainly not now. But what if he'd gotten *her,* not just *it,* out of his system?

She wouldn't think about it. Having sex had changed everything. And more had happened between them than Holden wanted to admit. She could feel it. She wanted that sunrise to happen again and again. She hoped he wanted it, too.

MERRY WISHED she'd asked Holden what time he would be over the following morning, for she found herself watching the clock like a school kid in detention. Holly picked up on her anxiety.

"Are you nervous about something?" she asked Merry as they ate breakfast. "You seem kinda jumpy this morning."

Merry didn't want to admit to the thirteen-year-old the true reason for her anxiety. She felt like a jittery teenager waiting for her date to show up. But Holden wasn't her date, and they certainly weren't teenagers experiencing puppy love.

"I'm hoping Holden remembers you have to be at school by eight o'clock," she answered.

"Aren't you taking me?"

"Yes, but he's going to come along."

"Why?"

Merry kept her face turned so Holly wouldn't see the way her cheeks flushed at the memory of the night before. "We need to run some errands afterward."

"Oh."

Before the girl could pose any more questions, Merry changed the subject, asking her about her class schedule.

It was while Holly was finishing her breakfast that Julia arrived, bearing a gift—a red-foil-wrapped box with a big white bow on top.

"This is for you," Julia said, handing Merry the package. "Dad told me you weren't coming over for Christmas. I wanted you to have this, so I thought I'd drop it off on my way to school."

Merry's stomach squirmed. "He told you what happened?"

Julia nodded. "I'm really sorry, Merry. You know how much Renée and I wanted you to be a part of our family."

"I know, but it isn't going to work out." Merry rubbed her arms absently. "I wish you hadn't bought me anything. It doesn't seem right, considering the circumstances."

"Are you sure it's over between you and my father? I mean, I know you have some problems, but can't you work them out? He's miserable, Merry."

Merry shifted from one foot to the other. "Look, this is rather awkward. I know you mean well, but I don't think we should be discussing this."

Holly chose that moment to stick her head out of the kitchen. Seeing her inquisitive look, Merry said, "Why don't you get your things together for school?"

Holly's dark head quickly disappeared into the bedroom.

"Is that the foster child you want to take in?" Julia whispered.

"Yes," Merry answered proudly. "Her name is Holly."

Julia didn't ask any more questions about Holly, for her thoughts were clearly elsewhere. She glanced around Merry's living room. "Where's Holden?"

"He's not staying here."

"He isn't? I thought my father said he was spending Christmas with you."

Holden chose that moment to arrive. Just what Merry didn't want—Julia to be present the first time she saw Holden after their lovemaking. She was feeling uncertain enough without that.

When Julia caught sight of him, her face lit up. Merry experienced a surge of jealousy when the blonde rushed over to take him by the arm and pull him into the living room.

"Holden, hi! I'm glad you're here. You have to talk to Merry and convince her that just because she and my father have decided to postpone their wedding, it doesn't mean the two of you shouldn't spend Christmas with us."

So that was why she'd come, Merry realized. She wasn't as concerned that her father had lost his fiancé as she was that Holden wouldn't be at their holiday festivities.

"I've never been able to tell Merry what to do," Holden answered with a wry grin. The words were delivered with a polished charm that had the younger woman staring up at him with doelike eyes.

"It's really not a good idea, Julia," Merry said, annoyed that Holden was wasting his charm on Steve's daughter. Why didn't he remove Julia's hand from his arm?

"If I can't talk you into coming for Christmas, you're at least going to have to stop by the house." This comment was directed at Holden. "I have a gift for you."

Merry didn't get to hear Holden's response, for Holly called out from her room and she went to see what she needed. All she heard was Julia's tinkling laugh. As she listened to Holly complain about not being able to find her history book, Merry's thoughts were on the couple in the living room.

"Holden, we'd better leave if we don't want Holly to be late," Merry announced as she swept back into the living room after a moment. "I'm sorry, Julia, but we have to go."

With lips pursed in a pout, Julia eyed Holden predatorily, then glanced at Merry and said, "Please think about what I said. Dad is miserable without you, Merry."

To Holden, she winked and said, "Call me."

In the car, Merry avoided looking at Holden, preferring to give her attention to Holly, who was not at all happy to be returning to school. Holden said little, keeping his eyes on the road and only speaking when he needed directions.

"I'm going to go inside with her," Merry told him when he pulled the car up in front of the school building.

"Okay. I'll park across the street and wait there."

Merry could see that Holly was dreading going inside. With as much optimism as she could muster, Merry walked her up the concrete steps, through the front door and down the noisy halls to the principal's office.

It only took a few minutes for Holly to be reinstated. Merry had conversations with several of the staff, including the guidance counselor and one of Holly's teachers. When she got back to the car, Holden was reading the morning paper. When he saw her, he folded it and put it aside, then started the car.

"Everything all right?" he asked as she got in.

"Yes."

"Good."

They drove in silence for several miles until finally he asked, "Where are we going?"

"I thought I'd take you to breakfast."

"I've already eaten," she answered, wondering why they were talking about breakfast when they should be talking about what had happened between them last night.

"I haven't and I'm starved."

She didn't ask him what restaurant he was going to and was surprised to find they were in downtown Minneapolis. When he pulled the rental car into the valet parking in front of his hotel, her heart began to beat faster.

"We're having breakfast at your hotel?"

"Do you mind?" he asked, a sexy glint in his eye.

She could only shake her head.

A bellman opened her door and helped her out. Holden came around and escorted her inside. Instead of heading toward the restaurant, he led her to the elevators.

As they waited for one, he asked her about Holly's school and what the principal and teacher had to say about her. He acted as if the two of them riding up to the fifteenth floor on the elevator was the most natural thing in the world.

When they stopped outside his room, she finally said, "I thought you wanted to have breakfast."

He unlocked the door and pushed it open for her. "I do."

She stepped inside and he followed. Before he closed the door he slipped the Do Not Disturb sign on the handle.

"Well?" She was waiting for his answer.

"You're breakfast."

CHAPTER FOURTEEN

"WAIT A MINUTE. We can't do this," Merry said as Holden moved toward her.

"We can't?" The gleam in his eye told her he disagreed.

"No." She closed her eyes and willed the trembling inside her to stop. It didn't.

"Don't you mean we can't *not* do this?" he asked, stepping so close to her she could feel his breath on her cheek. "Open your eyes, Merry."

His husky voice had a seductive quality she couldn't ignore. As she looked into his eyes she could feel her resistance melt.

"The only thing that kept me from following you home last night was Holly. I knew I wouldn't be able to keep my hands off that beautiful body of yours." He didn't touch her, but stared at her with such a hunger in his eyes Merry could feel her limbs weaken. She knew she should turn away from him, but felt incapable of movement.

"Holden, I—" she began, only to have him silence her with a kiss.

It was a deep, probing kiss, and when it ended, he said in a trembling voice, "I think last night was the longest night of my life. I couldn't wait for morning to come."

His eyes conveyed the same message as his kiss. He wanted her. Badly. Excitement made Merry gasp, and once again his lips found hers. As his tongue slipped into her mouth, desire pushed all thoughts of talking from her mind. In his arms she felt as if she'd finally come home. This was what she'd been searching for all of her life. Never again would she feel alone as long as she was loved by this man.

From the very first time he'd kissed her fourteen years ago, she had wanted him to be the only man in her life. Nothing had changed. Not only was it the reason she'd hated all the women he'd dated, it was why she hadn't had any satisfactory sexual relationship, why she'd valued her engagement to Steve for all the wrong reasons.

She was in love with Holden, plain and simple. There was no point pretending it was just a physical attraction that would gradually run its course. What she had with Holden went beyond desire. She slipped her arms around his neck, urging his strong, hard body closer to hers. She needed to hold him, to make him quiver, to become one with him, body and soul.

Fueled by the same passion, she arched against him. "Oh, Holden. This is so right," she whispered.

"I need you, Merry," he said between kisses. "I've never needed anyone like this before."

For her, his words were the pot of gold at the rainbow's end. All of her life she'd waited to hear them. Her hands moved down the front of his shirt, impatiently tugging at the tiny buttons.

She voiced her thoughts. "I've waited so long for this," she said, pressing kisses to his hot flesh as she opened the shirt. "I still can't believe it's happening. Oh, Holden, I love you so much."

The minute she uttered the words, Holden stiffened. Fingers that had been tenderly caressing her breasts froze. It didn't take but a moment for Merry to realize that even though he still held her in his arms, he'd withdrawn from her emotionally.

"Holden?" Eyes misty with passion, she looked to him for an answer.

"You're right, Merry. We can't do this," he muttered, raking a hand through his hair as he turned away from her.

"Why? Because I said I love you?" Fear rose in her chest.

"This isn't about love, Merry."

The fear threatened to choke her. "What are you saying? That you only want my body? That I'm just another one of your playthings?"

"No, it's not like that at all," he denied gruffly. "I care about you. It's why I'm not going to take you to bed."

"Spare me the 'I'm doing this for your own good' routine," she said mockingly.

"It's true."

"Pig's ass. You can't honestly expect me to believe that because of your great affection for me I don't have to be a victim of the usual 'love 'em and leave 'em' Holden Drake treatment."

She'd gathered momentum now and wasn't about to be stopped. "Well, let me tell you something, Holden. It's too late for you to have a conscience. You made love to me last night. Call it whatever you like, but to me it was making love."

"It shouldn't have happened," he said quietly.

The words were like physical blows to her. Still, she went on. "But it did. Right here. In this room." She paused to take a deep breath and ask in a pained voice, "Why, Holden?"

"We both know why."

"What are you trying to say? That it was simply something physical we couldn't ignore?"

"Merry, don't do this," he pleaded.

"Don't do what? Analyze what happened last night?"

"We had sex, Merry. We've been attracted to each other for a long time, and it probably would've happened sooner if you hadn't been engaged."

"But now that we've gotten it out of our systems, we don't need to do it anymore, is that it?" Her eyes flashed.

"That's not what I mean . . ." he started to explain, but she wasn't about to stand around and listen to him tell her she'd made a fool of herself. She reached for her coat.

"Merry, wait. Will you let me explain?"

"No, you've already explained more than enough!" She headed for the door. "You forget, Holden. I've known you longer than any other woman on this earth. I know exactly what you mean." And with those words she stormed out the door.

Holden followed her to the elevators. "You don't have a car. I'll take you home."

"Don't bother. I'll grab a cab."

He followed her down to the lobby, anyway. Before the valet could retrieve his car, however, she'd jumped into a taxi and was gone.

AFTER THE SCENE with Holden, Merry looked forward to going to work at Braxton's. At least she would find solace in her music. Despite the ache in her heart, she managed to put on a smile and entertain the crowd of Christmas shoppers.

However, throughout her performance she never gave up hope that Holden would appear and tell her he'd been wrong this morning. She wanted him to say he'd been mistaken about his feelings, that he loved her and didn't want her to be like all the other women in his life.

He didn't. Nor were there any messages from him on her answering machine when she got home. As she and Holly ate dinner, she debated calling the hotel to see if he'd checked out.

She didn't. She was afraid she'd discover he'd left without saying goodbye.

Later that evening, she pulled out the pieces for the green velvet dress, and the two of them went to work. As they pinned and sewed, Merry kept the conversation light, talking about music and some of the funny things that had happened to her during her school days. At one point, her cheerful facade must have slipped, for Holly picked up on her mood immediately.

"Did I do something wrong?" the teenager asked.

"No, why?"

She shrugged. "Just wondering." She eyed Merry curiously, then said, "You won't be mad at me if I ask you something, will you?"

"Of course not. What do you want to ask me?"

"Did you and your boyfriend have a fight?"

Merry, who'd been kneeling on the floor, sat back on her heels. "What makes you think we did?"

"He sounded kinda mad yesterday when he was here." Noticing Merry's eyebrow lift, she added, "I overheard you fighting with him. I couldn't help it."

Merry realized Holly was talking about Steve, not Holden. "Did you hear what we were fighting about?"

"I only heard a couple of words."

Merry knew there was no point in lying. "Steve was angry yesterday. It was because we decided to end our engagement."

"So that's why you're not wearing your ring."

"Uh-huh."

There was a brief silence as Merry finished pinning the seams of the dress. Then she draped it over Holly, who stood perfectly still while she made some adjustments.

When Merry announced the seams were ready to be sewn, Holly stepped out of the dress and asked, "Are you sad you and Steve are broken up?"

"A little," Merry answered truthfully. "He's a nice man."

"How can you say that after he left you?"

Merry realized then that Holly couldn't have overheard very much of her conversation with Steve. "Why do you think *he* left *me?*"

Holly shrugged. "My mom said men are jerks, and sooner or later they all leave."

In her present state of mind, Merry could have easily agreed with her, for that was exactly what Holden was going to do to her. Yet she didn't want to encourage this already troubled teenager to have such a jaded view of male-female relationships.

"I know sometimes it looks as though men always leave, but that isn't necessarily true," Merry explained carefully. "I have several friends who are happily married. They believe they are the luckiest women in the world, which just goes to show that there are nice men out there. The problem is, I think they're hard to find."

"What about Holden?"

"What about him?" Merry asked innocently.

"Is he one of the nice guys?"

The question put Merry on the spot. What should she tell the teenager? That until this morning she'd thought he was nice but now he fell into the jerk category?

"I think it's better if we don't talk about Holden," she answered, which of course, only made the girl more curious.

"Why? Did he go back to California?"

"Because it's late and you have school in the morning and I have a lot of cleaning up to do before I can turn in," Merry answered in a rush, scooping up the scraps of fabric on the floor.

Holly didn't press the subject, but helped Merry put away the sewing supplies. As soon as they'd straightened the bedroom and had a light snack, Merry said good-night to the teenager.

Only then was she able to retreat to the privacy of her own room and do what she'd wanted to do for the past twelve hours. She lay down and wept.

What she didn't know was that her sobs could be heard in the other bedroom by the girl who'd heard her arguing with Steve.

THE FIRST THING Merry needed to do the following morning was get rid of her puffy eyes. While Holly showered, she rested a tea bag on each eyelid and prayed that her makeup skills would hide the results of her sleepless night.

There was little time for conversation between Merry and Holly at breakfast because the phone rang repeatedly. Each time Merry had jumped up, hoping it was Holden, but not one of the calls was from him. They were all from her piano students, calling to wish her a happy holiday. Because of her restless state of mind, Merry didn't notice the pensive look on Holly's face as she ate her cold cereal.

Merry assumed Holly's silence was caused by the apprehension she experienced every day at the thought of seeing her peers. She didn't know that while she'd been in the shower, Holly had heard Steve Austin's voice leave a message on the answering machine—a message meant for Merry's ears only.

Nor would Merry ever hear that message, for Holly had erased the tape, wanting to spare her music teacher any more heartache. Unfortunately more than one heart was breaking this morning; Holly's was, too. For with Steve's phone call, her suspicions had been confirmed.

Now she knew she was responsible for Merry's broken engagement. Once again she had hurt someone. She really was bad. She was going to have to do something before Merry was hurt again.

WHEN MERRY RETURNED HOME from driving Holly to school, the message light was blinking on her answering machine. This time there was a message from Holden. He wanted to see her.

Merry's hand shook as she punched in the phone number of the hotel. "Hi. It's me."

"I'm going back to California this afternoon. I'd like to stop by before I go," he told her.

"I'd like that, too."

"Good. I'll be right over." And before she could say another word, he'd hung up.

Quickly she checked her makeup, making sure there were no traces of the puffiness. Lying awake last night, she'd thought about what she would say to Holden when they finally met again. Now she knew. The minute she'd heard his voice on the phone she'd known there was only one course of action she could take.

While she waited for him to arrive, she relaxed by playing a medley of Elton John hits. Any composure she gained by playing, however, disappeared at the sound of the doorbell. She quickly went to the phone and muted the ringer, turning on her answering machine to record any calls. She wanted no interruptions while Holden was here. She took a deep breath and went to let him in.

HOLDEN WASN'T feeling well. The last person he'd wanted to hurt was Merry, yet here he was standing on her doorstep knowing he'd hurt her and searching for the words to tell her how sorry he was.

Since the moment she'd stormed out of his hotel room, nothing had been the same. He hadn't been able to eat, he hadn't been able to sleep, and he hadn't been able to work. If he was ever to have peace of mind, he needed to hear her say she understood why their relationship couldn't be a sexual one. Then life could get back to normal. He could return to California and they could be friends again.

"I'm glad you came," she said when she opened the door to him.

He figured that was a good start anyway. He smiled at her as he stepped inside, but she simply looked away. He knew her well enough to know she was still angry.

"I couldn't leave without apologizing to you," he said, getting straight to the point as he followed her into the living room. "I hurt you and I'm sorry."

He wanted to reach out and touch her, but he was afraid she'd rebuff him, and that was the one thing he couldn't bear.

"There's no need to apologize, Holden," she told him in that voice that could make him forget he possessed self-control.

"Are you saying you understand why I said what I did yesterday?"

She held his gaze. "I think I might understand you better than you do yourself." The challenge in her eyes was unmistakable.

He could feel his muscles slowly begin to relax. This was Merry. The one woman he could tell anything to, the one who'd always understood him. Everything was going to be all right.

A grin tugged at the corners of his mouth. "Maybe not better, but certainly well. We've been good friends

for too many years to let something like sex come between us now."

"We didn't have sex, Holden. We made love." Her
gaze didn't waver.

The grin slid from his face, and his muscles tightened once more. How did he tell her it was great sex,
but not love?

"That's why I told you I loved you," she continued, not waiting for him to comment. "I know you
think it was just something physical, which had been
between us since we were teenagers, but it was more
than that."

He looked away. He didn't want to see the disappointment in her eyes when he told her she was wrong.

"I wish you wouldn't do this," he murmured.

"Do what? Tell the truth?"

"No, go reading more into what happened then
what was there." He hated to say the words, but he
couldn't let her create false hopes, either.

"You think we just had sex?" she asked, not in anger, but with an almost gentle tone.

"It was *great* sex, Merry," he told her, experiencing a quick jolt of excitement as his body automatically responded to the memory.

She must have been thinking along the same lines,
for her cheeks turned a deep pink. "Real arousal has
to do with the soul, Holden, not with the flesh."

"Merry, you don't want my soul," he said.

"And if I do?" Once more he saw the challenge in
her eyes. She was not going to make it easy for him.

"You'll only be hurt again." He expected her to argue with him, but she didn't.

She simply said, "It's too bad. We're a perfect fit." She folded her arms across her chest and asked, "So where do we go from here?"

He studied her for several moments, unsure why she was taking everything so calmly. "I'd like to think we can go back to the way things were. Close friends who are always there for each other."

She shook her head, a smile of regret on her face. "Sorry. It won't work."

Her answer didn't really surprise him. He was thinking the same thing.

"You've been a part of my life for twenty years. I don't want to see that end," he told her sincerely.

"I'm not sure we can be friends and not lovers, not now," she said. He saw a certain vulnerability creep into her eyes.

"And if we're lovers, we won't be able to be friends? Is that what worries you?"

She nodded.

"You don't need to worry. I'll make sure we stay friends and nothing more."

"No, Holden. I don't want to be your friend."

She might just as well have taken a knife and cut off one of his fingers. "Come on, Merry. Don't say that," he begged.

"And what do I get out of this long-distance friendship? A trip to California once a year?" Again there was no hostility in her tone, just . . . sadness.

"What do you suggest we do? Forget everything we've meant to each other?"

"Maybe it's time we moved on," she suggested soberly.

"I don't want to move on without you. You're one of the few bright spots in my life. Tell me what it is you want me to do and I'll do it."

She stood silent for several moments, staring at him, her face filled with myriad emotions. Finally she said in a clear, calm voice, "I want you to marry me, Holden."

CHAPTER FIFTEEN

As THE FLIGHT ATTENDANT passed out headsets to the passengers in first class, Holden stared at his laptop computer. Ever since he'd opened the "notebook," the screen had remained blank except for the blinking cursor, which hadn't moved one inch. All the mental notes he wanted to file were still trapped in his head.

He looked at his watch and grimaced. Between the turbulence over the mountains and the screaming pair of toddlers across the aisle, this was the flight from hell. No wonder his concentration was impaired. He pulled a copy of the *Minneapolis Star Tribune* from his briefcase and perused the world news.

After several minutes of staring at the same headline, he folded the paper and stuffed it back into his briefcase. It wouldn't matter what he read, what he watched or what he listened to. He was totally preoccupied with one subject. Merry.

He leaned his head back against the seat and closed his eyes, giving in to the temptation to think about her. Ever since she'd proposed to him, his insides had been as turbulent as the unfriendly skies. He still couldn't believe she'd asked him to marry her without batting an eyelash.

He'd had women hint that they wanted to get married, but in all his thirty-three years, he'd never had one actually propose to him. Actually it was more of an ultimatum than a proposal. The thought brought a frown to his face.

How could she possibly think he was suitable marriage material? She knew better than anyone else his opinion on the subject of marital bliss. It didn't exist.

She thought his attitude was a burden from the past. "Get over it, Holden," she'd urged him in her eternal optimistic manner after he'd reacted in horror to her proposal. "Let go of the bitterness."

How could he? Didn't she know that his biggest fear in life was that he'd turn into the same kind of man his father had been? That he would one day tire of the woman he claimed to love and move on? No, she didn't know, because he'd never told her.

Of all the secrets he had confided in her, that was the one piece of information he could share with no one. She thought he was commitment shy, that it was women he feared. She was wrong. What he feared more than anything was himself and the possibility that he could become just like his father.

He shook his head as if he could clear it of such unwelcome thoughts. But they continued to torment him, as did thoughts of Merry.

He'd made a royal mess of her life. Sweet, resilient Merry, who'd always taken on the challenges life tossed at her, rather than buckle under in weakness and self-pity. There was nothing she wanted more than a husband and children. And now she wanted those things from him.

He couldn't give them to her. And he shouldn't have snatched away her opportunity to find that happiness elsewhere. If he hadn't gone to see her and met this Austin character, she might still be engaged to be married.

He grimaced. That was just as disturbing a thought as her proposal. He didn't want her, but he didn't want anyone else to have her, either. He felt like a first-class heel. He'd truly hurt the one person he cared for most in the world.

All he'd wanted was to make this Christmas special for her—to take her to London, to be with her. Now she was going to be spending Christmas alone with a thirteen-year-old foster child. That thought twisted his insides even further. More than anything he wanted to be with her over the holidays. He knew how difficult the season was for her, knew she had to fight off the same melancholy he did.

And had he not let his desire for her get in the way of his thinking, he *would* have been with her. For one night of pleasure in her arms he was going to pay dearly. It was a bitter pill to swallow. But even worse was the thought that he would never again hold her in his arms, never again kiss that lovely mouth, never again...

MERRY FINISHED the concerto, then slumped over the piano keys. Ever since Holden had gone, she'd been pounding out the music, searching for that tranquillity playing had always given her. But she hadn't been able to find it. Instead of feeling calm, she was exhausted.

And empty. When Holden left, he took part of her with him. Would it ever disappear, that hollow place, or was he the only one who could fill it?

She'd hoped that by forcing the issue of marriage, she could make him acknowledge his true feelings for her. Now she realized what a mistake that had been, for his true feelings were not love. She'd wanted so desperately to believe they were, but she'd been wrong.

She closed her eyes and bit her lip. She would not cry over him anymore. He didn't want her. He was gone. She had to accept that one glorious night of lovemaking was all she would ever have from him. Swallowing back the pain, she went to the kitchen to get a drink of water.

As she passed the phone, she saw that the message light on the answering machine was blinking. She immediately turned the ringer back on, then depressed the play button.

The first message was from someone at the studio confirming her recording schedule. The second was from the principal at Holly's school, who wanted to know if Holly's absence was excused. That made Merry sigh in disappointment—Holly was truant again—but it was the third message that had her clutching her stomach.

"Hi, Merry, it's me, Holly. I just called to say I'm sorry I ruined your chance at happiness. I'm leaving so you can get married and have children and I won't spoil everything. I'm going to find my mom. 'Bye."

There was a click and then nothing. Horrified, Merry replayed the message, her anxiety increasing as she listened for a second time.

Holly had called her, but from where? "Oh, Holden," she cried. "I need you!"

She glanced at her watch. He was somewhere in the air between here and California. There was no way she could get in touch with him. Which was probably just as well, she realized, as she grabbed her coat from the closet. He was no longer someone she could turn to for help. From now on she was going to have to resolve problems on her own.

Her first instinct was to call the police, but she quickly changed her mind. Involving the authorities would only create more problems for Holly with juvenile court. What she needed to do was find the girl herself and bring her back home.

"Think, Merry, think," she said aloud to herself, rubbing her forehead. "Where would Holly go if she was trying to get to her mother?"

It didn't take Merry long to come up with an answer. Holly had said she thought her mother was in New York. She didn't have enough money for an airline ticket; the train going east only left once a day, and that had been much earlier. That left the bus depot.

All the way downtown, Merry hoped she wasn't too late. That message had been sitting on her answering machine for at least two hours. Holly could be gone. She could be on her way to New York or, worse, been picked up by one of the undesirables who cruised the depot in search of young runaways.

When she entered the terminal, there was no sign of Holly anywhere. Not near the ticket counter, not along the row of chairs, not near the snack machines. Merry quickly checked the coffee shop, but all she saw were a couple of elderly travelers sitting at a small table. She was about to ask one of the staff if they'd seen a thirteen-year-old girl with grunge clothing when she noticed the ladies' rest room. She pushed open the door and nearly cried in relief when she saw Holly standing in front of the mirror applying eyeliner.

Unable to stop herself, Merry rushed over and hugged her. "Thank goodness I found you!"

"What are you doing here?" Holly asked, backing away from Merry with fear in her eyes.

"I came to get you," Merry answered gently. "I want you back."

"But I don't want you!" Holly cried, turning her back on Merry.

That was twice in one day, Merry said to herself, biting her lip in an effort to control her feelings. She took a deep breath and said, "Holly, listen to me. You didn't spoil my chance for happiness."

"Yes, I did! I cause trouble wherever I go."

"You haven't caused me any trouble. You've brought me joy. I want you to live with me." Merry spoke to her back, as Holly hadn't turned around.

"I don't want to live with you and I wish you'd go away," the girl answered, her voice cracking with emotion.

"All right, I will. But first you have to tell me why you think you're responsible for my not getting married." This time Merry put her hands on Holly's shoulders and slowly turned her around to face her. When Holly's eyes met hers, she said, "Tell me why, Holly."

"I heard the message."

"What message?"

"The one Steve left. He said he didn't want a foster kid to ruin his chance for happiness with the woman he loves. He was talking about me."

Merry's brow wrinkled. "When was this?"

"Yesterday—when you were in the shower. Then last night I heard you crying. I figured it was because of me."

"No, Holly. It wasn't. It was because of Holden."

"Holden made you cry?"

Merry nodded. "You see, the reason I broke my engagement to Steve wasn't because of you. It was because I realized I'm in love with Holden. I didn't tell Steve that at the time, because I didn't know myself that was the reason until after I'd given him back his ring."

"So if you're in love with Holden, does that mean you're going to move to California and live with him there?" Holly asked, her eyes clouding once more with fear.

"No, I'm not going to California to live with Holden," Merry said, trying to ignore the pain that accompanied that statement. "I'm going to stay right here...and I hope make a home with you."

Holly's shoulders slumped and she muttered, "I don't see why you want me."

"I think you know why, Holly," Merry answered. "I believe that buried beneath the makeup and grungy clothes is a beautiful spirit. I want that person to be a part of my life. Will you give me that chance?"

Holly shrugged. "I want to, but..."

"What are you afraid of?" Merry asked, for she knew it was fear she saw in those woeful eyes.

"I don't get to know many people, because once I get close to someone, all the problems start happening, and then they leave because they can't stand the pressure," Holly said in a small voice.

Merry pulled her into her arms. "Oh, Holly. I'm not going to leave because of a few problems. I'm great under pressure. You forget, I became a foster child when I was nine years old. And look at me now." She gave her an encouraging smile.

"You really want me to come back?" Holly said. Hope had chased away the fear in her eyes.

"Yes, I do."

"But you know I change foster mothers like I change socks," she reminded her.

"Maybe up until now you just haven't found the right pair of socks," Merry suggested, picking up Holly's duffel bag. "What do you say? Should we go home and finish that dress?"

"All right." And for the first time, Holly was the one to seek contact with Merry. She wrapped her arms around her and said, "Thanks."

"WHAT'S WRONG with you? You look terrible. Is it the flu?" Don Fredericks asked Holden the day before Christmas as they prepared to close the office early.

"I guess," Holden mumbled, knowing perfectly well his appearance had nothing to do with any virus or bacteria. It was Merry who'd caused him to lose sleep and his appetite.

"What are your plans for Christmas now that Merry's not coming out?" Don asked.

"I'm not celebrating Christmas. There's no point."

"Want to know what I think?"

"Not really," Holden answered, shuffling the papers on his desk to avoid his partner's eyes.

"You're lovesick."

"Well, Dr. Fredericks, I hate to disappoint you, but you're wrong."

"What happened between you and Merry when you went to Minnesota?" Don asked, curiosity gleaming in his eyes.

"Everything...nothing..." Holden threw down his pen in disgust. "I've got to get out of here," he muttered. He grabbed his coat and headed for the door.

"Go home and take two aspirins, then call Merry. You'll feel better in the morning," Don called out to his retreating figure.

If only it was as simple as taking a couple of aspirins and making a phone call, Holden mused later that evening. Unable to relax, he found himself in his bedroom, rummaging through his closet. Finally he found it. A small velvet box that Rosie had given him.

Inside was an exquisite cameo, the only piece of jewelry he'd ever seen his foster mother wear. When she'd told him she was leaving it to him in her will, he'd asked why she wasn't leaving it to Merry. Her answer had been, "Because I want you to give it to the woman who'll be your wife."

Holden had tried to talk her into leaving it to Merry, pointing out that it wouldn't be worn since he knew he was never going to head up the aisle. Rosie wouldn't listen. She'd told him the day would come when he'd listen to his heart and not his head.

Holden fingered the cameo. It was exquisite and delicate, and it made him think of Merry. For four long miserable days he'd ached for her. Nothing in his life seemed to matter anymore, not the fancy house, not the fancy cars and certainly not his work. All he really wanted was to be with her.

He took the cameo with him and set it on the small table beside the bed. Just as he was about to turn in, the phone rang. He hoped it was Merry. It wasn't. To his surprise it was Holly.

"I wanted to call and thank you for what you did for me," she said in a polite voice he hardly recognized.

"You're welcome, but I'm afraid I don't know what I did," he confessed.

"You went to see Chelsea Turner's parents, and now they're not going to press assault charges," she said with a hint of impatience, as if he should have remembered doing such a thing.

"That's great, Holly. I'm glad to hear it," he told her.

"Now I don't have to leave Merry," she said happily.

"How is Merry?" he couldn't resist asking.

"Fine."

"What are the two of you doing for Christmas?"

"Not much. Merry promised to play Christmas carols at some nursing home, and I'm going to try to cook something fancy, like pork chops or something. Merry's not a very good cook."

Holden smiled. "No, she's not."

"Well, I gotta go. I just wanted to say thanks. 'Bye."

And before Holden could ask another question about Merry, the girl had hung up.

As he sat there on the bed staring at the phone, Rosie's words echoed in his mind. *One day you'll listen to your heart, Holden.*

He went to the closet, pulled out his suitcase and started packing.

IT WAS SNOWING in Minneapolis when Holden's plane landed. Instead of renting a car, he caught a taxi and went straight to Merry's place.

As he stood on the doorstep, excitement swelled in him. He couldn't wait to sweep her into his arms and kiss her senseless.

Only it wasn't Merry who answered the door, but Holly. She was wearing the same apron Steve had worn the last time Holden had arrived, only on her it looked charming.

"Hi. Anybody else home?" he asked.

"Nope. Merry went to some charity thing at a children's center." Holly stood with a wooden spoon in her hand, looking as if she might throttle somebody with it.

"Can I come in?" he asked.

She shrugged. "I guess, although I'm not sure Merry wants to see you. She couldn't decide if you were one of the nice ones or a jerk."

Holden lugged his suitcase inside and stomped the snow from his shoes.

"Better take them off," Holly said, looking critically at his feet. "You'll get the carpet dirty."

Holden obeyed. As soon as he'd divested himself of his coat, he followed her into the kitchen. He watched her busily stir something in a big bowl, then asked, "Why didn't you go with Merry to the children's center?"

"Because I don't want or need anyone's charity."

Holden suppressed a smile. How many times had he heard Merry say those same words? "You know, Merry's not too fond of Christmas."

"I know. That's why we get along," Holly told him. "It's not an easy holiday for people who don't have family."

"Is that why the pine tree's still out on the deck?" he asked.

Holly nodded. "I kinda wanted to bring it inside, but I was afraid to ask Merry. I didn't want to upset her."

Holden glanced at his watch. "Do you think any stores are still open?"

She shrugged. "We could call around. Why?"

"I have an idea. Why don't you get your coat and come with me. I think we need to talk about a few things."

IT WAS A BLUE CHRISTMAS. Any way Merry looked at it, she came up with the same conclusion. Ever since Holden had left, she'd worked at keeping her spirits up—for Holly's sake—but tonight as she drove home to celebrate Christmas Eve with the teenager, she was having a difficult time fighting off the melancholy.

It would've been so easy to call Holden and tell him she'd accept him on any terms. Wedding ring or no wedding ring. But she knew that eventually the day would come when he'd leave again, and she couldn't go through another goodbye.

She forced a smile and carried the packages she'd kept hidden in her trunk into the house. It wouldn't be her best Christmas, but at least she could try to make it good for Holly.

"Mmm-mm, something smells good," Merry sang out as she stepped inside. "Holly? Where are you, and what's cooking?"

Wearing the green velvet dress, no makeup except for lip gloss and her dark hair in gentle curls, Holly presented herself to Merry. "What do you think?"

Emotions blocked Merry's throat. Gone were the eyebrow and nose rings. "You look lovely," she said, choking back the tears. "I thought you weren't going to get dressed up for tonight."

"I changed my mind," Holly said with a sly grin.

She extended a hand to Merry and pulled her into the dining room where candlelight revealed three place settings. "We're having a special dinner—bum-steads."

Merry's heart skipped a beat. "Bumsteads?"

"It's what families are supposed to have on Christmas," Holden said, stepping into view.

"Holden's been telling me all about the Christmases you had when you were my age. He said that families don't have to be people you're related to. They can be anyone you choose to be with and want to call your family."

"That's true," Merry said in a whisper, unable to take her eyes off the handsome figure Holden made.

Holly nudged Holden with her elbow and rolled her eyes heavenward. "Did you forget?" she whispered.

"Forget what?" Merry wanted to know.

"You're standing under the mistletoe," Holden told her, then wasted no time planting a kiss on her surprised lips.

It was a slow, tender kiss that probably would have lasted much longer had Holly not given a couple of polite coughs.

"We have another surprise for you, Merry" she announced and marched over to the patio door. With a twist of the wand, the louvers opened. "Ta-da!"

Merry gasped. Dozens of tiny white lights twinkled on the tree she'd banished to the deck.

"We would've brought it inside, but I didn't want to get the carpet all yucked up," Holly explained.

Merry turned to Holden. "Why?"

"Because I love you," he said simply. "You knew it before I did, but then, you've always known me better than I know myself."

"Does this mean . . ." She didn't know if she dared to ask.

PAMELA BAUER 293

"It means I'm one of the nice ones, not a jerk," he said with a crooked grin.

Holly chose that moment to interrupt. "Can we eat? I'm hungry!"

For Merry, the hot-dog bun with egg and tuna salad and melted cheese was the best Christmas dinner she'd ever eaten. She still couldn't believe that Holden had come back to her.

Later, when Holly could no longer stay awake and had gone to bed, Holden pulled a quilt from the linen closet and spread it on the floor next to the patio doors. He pulled Merry down beside him, so that they could look up at the twinkling lights on the tree.

"Are you sure about marriage, Holden?" she asked, as they lay quietly side by side.

"All my life I've listened to my head. For once I want to listen to my heart, and my heart is telling me I shouldn't live without the woman who's always been my best friend, the one bright ray of hope in the dark."

He reached into his pocket and pulled out the velvet box. "I didn't have time to get a ring, but Rosie told me I should give this to the woman I marry. I think she knew that woman was going to be you."

Merry opened the box and felt a rush of delight at the sight of the cameo. She fingered it lovingly, then leaned over to place a kiss on Holden's mouth.

"We'll be a real family," she whispered.

"A wife and kids... I'd thought those were things I'd never need, Merry, but now I realize I do. I need you and I never want us to live apart again."

She loved lying in the circle of his strong, protective arms. "What about your job?"

"I'm tired of working with the jaded and cynical, Merry. When I was here, I did a lot of talking with Tom Harvey. Remember that call I got that evening a couple of weeks ago, the one that, uh, interrupted us? It was Tom's new secretary calling to make sure I went in to see Tom first thing in the morning. I'm pretty sure I can get a position with his firm."

"But what about your house?"

"It never gave me the pleasure I thought it would. You know what Rosie always said . . ."

"Bigger and fancier doesn't make it better," Merry supplied.

"For so many years I've searched for answers in material things, Merry. Money, a big house, a fancy car. Now I realize that the answers weren't in any of those things."

She sighed. "Oh, Holden, you don't know how long I've waited to hear you say that."

"Whatever the future holds, Merry, I'll survive as long as I have you by my side. Merry Christmas."

EPILOGUE

"WE'VE BEEN in the car a long time. Aren't we there yet?" Merry asked from the passenger side of her husband's dark blue Lincoln.

"Just a couple more minutes," he answered, turning off the two-lane county highway to follow a single set of tire tracks down a snow-covered dirt road.

"We aren't going to get stuck, are we?" she asked as the car's wheels spun ominously.

"Nope. Everything's fine."

When they came to a red barn, Holden parked the Lincoln beside a yellow pickup as he'd been instructed to do. He could see Ned Robbins, owner of the farm, checking the harness on one of his horses. As Holden got out of the car, he waved at the farmer, then hurried around to Merry's side.

"You can come out now," he announced, opening her door.

"Don't I get to take off my blindfold?"

"In a minute. Here. Give me your hand." He bent to slide his arm around her shoulder and help her from the car.

As her feet touched the ground she let out a tiny yelp. "The snow's deep here!"

Before she could take another step, Holden scooped her up into his arms. "Is this better?" he asked, his boots crunching on the frozen snow.

"Mmm, lovely," she said, although of course she couldn't see the beauty of her surroundings. Not the bare limbs of the oak and birch trees, nor the shadows created by dusk, nor the horse-drawn sleigh that waited for them.

"I'm getting too big for you to be carrying me," Merry told Holden as his breathing became labored.

"I can manage," he said unevenly. "Are you sure you don't have quintuplets in there?"

She giggled. "The doctor said there's only one little baby."

"He doesn't feel so little."

"He?"

"Okay, she," he conceded, then added, "Maybe." His breath formed little clouds of white in the crisp winter air. He deposited Merry on the leather seat of the sleigh, then climbed in alongside her. Gently he untied the bandanna that had been covering her eyes.

"Oooh," she crooned with delight. "A sleigh ride! What a lovely surprise! And it's just starting to snow again..." Huge perfect flakes had begun to drift down, and Merry felt as if she'd become part of a Christmas card scene.

"You have Ned to thank for making this all possible." Holden introduced her to the burly man holding the reins.

Merry gave him one of her dazzling smiles. "Thank you, Ned. I love a sleigh ride. I can't think of a nicer present."

The farmer tipped his hat and wished them both a merry Christmas.

"This is only part of your surprise," Holden told her as he spread a plaid woolen blanket across their laps. "Since you wanted to have an old-fashioned Christmas, I thought this would be a good start."

The sleigh glided over the gently rolling, snow-covered hills, and Holden and Mary snuggled closer together, enjoying the scenery. As they passed a grove of conifers, she asked, "Are we going to cut down a tree? Because if we are, we should've brought Holly along."

"Don't worry about Holly. She approves of my plan," he said smugly, then stole a quick kiss.

When the sleigh carried them across wooden planks bridging a frozen creek, Merry caught a glimpse of a house nestled in the trees. It had shuttered windows, a gabled roof and a veranda that spanned the entire front. Smoke curled from the chimney, but it was the bright red ribbon tied in an enormous bow and attached to the front door that brought a lump to her throat.

Only a few weeks ago, a real-estate agent had shown them this country property. Merry had fallen in love with the two-story farmhouse immediately and had begged Holden to reconsider his opposition to buying an older house. His response had been to insist that they wait for spring, when they'd build a brand-new place with all the latest conveniences. Now she knew that it had only been a token resistance. The For Sale sign was gone and the name on the mailbox was Drake.

The sleigh pulled up in front of the house, and Holden looked at his wife. He saw that her eyes were misty. "Welcome to your new home, Merry."

She hugged him close and murmured, "I do love you, Holden." As they kissed in the fading twilight, the porch light came on. Standing in the doorway was Holly, a grin on her face.

"Hey! Enough of that smoochin' stuff. We have a tree to decorate," she called out.

Holden gave Merry one last kiss, then jumped off his sleigh. He lifted her down, then swept her into his arms, carrying her up the wooden steps and through the door Holly held open.

"How do you like your present, Mom?" Holly asked.

Sudden tears stung Merry's eyelids. It was the first time Holly had called her Mom; somehow that seemed to complete the lengthy adoption procedure. Holly was her daughter now, hers and Holden's. "It's perfect—just like the family that comes with it," Merry answered.

"It's going to need some fixing up," Holden warned, taking Merry's coat from her outstretched arms.

"I know," Merry replied. "But it'll be fun. You'll see."

"Dad says there's room in the barn for horses," Holly said, her eyes sparkling with enthusiasm as she led Merry into the living room. "And we can get a cat and a dog. And look at how big our Christmas tree is!"

Standing straight and tall in the otherwise empty room was a Scotch pine. On the floor beside it were boxes of ornaments and the twinkling lights Holden had purchased the year before.

"I thought we ought to have our tree *indoors* this Christmas," Holden said as Merry fingered the glittering ornaments.

"I'll sweep up the needles," Holly offered.

Merry didn't say anything. She couldn't, because she was choked with emotion. She remembered the previous year, when she'd put the tree on the deck—not so much because of the mess than her ambivalent feelings about Christmas. Feelings that were ambivalent no longer.

Seeing the tears in her eyes, Holden said, "It's not too late. We can still move it outside."

"Don't you dare," Merry told him, swallowing back the tears. "We're going to string popcorn and make paper chains and put whatever else we want on it. But first, we have to hang the lights."

"Does this mean I need to go buy sleeping bags?" Holden asked.

"You promised me an old-fashioned Christmas," Merry reminded him. "And to me, that means the kind of Christmas we had at Rosie's."

"But what about the baby?" Holly wanted to know. "You shouldn't be sleeping on the floor, being pregnant and all, should you?"

Merry placed her arm around Holly's shoulders and gave a reassuring squeeze. "As long as your father brings extra pillows, we'll be fine. What's important is that we establish some Drake family traditions. Because that's what we are. A family."

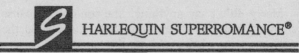

HARLEQUIN SUPERROMANCE®

A Superromance *Showcase* book.

His Friend's Wife
by
Janice Kay Johnson

Obsessed with another man's wife!

Jake Radovich had tried to be a good friend during Don Talbot's illness. He'd provided a shoulder for Clare, Don's beautiful new wife, to cry on; he'd been a surrogate uncle to Don's young son. Still, Jake wasn't fooling himself about his motives—Don was his friend, but Jake was in love with Don's wife. And Don knew it. Did Clare?

Now Don is dead—but the passions and resentments friendship once held in check are alive. And about to flare out of control....

Watch for *His Friend's Wife* by Janice Kay Johnson
Available in January 1996
wherever Harlequin books are sold.

SHOW7

MILLION DOLLAR SWEEPSTAKES (III)

No purchase necessary. To enter, follow the directions published. Method of entry may vary. For eligibility, entries must be received no later than March 31, 1996. No liability is assumed for printing errors, lost, late or misdirected entries. Odds of winning are determined by the number of eligible entries distributed and received. Prizewinners will be determined no later than June 30, 1996.

Sweepstakes open to residents of the U.S. (except Puerto Rico), Canada, Europe and Taiwan who are 18 years of age or older. All applicable laws and regulations apply. Sweepstakes offer void wherever prohibited by law. Values of all prizes are in U.S. currency. This sweepstakes is presented by Torstar Corp., its subsidiaries and affiliates, in conjunction with book, merchandise and/or product offerings. For a copy of the Official Rules send a self-addressed, stamped envelope (WA residents need not affix return postage) to: MILLION DOLLAR SWEEPSTAKES (III) Rules, P.O. Box 4573, Blair, NE 68009, USA.

EXTRA BONUS PRIZE DRAWING

No purchase necessary. The Extra Bonus Prize will be awarded in a random drawing to be conducted no later than 5/30/96 from among all entries received. To qualify, entries must be received by 3/31/96 and comply with published directions. Drawing open to residents of the U.S. (except Puerto Rico), Canada, Europe and Taiwan who are 18 years of age or older. All applicable laws and regulations apply; offer void wherever prohibited by law. Odds of winning are dependent upon number of eligibile entries received. Prize is valued in U.S. currency. The offer is presented by Torstar Corp., its subsidiaries and affiliates in conjunction with book, merchandise and/or product offering. For a copy of the Official Rules governing this sweepstakes, send a self-addressed, stamped envelope (WA residents need not affix return postage) to: Extra Bonus Prize Drawing Rules, P.O. Box 4590, Blair, NE 68009, USA.

SWP-H1295

CAN'T FORGET HIM
by Cara West

Nate Kittridge could kick himself.

While he was sowing his wild oats, his best friend's youngest sister, Megan Grant, had grown up.

She was no longer the little tomboy, content to hang around and hero-worship her big brother and his friend. Megan had become a beautiful and interesting woman. A woman who'd seen too much of Nate's love-'em-and-leave-'em attitude in the past to trust him now. And the entire Grant family—who'd always treated him as a son—wanted no part of him as a son-in-law.

Determined to prove himself worthy of Megan, Nate uncovers a secret that will change his life.

Reunited

First Love, Last Love

UNLOCK THE DOOR TO GREAT ROMANCE
AT BRIDE'S BAY RESORT

Join Harlequin's new across-the-lines series, set in an exclusive hotel on an island off the coast of South Carolina.

Seven of your favorite authors will bring you exciting stories about fascinating heroes and heroines discovering love at Bride's Bay Resort.

Look for these fabulous stories coming to a store near you beginning in January 1996.

Harlequin American Romance #613 in January
Matchmaking Baby by Cathy Gillen Thacker

Harlequin Presents #1794 in February
Indiscretions by Robyn Donald

Harlequin Intrigue #362 in March
Love and Lies by Dawn Stewardson

Harlequin Romance #3404 in April
Make Believe Engagement by Day Leclaire

Harlequin Temptation #588 in May
Stranger in the Night by Roseanne Williams

Harlequin Superromance #695 in June
Married to a Stranger by Connie Bennett

Harlequin Historicals #324 in July
Dulcie's Gift by Ruth Langan

Visit Bride's Bay Resort each month wherever Harlequin books are sold.

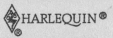

BBAYG

You're About to Become a *Privileged Woman*

Reap the rewards of fabulous free gifts and benefits with proofs-of-purchase from Harlequin and Silhouette books

Pages & Privileges™

It's our way of thanking you for buying our books at your favorite retail stores.

PROOF OF PURCHASE

HS-PP82

Offer expires October 31, 1996

Pages & Privileges ™

**Harlequin and Silhouette—
the most privileged readers in the world!**

For more information about Harlequin and Silhouette's PAGES & PRIVILEGES program call the Pages & Privileges Benefits Desk: 1-503-794-2499

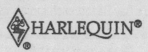

HARLEQUIN®

HS-PP82